SEASIDE
Whispers

*Seaside Summers
Love in Bloom Series*

Melissa Foster

ISBN-13: 9781941480564
ISBN-10: 194148056X

SEASIDE WHISPERS

Cover Design: Natasha Brown

EVERAFTER ROMANCE
PRINTED IN THE UNITED STATES OF AMERICA

A NOTE TO READERS

Keep up to date with the Love in Bloom big-family romance collection by signing up for my newsletter so you never miss a release:
www.MelissaFoster.com/Newsletter

Readers of the Seaside Summers series are in for a treat! After receiving hundreds of requests for more Seaside Summers characters, I have decided to write a spin-off series called Bayside Summers, also set on Cape Cod. You'll meet a few of the incredibly sexy, flirty, and fun characters from Bayside Summers in Matt and Mira's book, and of course you'll see our lovable Seaside characters in the Bayside series (they are neighbors, after all!). Be prepared for some wild, sexy fun!

The Seaside Summers series is just one of the subseries in the Love in Bloom big-family romance collection. Characters from each subseries make appearances in future books so you never miss an engagement, wedding, or birth. Keep track of your favorite characters with the essential Love in Bloom Series Guide:
www.melissafoster.com/LIBSG

Love in Bloom Subseries Order
Snow Sisters
The Bradens
The Remingtons
Seaside Summers
The Ryders
Wild Boys After Dark
Bad Boys After Dark
Harborside Nights

Get your FREE first in series Love in Bloom ebooks here:
www.MelissaFoster.com/LIBFree

CHaPTeR One

MATT LACROUX NEEDED a shower, a vacation, and to figure out what the hell he was doing with his life—in that order. And sex. Sex would be good. It had been a long time since he'd had a warm, willing woman in his bed instead of a research project to work on, papers to grade, or notes to coordinate on the book he was writing. In fact, now that he was thinking about it, he might move sex up to the top of his list— if he didn't have someone else's blood on his hands.

He tugged off his torn shirt, tossed it in the hamper, and turned on the shower. He'd been back on Cape Cod for less than three hours and had already broken up a fight between drunken college kids over by the Bookstore Restaurant, where he'd eaten dinner and *thought* he would write for a while. Maybe he should have done what so many other professors did when they took a sabbatical and gone to a nice resort somewhere, or holed up in a mountain cabin. He could have stayed at his cottage on Nantucket, but he missed his family, and his father wasn't getting any younger. Plus, his siblings' joint wedding was only two months away. It was taking place on their mother's birthday, to honor her memory. It was time to reconnect.

His mind drifted to the other person he'd like to reconnect with, Mira Savage, his father's employee and the woman who had been occupying Matt's thoughts since he met her last summer at his younger brother Grayson's engagement party. They'd spent the entire day together with her adorable son, Hagen. He'd seen her half a dozen times since, during brief visits home. They'd taken Hagen to the park together and a few other places, although they'd never gone on an official date. They'd exchanged occasional texts over the weeks in between, but that was as far as it had gone. *It* being Matt's attraction to a woman who lived too many hours away to get involved with. Mira wasn't the type of woman whose life he could complicate with intermittent encounters. She was a selfless woman who put her son and others first. The type of woman who blushed when he got too close. The type of woman a man took the time to get to know—*almost a year, that's pretty damn long*—to show her she could trust him, a woman who should be taken care of and protected but not smothered. And she was the only woman he'd like to undress slowly, loving every inch of her incredible body until she was trembling with need and slick as a baby seal. Keeping himself in check had been like dancing on hot coals, but he'd never stopped thinking about the sexy single mother and her inquisitive son.

He stripped off his slacks and stepped into the shower, turning the faucet to cold now that he was hot and bothered over Mira. He closed his eyes and exhaled a long breath. *One thing at a time.*

The water shifted from his head to his back, and Matt looked up at the faucet, which promptly fell, clipping his cheekbone.

"Ouch! What the—" He grabbed his cheek and pulled away from the water spraying in all directions from the broken spigot. *Perfect. Just perfect.* He washed the fresh blood from his fingers and quickly rinsed off.

He stepped from the shower and dried off, eyeing the offending fixture. The damn thing had a crack around the housing and rust on the inside. He'd rented his friends' cottage in the Seaside community for the summer. The place was in great shape, but things like showerheads were easy to miss when renovating. It was after nine o'clock, and Amy and Tony had a little girl. Matt wasn't about to bother them about a freaking bathroom fixture. He pulled on clean clothes and called his father, who owned Lacroux Hardware Store.

"Hey, Pop. Is the electronic code to your shop still Mom's birthday?" His father had been talking about retiring lately. The hardware store was meant to be the family legacy, passed down to one of his five children, only none of them wanted to take it over. But right this very moment, Matt had never been so glad that his father was in the hardware business. The Cape wasn't big on chain stores. The closest Home Depot or Target was a good forty minutes away.

"Yes. What's wrong?"

"I need a showerhead for Tony's place."

"Want me to run one up to you?"

Neil Lacroux would do anything for his children—even though they were all grown up. Matt knew he'd been lonely since their mother passed away unexpectedly from an aneurysm a few years ago, which was another reason he'd chosen to come back home during his sabbatical. He made a mental note to stop by the store and visit with him.

"I've got it, Pop. Sorry to bother you."

The drive to Orleans took only a few minutes. Even though Matt had grown up on the Cape, it always took him a day or two to adjust to being out of the city. Slacks and button-downs were replaced with shorts and tank tops, people moved at a more relaxed pace, and no matter how far from the beach he was, sand was ever-present. Sand in the grass, sand on the floors, sand on the seat of his car—and he hadn't even been to the beach yet.

He punched in the code to the security keypad, and the minute he was inside the dark store, he heard it. *Tap, tap, tap.* He froze, every neuron on high alert, and listened. *Tap, tap, tap, tap*, pause, *tap, tap, tap.* It was coming from his father's office. His arms instinctively flexed, preparing for a fight. He moved swiftly and silently to the office door and listened to the incessant tapping. *Dad's calculator?*

He pushed the door open, and his body flooded with awareness at the sight of Mira sitting at the desk, her fingers flying over the calculator. Maybe this was his lucky night after all.

Her hand flew to her chest. "Matt...?" His name came out all breathy. "You scared me. I had no idea you were in town."

Because I made a point of wanting to surprise you, although not exactly like this.

"Sorry about that, sunshine. I just got in a little while ago. I came to get a showerhead." He walked into the small office, taking in the ledger on the desk, illuminated by his father's ancient single-bulb lamp, and the family photos thumbtacked to the wall. He noticed a new photograph front and center, a picture of Hagen holding a fishing rod with a little sunfish dangling from the line. He knew how much Mira and Hagen meant to his father, but seeing Hagen's photo among their family's brought the full impact home. He shifted his gaze to Mira, and as the shock of his arrival wore off, a beautiful smile spread across her face. There it was, the brightness that had hooked him all those months ago. The sweet look of innocence and rebellious I-can-take-on-the-world confidence in her gorgeous eyes. She had no idea what she did to him.

"Sunshine," she whispered, and shook her head.

"You can't deny the way you light up everything around you." He'd given her the nickname last summer because she had such a positive outlook on life.

"You should see me before I have coffee in the mornings."

I'd like that more than you know.

"A showerhead? Let me show you where they are." She pushed to her feet, nearly bumping into his chest in the close quarters. Her chestnut hair tumbled sexily over her shoulders as she stood before him, one hand perched over his chest, the other reaching up to touch his cheek. "What happened?"

Their attraction had been immediate and intense last summer and had only grown stronger with each subsequent visit— at least he knew it had for him. For months he'd buried any hope of exploring their connection beneath classes and research papers. Now, as she gazed into his eyes, all those heated memories came rushing back.

"I was assaulted by the old one."

"Ouch." She grimaced, and the spray of freckles on the bridge of her nose rose with the effort.

He hadn't been able to get that cute mannerism out of his head when he'd gone back to Princeton, and damn, did he like seeing it again.

"You might need a stitch." Her fingers lingered on his skin, warm and soft.

He covered her hand with his, pressing it to his cheek. "It's nothing, really."

She nibbled nervously on the corner of her mouth. "I'll

just..." She pointed out of the office, and her hand slid from beneath his. Her breasts brushed against his arm as she walked away, stirring more of that same dark attraction.

There was no shortage of women vying for Matt's attention. From coeds to faculty, he could have his pick back in Princeton, and the choices were just as plentiful here at the Cape. But the only woman he saw when he closed his eyes at night was heading down aisle seven of his father's hardware store.

"Where's Hagen?" He told himself not to stare at her hips swaying seductively in a pair of skimpy cutoffs, but it was a tough reprimand to heed, considering she had gorgeous long legs—*the type of legs that would feel really good wrapped around my waist.*

In an effort to dissuade his dirty thoughts, he asked, "Why are you working so late? I thought you worked daytime hours." He'd have to mention something to his father. Orleans was a safe town, but he didn't like the idea of Mira working alone at night.

"Hagen is at a slumber party," she said, as if that explained everything. She planted her hands on her hips as he looked over the showerhead selections. "If I sit around at the cottage I'll just drive myself crazy worrying about whether he's okay, or if he'll get any sleep. It's better that I'm distracted with work."

"Is this your first night apart?" He grabbed a shower fixture, taking in her thoughtful expression.

"At almost seven? Goodness, no. I mean, we don't spend many nights apart, but he's not babied by any means. He'd never stand for that. You've met him. He'd probably read a book on how to escape from under Mommy's thumb and devise a plan." She sighed and stared absently over his shoulder, like she was reliving a memory. "It's funny how things change.

When he was a baby I couldn't bear to part with him." She shrugged. "But life can be crazy, and I think to be a good mother—especially a good single mother—you have to occasionally give yourself a break to rejuvenate. Hagen loves spending the night with my brothers and my friend Serena. I don't usually worry when he's with family, but when he's with friends I worry. It's silly, I know."

"That's not silly. It's the mark of a loving mother." He should know. His mother had been just as protective of him and his siblings.

She laughed and headed back toward the office. "You make it sound normal that I've got my nose stuck in a ledger all night because my son's at a friend's house."

He laid two twenties on the desk for the showerhead.

She gave him a deadpan look. "Seriously? You know your father won't accept your money."

"Then use it to buy coffee for the store and don't tell him." He left the money on the desk. "I spend most nights grading papers and working on research, so I'm not really sure what *normal* is anymore. But if this is your one night of freedom, let's go enjoy it."

She squinted up at him. "Like a pity date?"

He laughed and grabbed her purse from the back of her chair. "Hardly. Like two friends hitting the town to figure out what normal people do on Friday nights." Taking her hand, he said, "Let's go, sunshine. You can brighten up what was sure to be a very grim evening."

SUNSHINE. HOW MANY times had she dreamed of him

whispering that in her ear since last summer? *A shameful amount, that's how many.* That was not something she was proud of, but with her busy life, fantasies were all she had time for. Well, that and the fact that the guys who usually asked her out were not the type of men she could see herself getting serious with. Having a son changed everything. She needed a man who was reliable and patient, but selfishly, she also wanted a man who would treat her like a woman. A man who would understand that she hadn't had sex in years and not be turned off to reacquainting her to the dark pleasures of life.

She tried to keep up with the six-foot-plus hunka-hunka academic hotness dragging her out the back door. Matt was an intriguing mix of proper gentleman and flirtatious bad boy. She'd seen him at barbecues when he was in town visiting his family, and they'd gotten together a few times and taken Hagen to the park and the movies. They'd texted sporadically, and Mira had often hoped those friendly, sometimes slightly flirtatious texts might lead to something more, but they never had. It was just as well, because his world was a lifetime away from hers—in both miles and lifestyle.

"Where are we going?" She laughed as he tugged her along.

The door locked behind them, and he released her hand to check it. She'd heard rumors about Matt spending evenings prowling around saving little old ladies or something crazy like that. Her friend, and Matt's soon-to-be sister-in-law, Parker, called him the *secret savior*, and Mira knew firsthand about his propensity for being careful and protective. They'd first met at Grayson and Parker's engagement party, and sparks had flown from the moment their eyes connected. And the way Matt had treated Hagen, as if he were his to protect, had made him that much more appealing. When Hagen had played by the water,

Matt had watched over her son like a hawk. The two of them had clicked as quickly as Mira and Matt had. And their amazing connection hadn't ended there. During another visit, when they'd gone to the park and Hagen wanted to take a walk in the woods, Matt had watched his every step. The two had spent the entire time discussing bugs and snakes. The whole conversation had made her skin crawl, but Hagen had been in little-boy heaven. He'd finally met a man who treated him like he wasn't just a child talking nonsense, but an important person who knew what he was talking about. And he did. Even before he could read, he'd preferred being read to from *National Geographic* and the dictionary over fairy tales. "But, Mom," he'd insist. "You said we look up words we don't know. So *teach me* the words we don't know." Spoken like a boy of twelve, not four.

Matt pointed across the dark parking lot. "The Chocolate Sparrow. Perfect," he said with a too-sexy grin. "Didn't you tell me it was one of your favorite places?"

"That place is like the devil's playground. I'd like to melt all their chocolate and bathe in it."

Matt's eyes went darker than a little black dress, and her temperature rose fifty degrees. He clenched his jaw, then took her hand and led her toward the Chocolate Sparrow, walking so fast she stumbled trying to keep up. He held the door open and she inhaled the heavenly scent of calories waiting to land on her hips. As the door closed behind them, a whoosh of air carried the spicy, male scent of Matt. *Delicious.*

They wound through the crowd to the line in front of the baked goods. Cakes, brownies, cookies, pastries…The possibilities were endless. Mira leaned around Matt, eyeing the fudge in the glass displays across the room. He stepped to the side, allowing her a perfect view, and released her hand. No amount of chocolate was worth not having that big, strong hand touching her. That was as close to a man's touch as she'd come since her last dental appointment. She swallowed that sad thought, and seconds later, Matt's hand pressed against her lower back and he leaned down until his face was beside her ear. If she turned, she could taste his very tempting lips.

"A tubful of fudge to melt later, perhaps?" he whispered.

When she met his gaze, it was swimming with heat. Molten lava. Temptations of the naughtiest kind. *Holy cow.*

Before she could form a response, he said, "We'll get some of that, too."

How would she ever eat chocolate again without seeing *that* look? Where did it come from? Oh Lord, she must look as lustful as she felt.

They stepped up to the counter, and Matt waved at the display of desserts. "What would you refrain from eating if you were with Hagen?"

"How did you know…?"

"You said he can only take so much sugar before he turns into a factoid chatterbox and you can't keep up. More specifically, I think you said the equivalent to one kiddie-size ice-cream cone was his limit."

You remembered?

"*Said with the love of a mother*, of course," he added with a warm smile.

She banged her forehead on his hard chest, which she'd done a few times before. They were friends; it wasn't so weird of a thing to do. But now it felt intimate. She forced herself to take a step back. "You remembered that, too?"

He tapped the side of his head. "Hear it, read it, see it. Once is all it takes. Like that brilliant boy of yours. Now pick out all your mouthwatering treats before the hungry crowd behind us riots."

She stared into the display, but her mind was still on *that brilliant boy of yours.* People outside of her family called Hagen a lot of things—nerdy, quiet, different (the one that bothered her the most)—but *brilliant* was never tossed his way, except by her, which didn't really count. Her brothers called him smart, and bless their hearts, they talked about manning him up when he was older. Of course, as much as she appreciated their efforts, they couldn't know that the suggestion also stung. She loved her boy just as he was. She liked that he enjoyed learning more than he liked kicking a ball.

Matt's hand pressed more firmly against her, bringing her mind back to the moment.

"How about we choose together?"

"Yes, *please.*" *Anything to get my mind to behave.*

He pointed to a piece of decadent chocolate cake, chocolate-covered strawberries drizzled in white chocolate, and raspberry cheesecake. "What do you think?"

"Um…" Her mouth watered as she tried to decide. "Which do you want?"

"Which? I was thinking we'd get all three and share."

"All three?" She imagined smearing all that richness on her hips, where it was all going to end up anyway. That led to her thinking about Matt spreading it on her hips and his big hands moving along—

Gulp.

Time to shut her brain up.

"And a piece of milk-chocolate fudge," he added casually, sending her brain right back to the gutter.

"Or should I order a bucketful?" he said into her ear. Then a little louder, he asked, "Is water okay?"

"Yes. With ice. Extra ice, please." Chocolate and Matt together kicked off an avalanche that caused her brain to tumble south. Although his very impressive *south* was outlined nicely by his jeans.

She tore her eyes away. She was an educated, responsible mother, and it was time to act like one. *This* was the trouble with being around him. Other guys were easy to ignore, or at least resist, but Matt was different. She knew his family and friends. She'd seen him with her son. He was the epitome of a good friend, and a reliable, smart Princeton professor—which was probably where her naughty coed fantasy came from, considering she'd never had that particular fantasy while she was in college.

Pushing that thought away took many hard swallows and thoughts of butterflies and puppies, and...*Hagen*. Once again clear-headed, she focused on having a night of clean fun.

The tables were all taken, so they headed outside to the patio.

"What do you think, sunshine? Would these taste better on the beach? Or do you have someplace else in mind?"

Her mommy brain kicked in. "Cell phones don't work on the beaches, and I want to be available in case Hagen needs me."

"I forgot about the cell reception issues around here. Sorry about that." With a hand on her back, he guided her toward the parking lot. "Provincetown? Cell reception is fine on those beaches."

"P-town? You don't have to drive that far. We can—"

"That *far*? On your one free night? No such thing as too far, unless I'm boring you already?"

"No, definitely not. I'm just not used to having free rein over my time. P-town sounds great."

They headed across the parking lot toward his car. Between Mira's job at the hardware store and the bookkeeping she did on the side, she made a solid living, but her Subaru paled in comparison to the luxurious Mercedes she was climbing into. She'd been in it before, but it was just another friendly reminder to her crazy hormones not to get too excited. She'd spent years dealing with daycare and menial part-time jobs that allowed a modicum of flexibility for her to miss work when Hagen was sick. Her life had finally become stable, thanks to Matt's father. Neil Lacroux was a wonderful, caring boss, and he understood the often-changing schedule of a single mother. The hardware store was already on shaky ground, trying to compete with bigger companies who could offer deeper discounts. She didn't need to further jeopardize her job by acting on her crush on her boss's son.

She stole a glance at Matt, and her stomach tumbled. Apparently her hormones hadn't gotten the memo.

CHAPTER TWO

PROVINCETOWN WAS AN artsy community that never slowed down, and tonight was no different. The pier was bustling with people from end to end. Mira and Matt crossed over the boardwalk and weaved through the crowd toward the beach. Mira glanced at Commercial Street, the main drag through town. Music and laughter carried in the air. Colorful lights lit up the eclectic shops, men dressed in drag waved cards undoubtedly promoting comedy clubs and shows, and couples meandered by taking it all in.

Mira and Matt took off their shoes and carried them down to the water. How Matt managed to carry the bakery box, his shoes, and still put a hand on her back was beyond her, but she could see he was in protective mode. His eyes moved stealthily over the other people on the beach as he guided her a short distance away, where they sat by the water's edge.

Mira set their drinks in the sand and inhaled deeply, blowing out a long relaxing breath. "Boy did I need this. Thank you for dragging me out of the office."

"My pleasure. You do have me down as your date for the wedding, right?" He opened the bakery box, set it between them, and handed her a plastic fork from within the box.

Yes, please. "Your *date?*"

"I can't exactly show up as the only single Lacroux. Women

will be all over me."

"You want me to protect you from all those handsy women?"

"Yes," he said, dead serious. His gaze heated like it had in the Chocolate Sparrow. "I need you by my side, Mira."

Either he was full-on flirting or she'd lost her mind. She narrowed her eyes, feeling mildly daring. "What if *I'm* handsy?"

"You'll be my date, and my date can be as handsy as she wants."

Oh boy, did she like the sound of that. Just as her hopes soared, she remembered her little man. "But I'll have Hagen."

"Lucky for me I have two hands." He held up his hands as if to prove he owned two. "A double date, then?"

"Sounds great." A double date? With her son? That was so...*Matt.* He'd always included Hagen when he'd asked her out before, but this felt different, which meant she was clearly losing her grip on reality.

"Excellent. So what's on our agenda tonight? What's on your if-I-had-a-night-alone bucket list?"

She stabbed a hunk of chocolate cake with her fork. "I don't have that kind of bucket list. I have a *mom* bucket list."

He dug into the cheesecake and took a bite. His eyes widened and he scooped more cheesecake onto his fork and held it up by her mouth. "You have to taste this, and then I want to know about your mom bucket list."

She laughed and accepted the bite. The cheesecake and raspberry melted in her mouth. "That's better than an—" *Orgasm. Oh God.* He was totally messing with her head. She couldn't even remember what an orgasm felt like when it wasn't brought on by something battery operated. Of course, those were usually accompanied by visions of Matt touching her, licking her, perched above her while he was buried deep inside her.

"Than an…?"

"Ice-cream sundae," she blurted out.

He pointed his fork at her and narrowed his eyes. "That's only because you've never had one of *my* specialty sundaes."

"Funny. I was just thinking something similar." Their eyes held for so long she wondered if he could read her dirty thoughts. He picked up the fudge, broke off a piece, and fed it to her with his fingers.

Oh yeah, he could read them all right.

After a few minutes of flustered thoughts and forgetting how to speak like a normal person, Mira pulled herself together, and they *finally* fell into easy conversation, as they had so many times before tonight. What was it about tonight?

Matt continued feeding her bites of chocolate in between topics.

That's what it was about tonight. The flirting and feeding and treating her like she was more than a friend.

"You're trying to make me fat," she teased, taking a drink of water.

He lifted a chocolate-covered strawberry to her lips, and she bit right through the middle. An explosion of sweetness burst in her mouth.

"Nope, I just love the face you make after every bite. Like you disappear into a dark fantasy."

She felt her cheeks heat up and covered her face with her hand. "That's so embarrassing."

He lowered her hand with a sinful smile that made her insides melt.

"Why weren't you out on a date tonight?" He asked it so

passionately, he might as well have asked, *Why do you still have clothes on?*

Okay, maybe that was just lust turning her brain to mush.

"The dating pool on Cape Cod leaves a lot to be desired."

He scoffed and looked around the beach at groups of twentysomethings playing guitars, singing, and talking. "There are plenty of good-looking guys around here."

"Good-looking doesn't equate to worthy of dating." Hagen's father—*the lying, cheating bastard*—had taught her that men were even less reliable than the weather. She wasn't about to go the relationship route and chance Hagen—or her—getting let down again. She took another drink of water, hoping Matt would drop the subject, but his arched brow silently urged her to continue.

"Okay, fine." She rolled her eyes. So much for keeping her thoughts to herself. "Before I had Hagen I *might* have dreamed of finding Mr. Right. Being romanced with French restaurants and poetic gestures. All the immature fantasies girls are brought up to have." She shook her head and laughed softly, remembering how real and attainable that felt at one time.

"But that all changed when real life set in. A baby, sleepless nights, juggling schedules, dealing with colic, and…It doesn't matter why. Dating takes time and energy, and I don't have much of either left at the end of most days. I'm also a package deal. And more importantly, guys want attention, and I've never met a man who was worth diverting any of my attention away from Hagen." That was a tiny white lie. When she was with Matt she never felt like she needed to divide her attention between him and Hagen. The three of them blended together seamlessly. But there was a world of difference between spending a few hours with each other and a lifetime of togetherness.

"I guess that makes sense. I haven't been dating either." He paused, as if he wanted that to sink in, which it did, only to make her worry she was reading too much into it. "Tell me about your bucket list."

Glad for the change in subject, she said, "Only if you'll tell me yours."

She picked up a strawberry, and he wrapped his fingers around her wrist and held it still as he bit into the sweet treat, his eyes searing into hers. He licked his lips and took the stem from her hand, setting it in the box without ever breaking their connection. Silence had never felt so alive. Her mind traveled to those dark places she was trying to ignore. *Maybe we could be friends with benefits for just one night?*

"My bucket list in general?" he asked. "Or my one-night-of-freedom bucket list?"

Oh shit. What was she thinking? *Her boss's son? No. No benefits!* She needed the real benefits of having a job more than she needed sex with this gorgeous, fun, flirty creature.

"One night of freedom," she said quickly.

"That's a loaded question," he said in a low voice. "With dangerous answers. Let me think on it while you tell me yours."

Maybe the chocolate was laced with an aphrodisiac.

He glanced over her shoulder at a group of people by the pier playing guitars, breaking their connection. She inhaled a deep breath to rein in her out-of-control hormones.

"Okay, but you'll probably be disappointed. On my *mom* bucket list is making sure Hagen has a secure and happy future, which means eventually sitting for the CPA exam so I can make more money. Not that I want to leave your father's hardware store. You know I lost my dad when I was twelve, and your dad has become like family. He's really good to me, allowing me to work around Hagen's schedule and making other accommodations that I know would be impossible to find elsewhere. He's a good man, even if he is too stubborn to admit that the business is threatened by big businesses offering lower prices." She waved a dismissive hand. "Anyway, that's about it. I've got a great cottage at my brothers' resort, and a job I love. Right now my life is all about bringing up Hagen."

He settled his hand over hers with a serious expression. "That's a respectable mommy list. Now tell me about the list you apparently *don't* have. Your fantasy list."

You mean the one you're the star of?

"We have all night to do whatever you want, sunshine. What do you want to do?"

You, nearly slipped out. She cleared her throat and said the only other thing she could think of. "A ghost tour."

He laughed.

"Seriously." *If I can't have my real fantasy, I might as well have my top nonsexual fantasy.* "That's something I can't do with Hagen, and I have always wanted to go on one. Now it's your turn. What's on yours?" *And answer fast before some embarrassing confession slips from my lips.*

His eyes heated again. "This is it."

"Getting a sugar high in P-town? That's not much of a list."

"I disagree. Spending an evening alone with you is a very fine start to my list."

Oh my. Her heart fluttered at his words, his touch, and the tender look in his eyes. *Tender.* Not *rip my clothes off and take me for a night*, but *I want to kiss you until you can't see straight* tender. Yeah, that look, and boy did she ever want that kiss.

"Professor Lacroux, that was a very smooth line."

"It wasn't a line, and for the next three months I'm not a professor. I'm on sabbatical. Remember the article I wrote for the *New York Times* that went viral?"

It wasn't a line? You're here on sabbatical? "H-hard to forget. You were like a local hero." Her voice came out soft and shaky. She remembered the throngs of customers coming in to the store to congratulate his father more than she remembered the article itself, but she knew it was a very big deal.

"A hero? So ridiculous. Anyway, I've been wanting to do more than teach for a long time. There's so much administrative red tape, and between research papers, teaching, and applying for grants, I was losing my mind. When that article came out, I had two unfinished goals. Making dean of the School of Social Sciences would be the brass ring, the pinnacle of my career—and it's never going to happen, since the man who holds that position said they'll have to carry him out in a wooden box. And publishing a book. A substantial book deal came through as a result of the article. And as for the dean position"—he shrugged—"I guess some dreams aren't meant to be achieved. Or maybe we're simply meant to make tough choices. Anyway, I chose door number two. The book deal, reconnecting with family, and…"

His unsaid words lingered in the space between them, offering too many possible interpretations for her mind to grasp. Since that amazing day they spent together at his brother's engagement party, each of their brief visits brought them closer together, but he'd always been off-limits, which kept him very clearly in the fantasy-only realm. Knowing he was here for three months was giving her heart palpitations.

"Mira?" He ran an assessing gaze over her face. "You okay?"

"You kind of just blew my thoughts out of my head."

He laughed, a low, sexy laugh that vibrated between them.

"Let's see if I can reel them back in. I've never been so thankful for a broken shower before in my life, and I can't think of anyone I'd rather spend an evening with than you."

That was supposed to reel her thoughts back in?

"There is something else I've had on my bucket list." He pulled her to her feet, tucked an arm around her waist, and gathered her against him. "Dancing in the moonlight with a gorgeous woman who negates all thoughts of anything except the here and now."

Oh boy did he feel good. His body moved with grace and strength. Every brush of his hips was pure seduction, definitely not befitting of a respectable professor dancing with a responsible single mother. *For the next three months you're not a professor. But I'll always be a mother.*

She'd dreamed of being in Matt's arms for months, and this was *so* much better than her fantasies. She had never questioned her decision to have Hagen, and she didn't begrudge it now, but she had important responsibilities, like keeping her job. She couldn't afford to get as carried away as she'd like to. But as he held her against his hard body, his strong arms buffering her from the rest of the world, she closed her eyes and wondered if, just for tonight, she could allow herself to be something more than a responsible mother.

MATT'S HAND SLID down Mira's back, splaying across the width of her waist. The melody of the guitars and the sounds of young voices played around them like their own private serenade. He hadn't danced in years, and he couldn't remember the last time he'd told a woman he couldn't think of anyplace he'd rather be than with her, much less meant it. But there was something about Mira—no, that wasn't right. Just as he'd found last summer, and during all their interactions in between, there were *many* things about her that were reeling him in. As her enticingly soft body molded to his hard frame, he knew he was skirting a dangerous line. A line he desperately wanted to cross, but she hadn't taken the bait to any of his innuendos. Maybe she wasn't ready to cross that line with a man who might only be in town for three months.

They danced long after the song ended, with the wind at their backs and the gentle sounds of waves sweeping up the shore. Their bodies swayed sensually. Her embrace was enticingly *right*. When they stopped dancing, they gazed into each other's eyes, and a handful of silent messages passed between them. He saw her nervousness and her hunger.

His eyes moved slowly over her high cheekbones and the bow of her perfect, kissable lips. "You're so beautiful."

Her cheeks turned that rosy shade of pink he liked so much, and she shifted her eyes away, but not before he saw the lust brewing in them. He wanted to *taste* her positivity, to devour the passion feeding the hunger in her eyes, but he knew he shouldn't push too hard. His stay here was only temporary, and she was his father's employee.

When that reminder didn't take away the urge to lean down and kiss her, he took his thoughts one step further, because above all else, despite this impulsive night, Matt was a careful thinker. He wasn't a player like some of his brothers were before they'd settled down. In fact, he was just the opposite. Matt was selective about the women he was intimate with because he rarely did anything without his heart coming into play.

Knowing Mira hadn't been dating confirmed what he'd suspected. She lived her life in the same vein.

"Mira." Her beautiful hazel eyes were full of hope and desire. He took her hand and her fingers curled around his. He couldn't resist flattening his hand on her lower back, bringing all her lush curves tighter against him again.

She blinked up at him, her long, dark lashes sweeping over her cheeks. She nibbled her lower lip, and that simple act made her look sensual and innocent at once. The world around them disappeared in those magical seconds that preceded a first kiss. He felt their thighs brush and her chest lift against his with each anticipatory breath. They were both into this, ready, willing, and oh so able.

He nuzzled her neck, inhaling the scent of sinful promises. Desire swam in her eyes as her fingers pressed into his skin, but his mind wouldn't stop ticking off the ramifications of a night of passion with Mira. One night of being buried deep inside this incredible woman would never be enough. She deserved more than a few pieces of chocolate and landing in bed beneath him. This wasn't even a proper date.

Gritting his teeth against what he really wanted, he forced himself to take a step back.

"How about that ghost tour?"

CHAPTER THREE

WHEN THE GHOST tour began, Mira was sure it was all a hoax. Malena, their tour guide, a pretty redhead cloaked in a black hooded cape with red lining, gave out glow-stick bracelets to *ward off evil spirits*. Mira and Matt shared a few laughs over the neon jewelry. As their group of eighteen ghost seekers walked down Commercial Street, Malena described ghosts of sea captains, fishermen, and residents who supposedly continued to roam the streets of Provincetown. Mira wasn't frightened at all. At least not of ghosts. The incessant pounding of her heart caused by the tall, handsome man holding her hand, who smelled like musk and something she'd like to run her tongue all over, however, was a whole different story.

She'd wanted to kiss him *so* badly on the beach, but she'd also been flat-out, heart-stopping petrified. It had been *years* since she'd kissed a man in the way she wanted to kiss Matt. Not to mention that every time they were together her mind went directly to *sex*. She'd already envisioned them having sex in his car, on the beach, and embarrassingly, on the steps of Shop Therapy in the center of Provincetown. *Gah!* That was crazy, because like kissing, she also hadn't had sex in too many years to count. She'd probably forgotten how to do it with anything other than her battery-operated boyfriend. Was there a wrong way to have sex? She might have to take her friend Serena up on her offer to sex her up. Serena would be thrilled. She'd only been bugging her about it for the last few *years*, and right now Mira felt about a million miles behind the dating eight ball.

They followed Malena out of town and up a steep, desolate road that looked like it led directly into the night sky as she told an eerie story about a sea captain who was beheaded on this very street in the eighteen hundreds. Their only light was the lantern Malena carried at least twenty feet ahead of them and the silly glow-stick bracelets bobbing behind her like she was the pied piper. When she finished telling the story, silence fell over the group. The higher they climbed, the creepier the night became. The air felt like breath ghosting over Mira's skin.

Matt tucked her beneath his arm. "You okay?"

"Yeah." Her voice came out shaky, and he must have noticed, because he tightened his grip around her. Her skin was beginning to crawl with the idea of a headless ghost wandering around them.

When they reached the cemetery at the top of the hill, there was a collective gasp. A sea of cracked and crooked headstones was surrounded by sparse trees branching out against the night sky like skeletons swaying in the breeze. They reminded Mira of old black-and-white cartoons where trees wrapped gnarled branches around people as they passed by. A shiver ran down her spine with the thought, and she snuggled closer to Matt.

"We suggest you spread out and take pictures wherever you feel the presence of a spirit," Malena said. "If you're lucky, your pictures will reveal orbs that aren't visible to the naked eye. The quieter you are, the more focused you'll be, so take your time, and take a partner with you if you startle easily."

"That's our cue, sunshine." Matt guided her away from the crowd.

"Do you believe in this stuff?" She had one arm around Matt's waist, the other pressed against his stomach. She would have climbed him like a mountain and hung on for dear life if she weren't afraid of exactly what that would do to her very lonely girl parts.

"Spirits? Sure. Look how magnificent human beings are. I'd hate to think all this greatness simply ends after we die."

She looked up at him as they walked beside a row of headstones. "I figured as a professor you'd be more, I don't know, grounded than that."

"You mean stodgy?" He tugged her closer.

"No," she insisted. "More scientific, maybe."

"I'm plenty scientific." He reached into his pocket and withdrew his cell phone. "Let's get a few pictures and see about those orbs." He held the phone up, with the camera facing them.

"A picture of *us*?"

He grinned and clicked off a few shots. "To start."

They walked deeper into the cemetery, stopping beside a large tree with moss snaking up the trunk.

"Look," Mira whispered, pointing to mist rising from the ground around an old, unreadable headstone. "Get a picture!"

Matt took the picture, and she walked closer to the headstone, still clinging to him like a security blanket. She crouched to get a better look, bringing him down with her.

"Why is there mist only on this one?" she asked, looking around at the other headstones.

Matt moved away and frigid air engulfed her as he took a picture of her huddled there on the ground amid the mist.

"Get back over here!" She darted to her feet and wrapped herself around him again. "Something happened. As soon as you walked away the air turned cold."

"You missed my body heat." He shifted so she was pressed against his chest and thighs.

She laughed to cover up her agreement. "It was different. *Ghostly*."

"My body has been known to evoke *otherworldly* experiences."

Even in the darkness she could see the wicked look in his eyes, feel the hard heat behind his zipper. Her mind immediately pictured his naked body above hers, her legs wrapped around his waist as their bodies became one.

This was not good.

It was *marvelous*.

Marvelously *hot*.

A marvelously hot *fantasy* that was never going to happen because she wasn't about to risk Hagen's heart—or her own. Or her job. She banged her head on his chest and groaned, trying to reel her dirty thoughts back into submission. *Submission?* Oh yeah, she'd submit to him.

Hushed whispers filtered into her foggy brain. Other people from the tour were just a few feet away, and here she was having an erotic fantasy about the man who wasn't even her official date. She realized she was practically panting and clinging to his biceps. And he was looking at her like he knew *exactly* what she was thinking.

She forced herself to step away on wobbly legs.

Matt scrolled through his phone. "Sunshine? I think you're going to want to see this."

He held his phone out, and Mira looked at the picture of her crouched beside the headstone. Mist floated up from the ground like ghostly arms reaching for several startling visible orbs floating around Mira.

The hair on the back of her neck stood on end and goose bumps chased up her arms. "Matt!" she whispered urgently, pushing the phone away as she wrapped her arms around Matt's middle, then pulling the phone into view again. "I don't want to see it, but I *have* to."

Matt chuckled and rubbed his hands soothingly along her back. "They can't hurt you."

"How do *you* know? Maybe they can. Maybe they'll follow us home and watch us." She rambled, too nervous to stop, conjuring up all sorts of awful thoughts about ghosts and evil spirits, until Matt shoved his phone in his pocket and pressed his hands to her face, silencing her with a serious stare.

"How do you know they're bad? My mother and your father are gone. Couldn't the orbs be their spirits? Or maybe they're not spirits at all, but a symptom of the weather."

"Uh-huh," she mumbled.

They moved silently through the cemetery, awareness and heat twined with the eeriness of the evening, leaving Mira in a heightened state of hot, bothered, and frightened. The rustling of the leaves sounded like feet shuffling on pavement. Every noise brought her closer to Matt. He was eating up her clinginess, whispering scary stories to make her hold him even tighter. By the time Malena gathered the group for the walk back, Mira was a trembling mess of lust and ghostly thoughts—lust was winning by a mile.

As the group headed out of the cemetery, Matt pulled her against his chest. She felt his heart stomping out the same frantic beat as hers. She fisted her hands in his shirt, her mind reeling with questions. *What would it be like to kiss you? A simple press of our lips or a full-on tongue-lashing? Messy or proper?*

Sensual or tentative? Would you hold me against you as you are now or lay me back and take full control?

What am I doing?

No kissing. Kissing would lead to sex.

But she *really* missed having sex. She was *starved* for sex, and just thinking about Matt scratching that itch made her want him even more.

But he was only here for three months, which was great. Much longer than any other visit, but what would happen after that time? She loved their friendship and didn't want to have any regrets. Tonight had been unbelievable, and she'd treasure it forever, but once she kissed him? Once she felt all the power behind him? How would she ever keep from wanting more? And really, what more could there be? *Three months of fantastic sex?*

She needed a shock collar or *something* to zap her back into her responsible motherlike brain because three months of fantastic sex was sounding really good.

She forced herself to release his shirt, and he pressed his hands over hers, keeping them flat on his chest. His eyes blazed through her with an intensity that made her whole body shudder.

Kiss me.

She closed her eyes and all the fear of ghosts and spirits disappeared. Her mind wandered to the dark places she was struggling against, and the rivaling, practical thoughts came rushing in. What if they kissed? What if they did have sex? Then what? Where could that possibly lead? This was another reason she didn't date. She was a planner. She had to be to keep up with her and Hagen's schedules.

Oh God. What am I doing?

She opened her eyes and drew in a deep breath. She might not be able to hold on to the romantic notions of being swept off her feet by a man who adored her, like she had when she was younger, but she could still hold out for a man who would actually be there for more than a few weeks.

It took all her willpower, but she pushed past the wild, unfamiliar desires wreaking havoc with her brain and said, "We should go."

She turned away, instantly filling with regret for putting space between them. Gulping cool air into her lungs, she hurried toward the group.

Then Matt was beside her, tugging her against him again, protecting her from unseen threats—and maybe from her own head.

MATT WAS A lot of things—a careful thinker, a loyal brother, a studious professor—but he wasn't a *taker*. Until now. Until Mira. He *wanted* to *take*—her kisses, her body, her sweet, sexy laugh—and he wanted to shatter the tug-of-war lingering in her eyes. He was barely aware of the group as they came to Commercial Street and the group disbanded. He had one thing on his mind and one thing only, getting Mira alone.

The devil on his shoulder told him to *take, take, take*, but the voice of reason he lived by reminded him of all the reasons he needed to go slowly with her. The opposing voices were enough to make a man lose his mind.

By the time they reached the car, he was sick of thinking. He turned toward Mira and placed his hands on her rounded hips. *Perfect*. Their eyes locked, and he stepped forward, pinning her against the car with his body. His hand slid up her side, grazing the side of her breast. Her breathing hitched, and the sexy sound sent his hips pressing forward. It had been a long time since he'd wanted a woman so voraciously.

"Tell me to back off and I will," he said.

Her lips parted, but no words came. She wrapped her arms around his waist and her tongue swept over her lips. Holy hell, he was so tied up in her he felt the heat of her tongue between his legs. He touched her cheek. Her skin was soft and warm, and when his thumb brushed over her slick lower lip, her breath left her lungs.

He lowered his face, pressed a kiss beside her ear, and whispered, "I'm only here for three months. I can't make any promises."

Her hands tightened around him. "I know."

He kissed her jaw, her neck, and felt her swallow hard. The whimpering sound she made brought his eyes to hers. A sensuous tether formed between them, luring him closer.

"I've wanted you since I first set eyes on you last summer in that pretty pink dress smeared with Hagen's sticky fingerprints." He brushed his lips over her smiling mouth. "Tell me to stop and I will," he repeated more urgently, giving her a chance to do what he wasn't strong enough to.

She lifted her chin, meeting his gaze like a timid bird wanting to find its wings. *Oh yeah, sunshine. I'll help you find those wings.*

"One kiss," he promised, though he feared it was a lie.

His mouth descended toward hers—

"Matt!"

He froze at the sound of his sister's voice. Mira snapped upright, bumping into his chest with an *oomph.*

Scanning the lot, he saw Sky and her fiancé, Sawyer, jogging toward them. Cursing under his breath, he squeezed Mira's arm in apology for the intrusion and took a step back. Sky and Sawyer lived above Sky's tattoo parlor minutes from where the ghost tour disbanded, but it was after midnight, and he hadn't even considered that they might run into them.

"Matt!" Sky was his youngest sibling and only sister. Her skirt nearly dragged along the ground as she approached, her eyes moving curiously between them. "Mira? Hey, how are you?" She hugged Mira, who looked like she'd been caught naked. "What are you guys doing here? Matt, what happened to your cheek?"

He'd forgotten about the damn cut. "It's nothing."

Sawyer slapped Matt on the back with a knowing wink. "Having a good night?"

It was about to get even better.

"Yeah, we're…" He glanced at Mira and put a hand on her back, hoping to settle her nerves. "Celebrating. Tonight's Hagen's first slumber party, which means Mira has no curfew."

"Really?" Sky's eyes widened. Her long dark hair and ever-present smile reminded Matt of their mother. Sky liked to stick her nose into her brothers' personal lives, which was pesty, but she meant well. Sky loved to see people happy. That was her *thing*.

"Great, then you guys can come with us." Sky linked her arm with Mira's and began walking toward Commercial Street. "We're going dancing. Once a month Sawyer and I stay out all night just because we can. What a coincidence that you guys are up here, too."

Mira looked over her shoulder at Matt with so much longing in her eyes he felt it in his bones. He'd already shown their hand, so they couldn't really pretend they had to get home. He mouthed, *Sorry*, and she mouthed, *It's fine*, and flashed her sunny smile.

Sawyer sidled up to Matt as they headed toward the night-clubs. "You and Mira?" he asked quietly. "I had no idea you two were…"

"We weren't." *But we are. We so are.*

CHAPTER FOUR

DRINKS, MUSIC, AND a visual feast of seduction had been on tap since they'd arrived at the dimly lit nightclub, and Mira was mesmerized by *all* of it. Sweaty couples slithered against each other like mating snakes, groping and kissing with reckless abandon on the crowded dance floor. Mira had never watched porn, not one minute of it, but this *had* to be similar. It felt erotic and dark. She felt voyeuristic, but she couldn't look away from the openmouthed kisses and sexual possession before her, and it made her *want* deep in her core. She hadn't been dancing in forever, but tonight the music pulsed beneath her skin, alcohol warmed her blood, and the sexually charged atmosphere chipped away at her inhibitions. Sky and Sawyer had been on the dance floor for what seemed like hours, their bodies moving like they were made for each other. Embarrassingly, Mira envisioned their sensuality moving to the bedroom, like she read about in romance novels late at night after Hagen was asleep.

She wasn't usually a naughty thinker, but Matt unearthed those feelings in her, more so tonight than ever before. She blamed it on the aura of sex and lust and all things taboo going on around her. Matt slid a hand around her waist and pressed his mouth beside her ear, speaking just loud enough to be heard above the music. "Dance with me, sexy girl."

She hadn't felt sexy in years. She couldn't even remember if she'd shaved her legs that morning. Her life was so full of practicality it was a wonder she didn't have the days of the week embroidered in her underwear. But the way Matt's hand moved over her ribs in long, languid strokes and the seductive look in his eyes erased those worries. She let him lead her through the crowd until it swallowed them whole and she lost sight of Sky and Sawyer. The scent of testosterone and sex hung in the air. The heat was oppressive, making the bumping and grinding around her feel even more libidinous.

Matt kept a hand possessively around her, holding her against him as his hips moved with the smooth and powerful mastery of a man who had way more sexual experience than she had. His dark eyes held her captive, lulling her into a heightened state of arousal. Her nipples tightened with awareness and her body began to move without any cognitive thought. She couldn't think, could only *feel*—and *feel* she did. His impressive hard length brushed against her hips, and his hands moved beneath the back of her top, hot and strong against her flesh. Her fingers played over his muscular pecs, and in her mind she saw her mouth on his skin, tasting his salty sweat, feeling his muscles jump beneath her tongue. Her hands traveled up his shoulders, around his neck, then down his strong arms. She closed her eyes, reveling in his touch as his hands swam up her shoulder blades, then slid down to the low-riding waist of her shorts, then back up again. She felt the heat of his piercing stare through her closed lids. When she opened her eyes she felt braver, bolder, and slid her hands into the back pockets of his jeans, bringing them even closer together. *Oh yeah, this is so much better.*

Matt moaned beside her ear, his hips thrusting as if they were in bed. Heat pooled inside her. Beside them, two women were making out, groping each other's breasts and kissing. It was a beautiful, thrilling sight, and she was surprised at how much it revved her up. Matt turned her in his arms, bringing her ass against his formidable arousal. His hands slid up and down her body, caressing the sides of her breasts as he ground into her from behind. She had a momentary thought about this not being how a mother should act. They weren't even technically on a date, but having Matt's hands on her, feeling the effect she had on him, was too good to pass up.

Maybe it was the music, the environment, or maybe she'd just reached her breaking point, but this was it. She wanted him, for a night, for a week, for three months. She'd take whatever she could get and deal with the aftermath later. Tonight she wasn't just a mother. She was a *woman*.

She raised her hands over her head like she'd seen Serena do when it was just the two of them goofing around, and her body took over. Her hips swayed, her chest and shoulders writhed sensually, and her thoughts spun away. Then Matt's hot mouth was on her shoulder, kissing and tasting, making deep, guttural sounds that sent thrills thrumming through her. His hands splayed over her stomach, pressing her back against his powerful chest, and he slicked his tongue over the shell of her ear. She closed her eyes, arching her neck to the side and giving him better access. He didn't waste a second, and sealed his mouth over the sensitive skin where her neck met her shoulder, sucking the strength right out of her knees. As if he felt her stability fail, he tightened his arms around her.

"I've got you," he said, and pressed another kiss beside her ear.

He turned her toward him, and her hands instinctively wound around his neck.

"You're so damn sexy, sunshine. You're killing me."

"There you go calling me sexy again and making my stomach flip. I haven't felt sexy in years."

He leaned in so close she could practically taste him. "Trust me, sunshine. There's all kinds of sexy going on with you. The kind of sexy that makes a smart man go dumb."

He brushed the backs of his fingers down her cheek, and her nipples tingled with anticipation. Her skin was hot, her breathing ragged. Nameless people bumped into her on all sides and she didn't care. She was here, with the man she wanted, the man her son adored. The man she wanted to be taken by.

She had no idea how long they danced, gazing hungrily into each other's eyes, making silent promises for *more*, but when Sky tapped her shoulder, she was drunk with desire.

"Come on. We're heading out to watch the sunrise," Sky shouted.

Sunrise? Her brain—and panic—kicked into gear. They must have been there for *hours*. She wasn't ready for their night to end. How could it be morning already?

"What time do you need to get Hagen?" Matt asked.

Could he be any more wonderful? Even with all the heat smoldering between them, he was thinking of her son. "Ten. His friend's mom is bringing him home after they go out to breakfast. I'd like to watch the sunrise. I haven't done that since Hagen was a baby and I'd watch it through the window while I rocked him back to sleep."

Matt lowered his mouth beside her ear and said, "Anything you want, sunshine. But one day soon it'll be me who's tending to you as the sun rises, and it won't be to lull you back to sleep."

With a protective hand on her back, and a promise that made her knees weak, they made their way outside.

THREADS OF ORANGE and yellow crept over the horizon like mist rising from the bay. Colorful reflections danced off the endless water. From their perch on the cool sand, it looked like the bay spilled off the far reaches of the earth. Matt wished this night with Mira could be endless. She was nestled against his side fast asleep. She'd barely made it ten minutes out of the club, and he didn't have the heart to wake her.

Sawyer tapped his shoulder and nodded at Sky, in a similar position as Mira, also sleeping.

"Guess their men aren't very interesting after all," Sawyer joked.

Matt wanted to be Mira's man, although he knew that would be tricky considering his life was in New Jersey and hers was here. But people's lives changed. Who knew what would happen a week from now, much less a few months. Sawyer had been a professional boxer when he and Sky had fallen in love, and a head injury had led him to retire. Now he coached and wrote poetry with his father, and he seemed happy with his new and different lifestyle, and gloriously happy with Sky. Each of Matt's siblings had fallen in love over the past few years, opening Matt's eyes to what he was missing out on. He wanted what his siblings had, what his parents had enjoyed. Although he'd been growing tired of teaching, he wasn't sure he could handle leaving it behind. The sabbatical was a test.

"I should've taken her home hours ago. I know she's not used to being out this late." Matt touched Mira's cheek, feeling selfish for wanting to spend every possible second with her.

"So, when did this happen?" Sawyer asked. "Sky was ready to grill you two, but when she said you just got to town, I convinced her to give you a day or two."

"Thanks. I'm sure she'll grill me tomorrow." Matt smiled at the thought of his sister wanting all the juicy details. Hell, he wanted to *make* juicy details.

"The showerhead at the cottage broke and I went down to my father's shop to get a new one." He touched the cut on his cheek. "Mira was there working, trying to keep herself distracted from worrying about Hagen."

Matt paused, thinking about how his entire outlook had changed when he'd found Mira at the hardware store. A frustrating night that had begun with breaking up a fight had ended with the woman he thought he'd never have enough time to give what she needed and deserved asleep on his shoulder. Life worked in mysterious ways.

"Do you think it's possible to carry a torch for someone for months and not realize how hot it burned?"

"If you mean you and Mira," Sawyer said, "we all thought you'd hook up last summer."

"I had too much on my plate to put her in that situation. I've had too much on my plate for far too long." He shifted his eyes to the beautiful woman breathing softly beside him. "I had a hard time pushing thoughts of her away when I went back to Princeton, but I thought I'd done a pretty good job of it." He shook his head. "Boy was I ever wrong. The minute I saw her, all my feelings rushed forward like I'd opened the dam gates. I swear, her voice does funky things to my stomach, and that smile? Jesus, Sawyer, her smile…It's not logical, but when we were out tonight, I wanted to *claim* her." As his feelings poured out, he knew the night had affected him much more strongly than he'd even imagined. This was a very touchy-feely conversation for Matt to be having with another man.

"Nothing about relationships is logical." Sawyer glanced at Sky. "Look at me and Sky. We met on a fluke when I came in for a tattoo. I swear we fell in love in the first three hours we spent together, and it's only gotten stronger since. That's what love is. It changes everything you thought you knew about yourself. One look at Hunter should tell you everything you need to know."

Hunter, Matt's older brother, had been the biggest player of them all. Before falling in love with Jana, Hunter had been with a different woman every night of the week—*until he wasn't*. And then there was only Jana. In a few weeks Hunter and Jana, Grayson and Parker, and Sawyer and Sky would be married, and soon, starting families, chasing their futures with the people they loved, while Matt chased clarity and tried to figure out if going back to teaching meant chasing the wrong future.

"Yeah, I guess you're right," Matt said. "But I was never that way with women. My mistress was academics."

"Mine was boxing. Now I've got only one mistress." Sawyer glanced at Sky and said, "I'm the luckiest guy on earth, Matt. In eight short weeks, she'll be my wife."

Matt didn't know much about Hagen's father, but as Sawyer talked about becoming Sky's husband and eventually starting a family, and went on to describe how his relationship with his father, who had Parkinson's, had changed since they began writing together, Matt wondered what had happened. Had Mira ever been married? All it would take was one conversation with Sky to get all the facts, but Sky wasn't the one he wanted to talk to. He wanted to hear Mira's story from Mira. He wanted to look into her eyes and feel what she felt. He wanted to know what she'd been through to become the strong woman and mother she was. On the heels of that thought came thoughts of his father. He bound them together with Mira's earlier comment about the store having trouble competing with larger businesses and tucked them away to revisit soon. Tonight—*this morning*—was his and Mira's.

An hour later, Matt and Mira pulled into Bayside Resorts, the resort community her brothers owned. It was larger than Seaside, which had only a handful of cottages that had been owned by the same families for generations, a small recreation center, and a pool. Bayside Resorts had at least three times as many cottages of varying sizes, a restaurant, pool, tennis courts, a recreation center, and gorgeous views of Cape Cod Bay.

"This is great. I'd heard your brothers were fixing it up." Matt's oldest brother, Pete, owned a cottage at Seaside and a house on the bay just down the beach from Bayside Resorts.

"Drake and Rick bought it with their friend Dean Masters. They're all working hard to make it beautiful again."

As Matt drove through the community, he took in the renovations being done to the recreation center, the pool, tennis courts, and lush gardens throughout.

"They're making headway. The gardens are gorgeous."

"That's all Dean. He's got a gift for foliage. Follow the gravel road around the rec center." Mira pointed and yawned. "I'm sorry. I'm so embarrassed about falling asleep."

He reached for her hand across the console. "Don't be. It gave me a chance to strip you down and take dirty pictures, which Sawyer and I posted on MILF websites."

She laughed and swatted his arm. "That's not very appropriate coming from a professor."

"I told you I'm not—"

"A professor for the next three months. I know. But that doesn't give you free rein to turn into a teenager."

He couldn't resist waggling his brows and teasing her again. "You know what they say about teenage boys. They can go all night."

She laughed. "When you went on sabbatical, did you leave your adult brain behind?"

He was beginning to wonder that himself. Mira had that effect on him, making him feel freer, younger, more playful than he had in a very long time.

As he pulled up to her cottage, he said, "You're right. Sorry. I haven't slept in…" He looked at the clock on the dashboard. "Almost two full days."

"Seriously?"

"I had a lot of packing to do, and then I was lucky enough to spend an amazing night with this really sexy woman." He parked the car in front of her adorable cottage. Yellow shutters and flower boxes billowing with colorful blooms beneath each window accented weathered-gray cedar siding. The small yard was well kept, with typical Cape Cod sand and grass in the front and pockets of pretty gardens. It was easy to imagine Mira and Hagen strolling through the community to the pool, or hanging out down at the bay. He felt an unfamiliar longing to share in those moments.

Matt came around the car and helped her out. "Nice cottage."

"Thanks. It has a great view of the water." She yawned again. "I'm sorry. I'm usually in bed by nine thirty."

"Damn, you should have told me. I would have totally been up for that."

"Matt," she whispered.

She nibbled on her lower lip, and it cut straight to his heart. Sometime over the evening he realized that coming home had as much to do with Mira as it did with his family. He didn't want to rush her or make her feel uncomfortable, but he *wanted* her, and he wasn't about to pretend he didn't.

He slid his hand beneath her hair and massaged her shoulder, loving the moan it incited.

"It's almost eight. There's no way you'll be awake enough to hang out with Hagen. He'll probably want to talk about his first overnight adventure in exorbitant detail. Why don't you take a nap and I'll hang out here and write on the deck, spend time with Hagen, and then after you wake up, we can go get your car."

She unlocked the front door, and he followed her inside.

"I can't do that." She yawned again, her eyes wide with embarrassment.

"You can, and you will." He took in her cozy wine-colored sofa and colorful accent pillows, which matched the floral curtains. A wooden rocking chair sat beside the window with a paperback on the cushion. The coffee table was home to a laptop and two binders, as well as several *National Geographic* magazines, a book titled *Boat Building 101*, and a stack of Boxcar mysteries. *Hagen.* The kitchen was outfitted with white cabinets with yellow handles, matching her sunny disposition. The whole cottage felt very feminine. Very *Mira.*

"Matt, you need to sleep as much as I do." She yawned again, and he couldn't resist pulling her into his arms.

"Is that an invitation?"

"Not when Hagen's going to be here soon."

"Oh, the possibilities you've just left open." Her cheeks flushed, and he added, "Really, sunshine. I usually make do with only a few hours' sleep. Go take a nap. I'll go home and crash for the afternoon after we get your car."

"But I can take a nap while Hagen plays."

"He's going to be excited about his night out, and I'd like to see him anyway. I missed him these last few weeks, too." He was looking forward to hearing about Hagen's first sleepover. He'd lived with updates via texts for long enough. This was so much better.

"Really?" Mira asked tentatively. "He'll be over the moon. He adores you, but you've already gone above and beyond what a good friend should do. You've given me a night I'll never forget."

"Then let me give you more." He cradled her beautiful face in his hands. His entire body flamed with anticipation. "We never got our one kiss, and a kiss good night seems fitting, even if it's in the morning."

"Yes," she whispered breathlessly.

His heart sprinted toward the finish line, but he was in no hurry to take his first taste, a taste he'd remember forever. He brushed his thumb over her lower lip, and her needful sounds made everything sizzle—the air around them, the surface of his skin, the thick rod between his legs. He followed the curve of her lips with his tongue as he'd been dying to do all night, and she closed her eyes. *That's it, baby. Give yourself over to me.* He kissed the corner of her mouth, then the center of her upper lip, savoring every second as her breathing hitched and her fingers pressed into his sides. The anticipation was killing him, but he *had* to take a moment to look at her face, free from all worry, her soft, smooth skin flushed with desire. She was stunning, and when he closed his eyes tonight, this was the picture he'd remember. Mira, surrendering to their passion. She made a whimpering noise in the back of her throat, sending spikes of heat down his spine, and he couldn't wait another second. He kissed her softly at first, allowing their mouths to adjust, their tongues to find their way to that slow, drugging stride. He wanted this kiss to fill her dreams, to stay with her until she woke, and to tug at her throughout her days. He wanted this kiss to be the beginning of many, many more.

CHAPTER FIVE

MIRA BOLTED UPRIGHT in her bed and grabbed her phone. *Two o'clock? Shit.* She'd told herself she'd only sleep for an hour. She hurried into the bathroom to brush her teeth and wash her face, listening intently for Hagen and Matt. She looked like she hadn't slept in a week! She quickly ran a brush through her hair, washed up, put on a little blush so she didn't scare Matt away, and took care of her bathroom needs. She scrubbed her armpits with a washcloth—a shower would have to wait—and five minutes later, donning a clean sundress and a little perfume, she went in search of her little man.

And my big man.

Her mind careened back to their kiss. She could live forever with the memory of that one perfect kiss.

A breeze swept through the screen door that led to the deck, and she heard Matt's voice. She peered outside, but didn't see Matt or Hagen. She crossed the deck and saw them sitting on the dunes side by side—with Serena and Drake. Great. They'd probably already interrogated Matt.

She crossed the warm sand, hoping they hadn't completely scared him off—or turned him on, considering Serena looked like Rachel McAdams. Mira and Serena had grown up together, and when her brothers needed someone to temporarily manage the resort, Serena, who was between jobs, had been the perfect choice. She could be tough as nails or sweet as pie, depending on what a situation called for, and unlike most women, she didn't fawn all over Mira's handsome brothers. She'd gotten that out of her system when they were teenagers.

As Mira approached, Serena turned and mouthed, *I love him*, making Mira even more nervous.

Hagen jumped to his feet and darted across the sand. "Mommy!" His brown hair stood up every which way, and his normally serious blue eyes—the one physical trait he had of his father's—were gleaming with joy.

Matt rose to his feet with a warm and alluring smile, looking even more gorgeous in the light of day than he did last night. His hair was tousled, as if he'd run his hands through it. His cut had scabbed over and a peppering of whiskers had darkened on his chiseled cheeks, adding an edge to his normally clean-cut appearance. The sight of him brought goose bumps to her flesh.

Hagen launched himself into her arms, pulling her from her reverie.

"Hi, baby. Did you have fun?" She carried him to where Matt and the others were standing as Hagen chattered on about his slumber party.

"We had pizza and watched the movie *Robots* and stayed up until ten o'clock! Matt's going to make a robot with me. We got all the stuff, and Uncle Drake said he was jealous because no one taught him to make robots when he was my age. I wanted to build a boat, but Matt said I had to wait until he learned some things from Pete. Matt's going to talk to Pete, and maybe one day we'll build a boat with Pete's help. That's okay, right, Mom? You know Pete. He's nice, like Matt. We ate peanut butter and jelly sandwiches for lunch, and guess what?"

His chirpy voice was music to Mira's ears. He and Matt were going to make a robot? How? When? Matt was watching Hagen with the sweetest smile she'd ever seen, and her heart melted. "What, baby?"

"He likes chunky peanut butter like me," Hagen said proudly.

"I'll be sure to stock up."

Matt met her gaze and *sweet* turned to blazing heat. She caught an appreciative grin from Serena and a serious, though approving, look from Drake.

Hagen wiggled free from her arms and plopped down on the sand with a book. "Me and Matt were reading *All About Robots*, but Uncle Drake and Serena wanted to talk."

Matt leaned in close, eyed Hagen, and stopped short of kissing her cheek, squeezing her hand instead. His thoughtfulness stirred a swarm of butterflies in her stomach.

"Morning, sunshine," he said. "Hope you slept okay."

"Sunshine!" Hagen giggled. "He called you that at Grayson's!"

"I *love* the nickname," Serena said. Hugging Mira, she whispered, "Smart, great with Hagen, and I totally approve. If you don't go out with this man, I might."

"No," Mira said too fast and too loud. Her brother and Matt gave her quizzical looks. "Um, I mean, no thanks, Serena. Matt's going to take me to get my car."

Matt stifled a laugh, but not the knowing grin that told her his ears were buzzing. "Drake and I already picked it up."

"Um," was the brilliant response that popped out of her mouth. *You took care of Hagen and picked up my car?*

"Her mind's still fuzzy from sleep," Serena said in an attempt to save her.

Hardly. Lust maybe.

"Did Hagen do okay?" she asked.

Hagen called out, "Yes."

"He was fine," Matt reassured her. "I had to let him peek in on you to see that you were really sleeping, and once he did, we got right into guy stuff."

Hagen looked up at Matt with a wide smile, and Matt winked. *Guy stuff.* Hagen obviously loved being included as a *guy* instead of a *boy*. She wanted to give Matt a big kiss for that, but that would have to wait until a certain *guy* wasn't watching.

Mira turned her attention to Drake and Serena. At six two, with dark wavy hair and eyes the color of night, both of her brothers were mirror images of the young man their father had once been. Although Rick could be a hothead, Drake had a calm, confident demeanor, much like her son. Except today Hagen seemed like he might burst with excitement over building a robot.

"Did you guys give Matt the third degree?"

"Didn't have to," Drake said. "I know his brother Pete, and you work for his father. How bad could he be?"

"Matt's not bad," Hagen insisted.

"Thanks, buddy," Matt said. "He's just watching out for your mom, who looks beautiful today, by the way."

Wow, good answer.

Hagen giggled at that, too.

"I might have asked him a few questions," Serena admitted. "You know, just standard stuff, like where he lives, what he does for a living, and does he have any hot, single brothers."

As if Mira hadn't already shared all that information with her bestie multiple times over the past few months.

"I told her I'm the only single one left," Matt said.

"Which appears to be debatable," Serena said under her breath.

Debatable? No, he's definitely not available, thank you very much.

"Matt said you went *dancing*?" Drake knew what Mira's life was like—Hagen, work, Hagen, more work—and she could see that he was happy that she'd gone out and had some fun. When he or Rick watched Hagen, she and Serena usually hung out and watched movies, or went out to dinner, but they never went dancing.

"We did go dancing, and we watched the sunrise." Thinking about last night, and that magical kiss, she looked at Matt and said, "It was a perfect night, but I slept much longer than I intended to just now. I'm so sorry."

"I'm glad you got some rest. Hagen and I had a good time."

Hagen reached up and took Matt's hand. "Can we read this now, please?"

Hagen had taken to Matt instantly last summer, and all the times in between. She was glad nothing had changed.

"Hey, buddy," Drake said. "Maybe you should give Matt a break."

Her brothers had been her son's role models since the day he was born, and she wondered if it bothered Drake to see Hagen so taken with Matt. If it did, he wasn't showing it.

Matt lowered himself to the sand beside Hagen. "That's okay. I promised we'd get through what we could before I had to leave. We'll read one chapter, and then I've got to get home and fix my shower. Deal?"

She'd forgotten about his broken shower. He probably had a million other things to do, too, and yet here he sat with her son, with the patience of a saint.

Hagen nodded emphatically. "Deal."

Drake came to Mira's side and lowered his voice. "It's about time you went out and had fun, but next time maybe give me a heads-up?" She and Drake were close, as he'd stepped in as the male head of household when they'd lost their father. But lately, between the resort renovations and planning the opening of his fifth music store, she and Drake barely had time to catch up. Drake had always been into music. He, Rick, and their friends had formed a band years ago, and still played together. His love of instruments was what led him to open his chain of East Coast music stores, and now that he and Rick had bought the resort, he was on the hunt for a new location.

Serena rolled her eyes. "Doofus over here saw Matt's car this morning and his big-brother briefs got all knotted up. I calmed him with the promise of fresh coffee and doughnuts."

"Thank you," Mira said.

Serena grabbed Drake's arm and dragged him away. "You guys have fun. This one has to get on the phone with the contractor and raise a little h-e-l-l."

"Aw, Serena said a bad word!" Hagen called out.

"Do you have to be so smart?" Serena teased.

Hagen grinned. "Mommy says smart boys are the best kind of boys there are."

Matt met her gaze, and she swore the earth moved.

Boy, was Mommy ever right.

DESPITE HOW TIRED he was, Matt hated leaving Mira and Hagen. He'd forgotten how nice it was to be around an inquisitive child rather than surrounded by adults competing for head of the class. Hagen reminded him of himself as a boy. He'd wanted to know all the details about everything they read, and he seemed to catalog it and think about it, bringing it up long after they'd finished reading. And he knew that was all Mira's doing. A confident, inquisitive child was the result of strong, loving parenting.

He stepped from his car and heard, "Matt's here!"

Jenna, his sister-in-law, hurried across the quad—the community area between the cottages—with his adorable almost three-year-old niece, Bea, named for their mother, in her arms. Bea looked just like Jenna, with shiny brown hair that curled at the ends, big blue eyes, and even at her young age, a love of organization. She sorted her toys by color like Jenna matched accessories to her outfits.

Three of Jenna's sundress-wearing girlfriends, also cottage owners, appeared from different directions, descending upon him like ravenous gossipmongers. Obviously Sky had already spread the news of his night with Mira.

"Ladies," he said cautiously.

"We want the scoop." Bella, a ballsy blonde who was known for playing pranks and getting to the heart of matters in ten seconds or less, stepped onto the deck.

"Of course you do." Matt chuckled.

Amy, the quietest of the group, poked him in the stomach. "You didn't come home last night."

"Sorry, Mom."

Leanna, a feisty brunette jam maker, joined them with her pet labradoodle, Pepper, at her heels. "Hi, Matt."

"Hi." He crouched and loved up Pepper. What on earth made him think he should rent here at gossip central? In ten minutes they will have asked him a hundred questions, and by nightfall half of Wellfleet would know he and Mira had gone out.

Hm, maybe that's not such a bad idea.

"Unca Matt!" Bea reached for him with a toothy grin.

He lifted his niece into his arms and kissed her chubby cheek. "How's my favorite girl?"

Bea giggled and patted his cheeks with her hands. "Can I have a cookie?"

It seemed like she'd hardly known any words the last time he was home, and it struck him that he'd already missed too much of her life. He didn't want to be the uncle who missed out on everything. He just wasn't sure he knew how to step back from the career he'd worked so hard to build, or live a more carefree life like his brothers and sister did. He'd never been a carefree guy, but hell if he hadn't enjoyed every second of last night. He'd waited almost a year to spend real, meaningful time with Mira and one evening had only whet his appetite.

He looked at Jenna, who said, "She's had two already. No more cookies, sweetie."

Bea stuck out her lower lip.

"Aww," Amy and Matt said in unison.

"She's got you wrapped around her little finger, just like she does Pete." Jenna took pouty Bea from Matt and set her on the deck to play with Pepper. Pepper licked her cheeks, and she squealed with delight.

Everyone had thought Pete would be a strict father since he was so protective of Jenna and Bea, but when it came to Bea asking for things, he was a pushover. Even after just a few hours with Hagen, Matt could see how easy it would be to want to give a child everything. Hagen was so eager to learn, Matt could have stayed with him all day. That is, if he wouldn't have toppled over with fatigue.

He didn't have the stamina to get into gossip right now, either.

"You look tired," Bella observed. "Didn't you get *any* sleep last night?"

"No, as a matter of fact, I didn't."

Their faces lit up with interest. Matt laughed and shook his head. "But not for the reasons you dirty-minded scoundrels think. Jenna, is Pete around?"

"Yeah. He's fixing our sink," Jenna answered.

Matt headed in the direction of their cottage.

"Wait," Jenna called after him. "Why didn't you get any sleep if you weren't being a scoundrel?"

The girls and Pepper trailed behind him as he crossed the quad. He didn't think they expected an answer, though he knew they'd probably hammer him with questions until he gave them *something* to talk about.

He escaped their inquisition and walked into Pete and Jenna's cottage. His brother popped out from beneath the sink. Joey, his female golden retriever, trotted out of the bedroom with an excited *woof*.

"Hey, Pete. I need to talk to you about Dad." Thinking about his shower, he added, "And I need to borrow some tools."

Matt crouched to pet Joey, who slathered his face with doggy kisses.

Pete wiped his hands on his shorts, eyeing the girls out on the deck. "Sure. What's up?" He grabbed his toolbox and handed it to Matt. "Take whatever you need."

Matt rifled through the tools. "Has anyone talked with Dad about how the store is doing lately? Mira said something about his being unable to compete with big businesses." Grayson and

Parker were in California this week for an event for the children's foundation Parker started, and Hunter had been swamped with a commissioned piece of artwork for Grunter's Ironworks, the metalworking business he and Grayson owned. Matt hoped to check in with them soon, but he knew Pete would have heard if there was an issue.

"I don't think Grayson or Hunter have, and Sky's been pretty busy with her tattoo shop, so I doubt she'd be focused on much else. I haven't, although I know he's tried cutting prices recently. Is she worried? And more importantly, does she think he's drinking again?" Pete leaned against the counter and crossed his arms. Their father had fallen into the bottle after their mother died, and though it had taken a long time, Pete had gotten him into rehab, and he'd been clean ever since.

"No. She didn't say anything about him drinking. And it was just an offhanded comment about him being too stubborn to admit that there were issues. I'll talk to her and see what I can find out. I just wanted to see if you had heard anything." The last thing Matt wanted to do was get involved with his father's business, but his father had worked his whole life to build Lacroux Hardware *for them*. He didn't want to see all his years of hard work and dedication go down the drain because his father didn't want to face the changing world. His father's world had changed enough when they'd lost their mother. He didn't need the business crumbling down around him, too.

"Sounds good. Let me know if you want me to step in." Pete's lips quirked up. "You and Mira, huh? Sky called Jenna bright and early."

"I bet she did." Matt rubbed the ache of fatigue in the back of his neck. "We had a great night. I had forgotten what it was like to…" *What? Go out with an amazing woman? Cut loose for a night?* Yes, but those weren't the biggest things he noticed. Usually when he was out, he was on high alert, watching out for everyone around him, but last night his only concern was Mira, and today he'd felt the same way about Hagen, just as he had each time they'd been together over the past year.

Pete cleared his throat, as if to remind Matt he was expecting an answer. Joey curled up at his feet with a huff.

"I had forgotten how it felt to be with someone special," he finally answered.

"Maybe you should have taken this sabbatical sooner instead of dicking around with an afternoon together every few months."

He'd had a hard time figuring out the right time to take a break from teaching. On top of that, he'd known that spending any extended amount of time with Mira would make it even harder for him to return to the life he was no longer sure he wanted in New Jersey. He'd known he needed to make some big decisions *before* seeing her again. With his hopes of becoming dean put to rest, he was ready to give his all to the book—and to Mira.

"I couldn't have," he said to Pete. "I had too much to wrap up. Between teaching, overseeing grad students, and my research, I worked every day until I was ready to drop."

"Grayson told me about his visit," Pete said with the older brother fess-up seriousness he'd perfected over the years.

Matt ground his teeth together. When their younger brother had visited him, Matt had arrived late, looking like he'd just been in a fight, which he had, after stopping a carjacking. "Gray's got a big mouth. On the *rare* occasions I had a free evening, I might have helped a few people."

His brother knew him too well to believe the simple confession. The truth was, in the little free time he'd had, Matt had gone to the seedier parts of town seeking a way to release his pent-up frustrations—taking down drug dealers, car thieves, and bastards who beat on women were his go-to late-night activities since college. But as his brothers and sister had each fallen in love, it had become harder and harder to pretend he wasn't missing out on what he'd secretly always wanted. The more he'd thought about what he really wanted in life, the more unfulfilling the things he was doing became. He'd been nearing his breaking point for quite some time, and when the economics article he wrote for the *New York Times* went viral and he was offered a major book deal, he knew it was time to reevaluate his life.

"Is that what you tell yourself, Matt? You might have *helped* a few people?"

Matt shrugged, having zero interest in talking about this.

Pete put a hand on his shoulder, the way he had throughout Matt's entire life. Pete had always been his stabilizing force, even in the most difficult of times.

"Matt, you put your life in jeopardy like you're Clark Fucking Kent. You're a mild-mannered professor during the day and a secret savior at night. How long are you going to torture yourself?"

Matt scrubbed a hand down his face. He'd been asking himself that for the past two years, and he still didn't have an answer. Guilt was a powerful thing, and Matt was a master at carrying it around like winter layers. He piled the guilt of not being home when his mother passed away on top of the horrible event that had changed his life—the one he'd never admitted to anyone other than Pete and hated admitting to himself. The night he'd been too bogged down with studies to meet a friend as he'd promised, and his friend had been attacked while walking alone on her way to her dorm. She'd never returned to school after that night.

"When you're done saving the world," Pete said, "we'll all be waiting for you to come home."

They stared at each other for a long moment. Pete wasn't being judgmental. Hell, he never was. Matt knew it killed his brother to know he was out there putting himself in harm's way. How many times had he gotten texts from Pete in the middle of the night—*Haven't heard from you in days. Just tell me you're still alive.*

"That's what I'm counting on," Matt finally answered. "I've got some major decisions to make. The advance for the book deal is enough for me to live on for three years, plus I have my savings, which is another two years at least. With the lecture circuit they're talking about setting up after publication, I'll be more than fine financially. I just don't know if I can do it."

"Write the book?"

"No. Step away from teaching for good. Give up on becoming the dean of the School of Social Sciences." Matt thrived on knowledge, and teaching had given him the opportunity to help others do the same. Every day presented a new challenge, and if he made a difference in the lives of even a few students, it was all the inspiration he needed to continue. But recently, as more of his teaching was guided by administration, wading through red tape had become exhausting. When he stood in front of the classroom, he saw himself at their age, felt the hope of the *past* and the desire for a different type of future.

"You said that guy was never stepping down, so that should be the easiest piece of the puzzle." Pete arched a brow. "And can you step down from the other?"

The other. Clark Fucking Kent. Hell if he knew. Matt shrugged noncommittally. That seemed like an even more difficult habit to break.

"That's what this sabbatical is for, right? Figuring out what you really want to be when you grow up?" Pete smiled and pointed to the cut on Matt's cheek. "Please tell me that didn't happen when you were with Mira."

"Nah. It happened in the shower. By the way, I promised Hagen we'd think about building a boat together, but I was thinking about starting with a raft. I'd love your help."

"Sounds good to me. You know that little brainiac will be telling us how to build it in no time. He's like you in that way. Cute as hell and smart enough to put some adults to shame. Give the kid a book and he'll figure out a better way to do things in no time."

Matt laughed. "Yeah. He's cool like that." He picked up the tools he needed and was hit with a wave of gratitude. Pete had come *home* after college. He'd refinished boats with their father. He'd held down the fort, taken care of Sky, and watched over their brothers at a time when Matt had been too entrenched with building his career and gaining tenure to be involved as closely as he should have been.

He set down the tools and embraced Pete. "Thanks, man."

"What for?"

"For sticking around, being here for the family while I was off building my career." He picked up the tools again, gave Joey a pat on the head, and pushed open the door.

"Unca Matt!" Bea squealed.

"Details, please," Jenna said.

"*Great*," Matt mumbled under his breath. He looked over his shoulder at Pete. "And for running interference for me."

Pete pushed from the counter. "I'm on it. They're just excited to add another hen and her offspring to the party. They adore Mira and Hagen." He patted Matt's shoulder on the way out the door.

Matt followed him out, and the girls swarmed. Joey and Pepper ran into the grass.

"When are you seeing Mira again?" Jenna asked, keeping pace with Matt's quick steps.

"Why on earth did you *behave*?" Bella quipped. "Don't you know she *needs* a scoundrel in her life? All women do!"

"Bella!" Amy chided her.

Matt shook his head without responding. He loved them all, even if they were chaos personified, but that didn't change the fact that this chaos was a world away from the quiet academic life he was used to. His mind traveled to Mira, reminding him that the quiet academic life wasn't all that he wanted any longer. He envisioned her here with the girls, laughing and carrying on, while Hagen played with the dogs or helped Pete fix the sink, because that boy's curiosity knew no limits, and it made Matt want to be right in the thick of it.

He definitely needed to get some sleep. He was supposed to be outlining his book, not fantasizing about a beautiful woman and her adorable son.

"We'll babysit," Leanna said, and Matt stopped cold.

The girls circled him, wide-eyed and eager, except Bella, who squinted with a serious look in her eyes.

"For a little juicy gossip," Bella offered.

Matt laughed and looked at Pete, who was busy giving Bea Eskimo kisses.

"Way to run interference, bro."

"I got sidetracked." Pete blew against Bea's cheek, making

her giggle hysterically.

Matt took a deep breath and faced the girls again. "What makes you think we need a babysitter? I like spending time with Hagen."

"Of course you do, but you can't exactly get amorous with him around." Bella pointed toward the pool where her husband, Caden, was holding their daughter, Summer. Tony and Kurt, Amy and Leanna's husbands, were also in the pool with their toddlers, Hannah and Sloan.

"Trust us," Bella said. "We know how valuable babysitters are."

She had a point, but Hagen was Mira's world, and the last thing he wanted to do was rock that boat—or *plan* to take things further. No matter how badly he wanted to be intimate with Mira, he preferred it to be a natural progression, not a scheduled event.

"Come on, Matt. We want to see you both happy. Give us some hope," Jenna pleaded. "Are you going to see her again?"

He was no match for their inquiring minds. "Okay, fine. Yes, I hope to."

"You *hope* to?" Amy tucked her golden hair behind her ear with a curious gaze. "That doesn't sound like you. Since when do you *hope* and not make things happen?"

"Look, I haven't slept in two days, I need to fix my shower, and you're making me question why I came to stay at the Real Housewives of Seaside instead of my nice quiet cottage on Nantucket. *Yes*, okay? If I have it my way, I'll see her tomorrow, and the next day, and the next."

As he walked away, he heard the girls whispering.

"We prefer to be called the 'Seaside girls,'" Bella called after him. "We're way cooler than the Real Housewives of *Any-*

where."

He lifted his hand and waved without turning around, lest they see his wide grin.

"FYI, you're here because you love it here," Jenna added. "And you're *family*. You *belong* here."

CHAPTER SIX

"HEY, SQUIRT." SERENA breezed through the doors of Mira's cottage Sunday morning carrying a big brown bag. She set the bag on the counter, sighed loudly, as if the bag were heavy, and tossed her hair over her shoulder before leaning down to kiss Hagen on the top of his head. "Figuring out how to overtake Bill Gates?"

"Who's Bill Gates?" Hagen glanced up from the robot book he was flipping through with a perplexed expression. "We're building the robot today."

"Are we, now?" Serena turned to Mira, who was making pancakes, and lowered her voice. "I came as soon as I got your SOS text. I'm so excited about Professor Hotness coming over. I brought *everything*."

Mira wondered what *everything* could possibly be. She hadn't been out of the dating scene for that long, had she? Were there accoutrements she wasn't aware of?

"I'm a nervous wreck."

"Don't be. I'll get you up to dating speed in no time. Feed the little scientist so we can get started."

Mira set a plate of pancakes and a glass of juice on the table. "Ready to eat, Hag?"

"Uh-huh." He carried the book to the table and opened it beside his plate. "Is it almost ten? I need Matt. I can't understand some of these words."

I need him, too.

She'd secretly worried that after they'd both gotten some rest, and some distance, they'd realize what happened was a mistake and write it off to the allure of the evening. But then he'd called a little after eleven o'clock last night—*I won't keep you up, sunshine, but I wanted to hear your voice.* He'd asked about Hagen, and they'd made plans for Matt to come over and build the robot with him. It was a simple two-minute phone call, and it put all her worries to rest.

Until this morning, when she realized *he was coming over.*

"We'll be in Mommy's bedroom if you need us, squirt." Serena grabbed the bag from the counter.

With a mouthful of pancakes and his eyes on his book, Hagen nodded.

"I knew you were holding out for Matt all these months," Serena whispered on the way to the bedroom. "You could have fessed up. I'm your best friend. It's not like I didn't notice how googly-eyed you got every time you talked about him."

"I did not."

"You did! And really, how many guys asked you out before him? You've turned down at least, what? A dozen guys? Then Matt spends one night with you and your vibrator has a new nickname."

"Ohmygod. Shut up!" *It had that nickname way before our midnight adventure.*

Serena laughed. "It's true. You've been hooked on him since last summer. So…it's only natural that you're ready to move to the head of the class and bang the professor."

Mira groaned. "Stop, please. Yes, I like him. A *lot*. He's my kind of guy. He's smart and funny and—"

"Hot as Hades?"

"Yeah," she said with a sigh. "There is that."

Serena dumped the bag in the middle of Mira's bed, and Mira began looking through the items. Makeup, perfume, clothing, Nair…

"Nair? That stuff smells worse than death."

"Trust me, you do not need razor stubble down there, and waxing hurts like a bitch. You want to be bare as Nair."

"What? I need to get rid of *all* my hair? Like a prepubescent child? What could possibly be sexy about that?" She'd shaved pretty closely down there already, leaving just a small tuft of curls. Did she really have to go bare?

Serena rolled her eyes. "Do you like pubes in *your* throat?"

"Ew! Serena!" She was used to hearing about Serena's random escapades, but it had been so long since she'd had her own to talk about, it brought this to an excruciatingly embarrassing level.

"What? You blew what's his name. Did he have hair down there?" She picked up a box of condoms and tossed it to Mira.

Mira dropped the Nair and caught the condoms, then frantically shoved the box under her pillow. "God, you're so raunchy. I don't remember what he had *down there*. I tried very hard to forget everything about him."

"I know, but really, Mira. Do you think a guy wants to wade through a forest to get to the promised land?"

Mira sank down to the bed.

Serena sat beside her, took her hand, and said, "Sweetheart, sometimes when a man and a woman spend a lot of time together, they get these tingly feelings."

They both burst out laughing.

"Tingly feelings? Really? Is that how your mom explained

it?"

"Are you kidding? Mother Teresa? She pretended sex didn't exist. Everything I learned came from hands-on experience. You know that. I shared them all with you."

"Another thing I tried to forget," she teased. "Seriously, though. I don't need condoms. You know I've been on the pill since Hagen was born. I wasn't about to leave *that* up to chance again."

"Diseases, baby. Use the condoms."

"Right. Between making a robot and serving lunch, me and Matt will find time to *do it*." The prospect of sex with Matt seemed impossible. She pushed the Nair under the pillow with the condoms. She didn't want to think about being bare as a baby any more than she wanted to think about having condoms. She hated the idea of planning sex.

"Mom?" Hagen called from the hallway.

Mira scrambled to cover up the loot Serena brought, and Serena laughed. "There's nothing sexual in there. I left the toys at home."

Hagen appeared in the doorway with his book and an ample amount of syrup on his shirt. "Can you tell me what a 'com-plant' robot is?" He handed her the book and peered between them at the bulky covers. "What's that?"

"Girl stuff," Serena said, as if that would satisfy Mr. Inquisitive.

"What kind of girl stuff? Mom has a bathroom full of girl stuff. Makeup, lotion, deodorant with flowers on it that smells like lemons."

Mira laughed. "Just clothes and makeup, honey. Nothing important. And this word is 'compliant.' A compliant robot would be a robot that behaves and follows instructions, but I think they're referring to a much different type of robot than the one you and Matt are going to build."

"That's okay. One day I'll build a compliant robot." Peering around her again, he reached toward the crooked pillow. "What's under thi—"

Serena dove on the pillow. "That's my secret girl stuff that isn't for little boys to see."

Mira covered her face with her hands, knowing what was coming next.

"Mom said we can't keep secrets. She says secrets are like lies, and lies turn good people into bad people. Mom says…"

Ten very long minutes was how long it took to sidetrack her curious boy. It took only half that time for Mira to decide that mothers were hypocrites. A hard pill to swallow.

Hagen went into the other room to play, and Mira flopped onto her back beside Serena, who was still lying across the pillow. "How am I going to manage this?"

"Hello? I babysit."

She turned toward her friend. "No, I mean *this. Everything.* Hagen's going to ask questions I'm not prepared to answer. And I can't have condoms in the house. What if he finds them? How do other single mothers do this?" She bolted upright. "I'm doomed to either a sexless life or lying to my son about where I am or what I'm doing, aren't I?"

"It's not like you're a serial killer. All moms have sex, and not telling your son about your sex life isn't lying. Ew. No child wants to know about that. You're a beautiful, sexy woman. You can't deny yourself this."

"Trust me, denying myself the man I've fantasized about for so long isn't something I want to do. I just don't know how to navigate dating and being a mother and working. There's no time as it is."

"You'll find the time. You did last night."

Mira gave her a deadpan look. "What about the rest of it? I haven't, *you know*, since I got pregnant with Hagen."

"I know. I've been trying to get you to get your sexy on for a long time. Sex is like eating cake," she said reassuringly. "You stress over wanting it, but when you're devouring it, nothing is more decadent. Afterward there might be a little guilt, or maybe you'll be angry at yourself for giving in to the lifeguard in the changing room at the beach..."

"Serena!" Mira laughed.

"Oh yeah, that was me. It could happen to you, too, you know. Anyway, you might feel all sorts of things, but with the *right* man, the biggest thing you'll feel is wanting to do it again."

Serena pushed from the bed and grabbed the box of condoms, and from beneath the covers, a tube of lube that Mira hadn't seen. Mira's eyes nearly bugged out of her head.

"Lube?" she whispered. "I'm not menopausal, you know."

"Anal," Serena said casually.

"Serena," Mira whispered. "Did you even hear what I said? I haven't had sex in *years*. Do you really think I'm going to go *there*? Do *you* go there?"

"Don't be a prude. With the right guy I would." Serena grabbed her hand and tugged her toward the bathroom. "Come on. Remember my high school hiding place? Even Hagen the detective can't find them there."

Serena climbed up on the sink and set the box of condoms on top of the cabinet. Out of sight, yes, but somehow Mira knew they would never be out of mind with Matt around.

"Now," Serena said as she jumped down to the floor. "Let's

get started on your 'aren't-I-sexy' attire."

Serena wanted her to wear a dress—*for easy access, in case you get time alone*—but it made Mira feel like she was dressing to get Matt to make a move, and she was already nervous enough about wanting him to do just that. They settled on a blousy purple spaghetti-strap top, a cute pair of denim shorts, and leather sandals. Serena insisted she wear dangling earrings, a necklace on a long chain, and an armful of bangle bracelets, which jingled like bells around a cat's neck with every step.

"I feel overdressed for a day of robot building."

"You're just not used to looking like a woman instead of a mom. You look sexy and sweet, which is exactly what you are, so *own* it." Serena hugged her and patted Hagen on the head on her way to the front door. "Good luck with your robot, mini-man."

Mira spent the next twenty minutes contemplating Nair, lube, and condoms, all of which made her both excited and really, *really* nervous.

A knock on the door sent her heart into a panic.

"Matt!" Hagen leapt from the couch and ran for the door— and Mira slipped off the bracelets.

"YOU'RE *FINALLY* HERE!" Hagen grabbed Matt's hand and pulled him inside right past Mira, and didn't stop pulling him until they were standing in front of the table where he'd spread out the pieces of the build-your-own-robot kit. "Are those flowers for my mom?"

Mira flashed an apologetic smile. "Hagen, don't be so pushy, honey."

Matt raked his eyes down Mira's body. How was he supposed to concentrate on building a robot with her prancing around in a pair of skimpy shorts that made him want to run his hands up the length of her long, lean legs?

"Yes, buddy. These are for your mom, but I brought you something, too." He reached into his back pocket and withdrew a piece of paper with a website address on it and handed it to him.

"What's this?"

"That's where we're going to learn about what it takes to build a raft, which isn't quite a boat, but it's a start."

Hagen gasped and threw his arms around Matt's legs. "A raft! Mom, we're going to build a raft!"

"First we're going to research how to build a raft, so it might be a while before we actually build it."

Hagen blinked up at his mother, his blue eyes narrow and serious. "That's guy stuff, Mom. But we'll tell you about it."

Matt stifled a chuckle and placed a hand on his shoulder. "Buddy, a bit of advice. Don't push the woman who loves you out of your life. I bet your mom is excellent at research. You should probably give her the option to be part of the adventure instead of making the decision for her."

Hagen's little brows knitted. He gave one determined nod and said, "Okay. Mom, if you want to do research with us you can. But you probably won't want to help build it. That's guy stuff."

"Sounds perfect," she said sweetly. "Why don't you go put that paper someplace where you won't lose it."

Hagen ran down the hall and disappeared into his room.

Matt slid a hand around Mira's waist and drew her against him. She smelled incredible, and felt even better. "I missed you, and you look utterly delectable." He kissed her neck and took a step away when he heard Hagen running down the hall, handing her the bouquet.

"Thank you. They're gorgeous." She smelled the pretty flowers as Hagen came to her side. "Mm. They smell like mint."

"They're gloxinia."

"Ready?" Hagen said impatiently.

"Oh yeah. I'm ready." The innuendo in his voice was lost on the little boy, but Mira's eyes darkened. Last night's kiss had only made him hungry for more. Much, *much* more.

The three of them set to work at the table assembling the robot, but Matt's attention was divided as his leg brushed against Mira's, and she returned the secret touch, her leg pressing enticingly against his. Hagen and Matt read the instructions together, with Matt filling in all the bigger words Hagen had trouble with.

"How did you get to be such a good reader?" Matt asked.

"Mom says I was born reading," Hagen answered.

"He's always loved to read." Mira smiled at Hagen. "I think he learned to read because he was frustrated when I had to cook dinner, do laundry, or anything else that impeded his story time. He didn't ease into reading like most kids do. I swear he made up his mind that he wanted to read, and by the time he was five, he was reading *everything.*"

"Because I'm a smart boy," Hagen said without looking up from the pieces he and Matt were putting together.

Hagen asked dozens of questions, wanting to know why things worked and what would happen if they tried to put pieces together differently. Matt loved his inquisitive nature, and Mira was patient with him. She didn't respond with answers that were only appropriate for little boys. She went into detail, and Matt respected that. He liked that she didn't quash his curiosity. As a teacher, he could always tell which students had been encouraged to research and explore and which had been either stifled or handed answers their whole life.

As the afternoon progressed, Matt continually had to stop himself from reaching out to hold Mira's hand or stroke her cheek. He wasn't sure what she felt comfortable doing in front of Hagen, and assumed she would let him know. They'd exchanged heated glances, and when Mira got up from the table, she touched his shoulder or ran her fingers along his back, heightening his anticipation.

They had lunch on the deck, and when they came back inside, Hagen was determined to finish their project no matter how long it took.

"Mom," Hagen said as he climbed into his chair. "You can do your work while we finish."

"Work?" Matt asked, hoping their night out hadn't set her back too far. "On a Sunday?"

"I have a few bookkeeping clients I work with on the side. I usually do it while Hagen does his homework or when he's sleeping." She lowered her voice as Hagen settled in at the table and said, "I think that's his way of telling me you're *his* for a little while."

He wanted to kiss her so badly he could taste it. He shifted his eyes to Hagen, who was busy fitting two pieces of the robot together. Matt leaned in closer and whispered, "I'd rather be both of yours. And when the time's right, *just* yours for a very long, very passionate while."

CHAPTER SEVEN

LATER THAT EVENING, after an intense afternoon of robot building, they took the robot out onto the deck and tested it out. Hagen mastered the remote control in minutes, and the boxy little robot with bolts for eyes and stickers for the mouth and nose was cruising along—and stopping at each gap between the decking boards.

"*Ugh*!" Hagen picked up the robot for the umpteenth time, and he plopped down on the deck with a sullen face.

"This isn't exactly the best place to use the robot, is it?" Matt crouched beside Hagen, who shook his head. "Where do you think would be a better place?"

"A road," he answered.

"Hm. That doesn't sound very safe, and the roads around here are gravel, so that won't work."

Mira was about to make a suggestion when Matt lifted his gaze and winked. She smiled, understanding that even after a long day of answering Hagen's questions and teaching him about all things electronic, Matt was still teaching.

Hagen's brow furrowed, and his little lips pressed together. Matt didn't rush him like other adults might. *Like I might.* He waited patiently for her little boy's very smart brain to figure it out.

"A parking lot is flat, right?" Hagen asked.

"Usually," Matt answered.

"The pier where we get ice cream is made of the same stuff," Hagen said, lifting his baby blues to Mira. "Cars don't drive on the pier. Could we try that?"

Mira and Matt both smiled. Matt arched a brow, deferring to her for the answer, which she found as endearing as his patience.

"Sure. If Matt doesn't mind."

Matt took Hagen's hand as he stood. "I think it's a fine idea. We can grab dinner at Mac's and eat while we test it out. What do you say, buddy? A celebratory dinner."

"Yay!" Hagen cheered. "I'm starved."

Forty minutes later, Hagen had scarfed down a hot dog from Mac's Seafood and was guiding the robot along the pavement at the Wellfleet Pier. Matt and Mira trailed a few steps behind, eating lobster rolls while they talked. The sun was just beginning to set, threading ribbons of pink across the horizon.

"Thank you for taking so much time with Hagen today."

Matt finished his last bite and tossed his paper plate in the trash. His hand came to rest on her lower back, warm and possessive. It was funny how much she missed his touch after just a few hours.

"He's a great kid. I don't know many six-year-olds, but I can't imagine most would sit still for that long."

"He's got a long attention span when he's interested. When he's not, it's a whole different story. But I feel guilty taking up your whole day. Don't you need to be writing?"

"I got up at five and wrote for several hours before coming over. I'm still in the research stage, so my writing is more planning, outlining, taking notes. At some point I'll probably have to head into Boston to visit the library there. The Cape libraries aren't quite as well stocked."

"The Boston library? That's on our list." Mira watched Hagen maneuver the robot around a young couple.

"Your list?"

"Mm-hm. Hagen loves libraries. We've never taken a real vacation. Mostly because of where we live." She gazed out at the sailboats in the distance, inhaled the salty bay air. "Sandy beaches, gorgeous sunsets. Hagen can run along the pier, go fishing, boating, swimming, or play inland. I've never felt like he was missing out on much. But he turned six in December, and I promised myself I'd do more to expand his horizons. I don't want him to grow up having never been off the Cape. So we made a list of four libraries we want to visit along the East Coast, and we're going to take a week and visit each of them. It's not Disney World, but it's something we'll both enjoy. That's why I took on the consulting work in the evenings. That money goes directly into an account for our trip."

"That sounds like quite a trip. Will he do okay in the car for that long?"

"He's a wonderful traveler. I get more restless than he does."

Music began playing in the distance, coming from the gazebo Matt's brother Grayson built for the community to use for outdoor concerts across the street from Mayo Beach.

"Mom! Matt! Watch!" Hagen maneuvered the robot and made it look like it was dancing. Its arms and legs moved up and down, and its body bent at the waist, then turned in a circle. He laughed and wiggled his butt like he was dancing, too. His hair stood on end from the breeze.

Mira tossed her paper plate in the trash and she and Matt clapped.

"You made one rockin' robot, baby."

"May I?" Matt offered a hand to Mira. When she took it, he began dancing in stiff movements like the robot, earning hysterical laughter from Hagen, who joined in on the fun.

"Look, Mom! We're all dancing!"

Matt pulled out his cell phone and snapped a few shots of her and Hagen, who hammed it up, making goofy faces.

"I think I found my new screensaver," Matt said with a wide smile as he fiddled with his phone. "I'm texting these and the pictures from the other night to you."

When they reached the end of the pier, they sat and talked while Hagen showed a group of kids his robot.

"Can I ask you a personal question?" Matt asked.

Her stomach fluttered nervously. "Sure."

Matt nodded toward Hagen. "His dad? Is he still involved in his life?"

She'd wondered when he'd get around to asking. "No." When she'd first had Hagen, people had asked her about Hagen's father all the time, and she'd thought about making up a story so she wouldn't feel weird when she answered. But after a while she realized it wasn't her who should feel weird about it. All she'd done was trust the wrong man.

"Do you think Hagen would mind if I held your hand?"

He couldn't possibly know how much his asking meant to her. "I don't think so. Thank you for considering him."

"He matters most in this equation. I'll always consider him." He brought her hand to his lips and pressed a kiss to it. "Were you married to his father?"

She shook her head. "No. He was married to another woman."

Matt's smile faltered a little, and she didn't blame him. She knew how it sounded.

"I didn't know he was married when we were dating, and when I found out, I broke up with him. It was right after college graduation. He lived in a neighboring town from my school, and we had been dating for a few months. I was busy with classes, so I never noticed the telltale signs of a cheater. He could only see me on certain nights, and he rarely stayed over." She paused as the familiar ache filled her.

She looked at Hagen, and Matt draped his arm around her shoulder. He didn't say a word, but he didn't have to. His support was evident in his actions.

"Two months later I found out I was pregnant. I told him, but he didn't want anything to do with the baby. He signed over all parental rights in exchange for my silence. After Hagen was born, I received a check for ten thousand dollars with a note that said, 'To tide you over until you're on your feet again.' I put that money in an account for Hagen's college and never heard from him again."

"That must have been very hurtful."

"Not for me, but for Hagen. I was so angry at being lied to that by the time I found out I was pregnant, I was over him. But Hagen has asked about him, and it's hard to lie to him."

Matt shifted his gaze to Hagen, his empathetic expression turning fiercely protective. "What have you told him?"

"I've tried to keep it vague, but you know Hagen. When he was younger I told him that some children have mommies and daddies and some have only one parent, and I loved him twice as much as any parent could." She laughed softly, remembering the day that no longer worked. "He bought that for a while, and then I told him the best truth I had. I said I didn't know where his daddy was, but that I was sure he loved him very much. I know he signed over all his rights, but I have to believe that part of him thinks about the child he's never met. I consider it a hopeful truth."

Matt clenched his jaw. "Do you mind if I ask what his name is?"

Mira hadn't said his name in so long, it felt strange bringing it up from her lungs. "Larry Manning."

LARRY MANNING. THE name rooted itself into Matt's mind like a disease as they walked back down the pier at a snail's—or robot's—pace. He kept a protective hand around Mira and couldn't resist putting a hand on Hagen's shoulder as well. The thought of what Mira had experienced made him sick with anger. No woman should be put through that type of anguish, much less given the responsibility of lying to her child about it. Hagen was a smart, loving child, and he deserved a father who adored him. There was no good answer for the little boy. Nobody wanted to feel unwanted, not even by a no-good scumbag like Larry Manning. The truth had the potential to scar Hagen for life, leading to trust and intimacy issues that could impact every relationship he ever had.

If Matt felt protective of them yesterday, he felt ten times as protective tonight.

"Can we get ice cream?" Hagen asked.

It took all of Matt's reserve to bite his tongue and let Mira answer. There was nothing he wouldn't give Hagen right now. Or maybe ever.

CHAPTER EIGHT

AFTER EATING ICE cream as they walked along Mayo Beach, they crossed the street and Hagen played on the playground until he tuckered himself out. It was almost nine thirty when Matt carried him from the car into Mira's cottage, fast asleep.

"You can lay him on his bed and I'll change him into his pajamas." Mira turned on a night-light by Hagen's door. It was quiet, save for the sounds of the bay seeping in through the open windows.

Matt gently laid him on the bed, brushed a kiss to his forehead, and whispered, "Good night, little buddy." He turned to Mira and asked, "Would you like help getting him changed?"

"No, thanks. I'm okay. I'm used to this, and he's a really sound sleeper. There's a bottle of wine in the cabinet above the fridge if you want to pour us each a glass."

He was so loving toward both of them, it seemed natural, like they'd been part of each other's lives in a much deeper way than just friends since last summer. But Mira was getting way ahead of herself. It was hard not to with a man like Matt. He made it easy to want more.

She found him standing at the French doors, gazing out at the water. He looked impossibly handsome in jeans that hugged him in all the best places and a short-sleeved button-down shirt.

His thick hair always looked finger-combed, brushed away from his face. His looks were striking in a natural way, like model David Gandy. She'd bet hundreds of coeds had crushes on him.

"Hey, sunshine." He smiled and reached for her, his eyes distractingly seductive as he gathered her against him. "Is Hagen okay?"

"Fast asleep. Once he's out, he sleeps like a log."

One hand slid up her back, the other pressed against the base of her spine, keeping her close. "Does that mean I can kiss his mommy now?" He kissed her neck. "You need to tell me the rules."

"Rules," she said absently, enjoying his warm breath tickling her skin and the feel of his soft lips as he kissed a path up her neck.

His hand slid beneath her hair, cradling her head as he brushed his lips over hers in a whisper of a kiss. Her body tingled with anticipation. He gazed into her eyes, his hard, tempting body flush with hers. She felt every inch of his arousal, melted beneath the heat searing through their clothes, and when his mouth came down over hers, she abandoned all thought, surrendering to the need that had been mounting all day. His lips were soft, despite the urgency of their kiss. She moaned, and he made a deep, guttural noise that weakened her knees. She stumbled backward with the force of their kiss, clawing at his arms, her entire body arching against his in an effort to get closer. Her back met the wall, and she threaded her fingers in his thick hair, clinging to him as they ate at each other's mouths wildly, though quietly, rocking and grinding with maddening precision. She was wet and he was hard, and she'd give anything to be naked in his arms. Then his hands were on her ass, sliding up the back of her shorts—*Oh God that feels good*—lifting her up, guiding her legs around his waist and using the wall for support. He took the kiss deeper, sending spirals of ecstasy winding through her.

His mouth left hers and her head tipped back, eyes closed. She drew in a lungful of air, trying to get oxygen to her brain, but he was kissing and licking her neck in the most exquisitely enticing long, slow strokes.

It took her a moment to realize they were on the move. He carried her to the couch and carefully laid her on the cushions, then came down over her. God, he felt good. His hard heat pressed against her center. She'd forgotten how the weight of a man changed the feel of her own body. She felt feminine and sexy as he smiled down at her and shifted his weight, lying beside her with his leg and arm over her, so his body blocked the view from the hall.

"Don't worry, baby." With one finger he moved a lock of her hair away from her face and kissed her softly. "We aren't going to get caught naked on the couch."

Do I look worried? How could she worry with *him* taking care of her? She knew he would never put her or her son in an uncomfortable position.

"I just had to be closer to you. I've spent so many months repressing my feelings just to make it through the day. Now that I'm here, now that we have time to explore what's between us, I don't want to hold back."

She could hardly believe what she was hearing. Her heart soared knowing he'd been holding back, too.

With a feathery touch, his fingertips brushed her knee, moved up her thigh, over her hip, and along her torso. Even through her clothing his touch gave her shivers. He cupped her cheek and kissed her again, deep and sensual. The strength of his hand on her cheek, the feel of his whiskers against her skin, and the strong strokes of his tongue exploring her mouth consumed her. Her hand wound around his neck, and her entire body reached for him. Her knee pushed between his, and her hips were on a mission to connect with the hardness straining behind his jeans. Her nipples tightened and burned as their chests came together.

He lowered her to her back, never breaking the kiss. *Oh, this kiss!* She could live inside this kiss! But a kiss was nowhere near enough. Her hand pushed beneath the back of his shirt, claiming his hot skin. She couldn't stop a greedy moan from escaping and felt him smile against her lips.

"Guys like you only exist in magazines and fantasies," she whispered.

Her hand moved over his soft skin and the hard ridges of his back, his muscles flexing as he leaned further into her and his hand snuck beneath her shirt. His thumb brushed over her nipple in slow, enticing circles through her lace bra. Thank God Serena had convinced her to go full-on sexy with her lingerie.

"I assure you, sunshine, I definitely exist." He lifted her shirt and pressed a kiss between her breasts.

She'd dreamed about sharing this intimacy with him for so long her stomach dipped.

"You have been my only fantasy night after night," he said between each kiss he pressed to the swell of her breast.

He lowered the cup of her bra and teased her nipple with his tongue. Her nails dug into his skin as she arched against him, craving so much more. *More* she knew she couldn't have, not here, not with Hagen sleeping just down the hall. But this tantalizing persuasion? Oh yes, she would allow herself this. She closed her eyes and allowed her mind to once again drift away as he teased and sucked and turned her into a writhing, wet bundle of bones. His fingers trailed down her stomach, and habit had her trying to suck in the belly that she hadn't been able to lose since having Hagen.

He lifted his mouth from her breast, and her eyes opened at the loss.

He gazed down at her with passion brimming in his dark eyes. "Please don't. You're gorgeous. All of you. *Breathe*, baby. Relax. Let me love you."

His words stole her breath, and he must have noticed, because his lips curved up in a sinful smile, and he brushed them over hers. "Breathe, baby, or I'll breathe for you."

And he did, slanting his mouth over hers and breathing air into her lungs, love into her heart, and lust into every crevice of her body. His hand pushed down the front of her shorts, and she had a moment of worry—about Hagen and about what Serena had said. Would he recoil when he felt hair down there?

"My back's to the hallway. I'm listening for Hagen. If he steps out of his bed, I'll move before he even gets to the hall."

Relief swept through her. He was just as aware as she was. Thank goodness, because she was certain that if he touched her there—where she hadn't been touched by anyone but her gynecologist in years—she might detonate.

"Or we can stop," he offered, and began withdrawing his hand.

"No." She touched his wrist, holding his fingers in place beneath her pants. She was willing to take her chances about not being shaved bare, and she knew he would honor his promise about Hagen. "If you don't touch me I might die right here on this couch."

He laughed, and she tugged him into a kiss to escape the

embarrassment over having admitted such a thing. He kissed like he spoke, confident and in control, like she could let go of all her worries and he'd take care of everything. And take care of everything he *did*. His thick fingers parted her wet flesh, teased over her achingly sensitive nerves with deadly precision. Her knees opened wider as he pushed those talented fingers inside her. She sucked in a sharp breath with the exquisite intrusion. His thumb pressed and stroked her clit as his fingers sought the spot that electrified her entire body. Her hips rose off the couch, and he took her deeper, devouring her mouth as he masterfully brought her to the edge of ecstasy—no batteries required. She clung to him, unable to move even her tongue to match his efforts as he ravaged her mouth or *give* anything back beyond her willing body.

He didn't seem to mind. He kissed and teased and whispered against her mouth. "Love touching you. Feel so good, baby. So sexy."

Ice and heat spread through her chest, down her limbs, all the way to the tips of her fingers and her curling toes. Rivers of lust consumed her as she rode his hand, moaning into their kiss, her orgasm clawing for release. He deepened the kiss and his fingers slicked over the magical spot that sliced through her last shred of control. Her hips bucked, an indiscernible sound sailed from her lungs, and her inner muscles convulsed like they never had before. *This…him…them…*There were no words…

WITH HIS MIND on the beautiful, trusting woman coming apart beneath him and his ears on high alert listening for Hagen, Matt drank in all the sweetness Mira was willing to give.

The heat between her legs, the sexy sounds coming from her luscious lips. As exquisite as it was, none of it was enough. He'd never been a greedy man, but when it came to Mira, he wanted it all. Her body, her heart, her future.

He kissed her softly as she came down from the peak, panting and mewing like she'd never felt anything so good, and that filled him with so many sensations—pride, lust, happiness. He kissed her lips, which were swollen from their kisses, her cheeks, her forehead, and then her mouth again. When her orgasm receded and her breathing calmed, he crushed his mouth to hers again, touching and teasing her right back to the edge. He was aching to be inside her, to feel all that heat wrapped around him, bringing them even closer.

She came hard, whimpering into their kiss, holding on to him like he was her anchor—and damn did he want to be—and when it eased, she dropped limply to the cushions. Eyes closed, she whispered, "Matt."

"I can't wait to taste you, baby. To have my mouth on you while you come apart, to look into your eyes and feel what you feel when I'm buried deep inside you."

Her eyes flew open, the blush splashing across her cheeks with his dirty talk. He kissed her again. "Get used to it, sunshine. I want *all* of you. Your sexy bare breasts against my chest, your sweet body swallowing every bit of me. Your fine ass in my hands. My mouth on *every* inch of you, my tongue inside you."

She sucked in a sharp breath, spurring him on. He shifted his weight over her, rocking his arousal against her center, self-inflicted torture he was powerless to resist.

"I want to see your mouth around my cock." He paused, testing the waters, giving her a chance to tell him he'd crossed a line, but her eyes darkened, and she licked her lips, like she wanted it as much as he did.

"What else?" she asked with a shaky breath.

"Baby, when I get you alone, when we don't have to worry about your sweet little boy, I'm going to take you from above, behind, and every which way in between." He laced his fingers with hers and pressed them beside her head, kissing her neck and feeling her erratic pulse against his tongue.

"Tell me your fantasies, sunshine. I want to make them all come true."

"I...can't." She closed her eyes, and he kissed her again.

"The brain is a powerful thing," he reassured her. "When you're ready. When you trust me wholly and completely, which you will one day very soon, then you can tell me."

"I forgot you're a psych *and* econ guy. It's so not fair. You have the upper hand." She let out a long breath as he moved beside her and they both sat up. Matt had a double major in psychology and economics, but his advanced degrees were in economics, and that's what he taught at Princeton.

"I don't want the upper hand," he assured her. He ran his fingers along her jaw and whispered, "I want to be one with you, sunshine, and soon I'm going to have my hands *all* over you."

CHAPTER NINE

MIRA STOOD IN the kitchen staring at the couch during breakfast the next morning. She'd never thought much about that couch, but now it made her smile, and her stomach went all sorts of crazy just looking at it. Matt's words whispered in her head, as they had all night after he'd left. *When you're ready. When you trust me wholly and completely, which you will one day very soon, then you can tell me.*

"Can I bring my robot to camp?" Hagen asked. "I want to show it to my friends."

She shook her head to clear her thoughts, but all it did was rattle more of Matt's words free. *I want to see your mouth around my cock.* He'd shocked her with his dirty talk, but hearing him tell her exactly what he wanted had turned her on and made her *want* to have her mouth around his cock.

She carried her plate from the table, forcing those tempting thoughts away to focus on her son. "Sure, but we have to hurry. I want to stop by and see Serena for a few minutes before we leave." Mira bent to smell the pretty gloxinias.

"Yay!" Hagen carried his plate to the sink, then ran down the hall to his bedroom.

Mira's phone vibrated. Her pulse quickened at the sight of Matt's picture on the screen. She'd made the selfie he'd taken of the two of them at the cemetery his profile picture. She quickly read the text. *Good morning, sunshine. I'd call, but I don't want to throw off your schedule with Hagen. Can I see you guys this week and take you out on a real date this weekend?* She smiled at his inclusion of Hagen and warmed at the thought of going out with him this weekend.

She sent off a quick reply. *Hi. Thank you for being mindful of our morning madness. Of course you can see us, and I'll check on getting a sitter for this weekend.*

Hagen came out of his bedroom carrying his backpack. "I got it, Mom. Ready."

Doing a quick sweep of her little boy's freshly combed hair and clothing, she asked, "Did you brush your teeth?"

"Uh-huh." He smiled, revealing his teeth.

"Good boy." She grabbed her purse and keys as her phone vibrated again. She read the text quickly—*If you can't find a sitter, I don't mind taking Hagen with us.* Smiling, she shoved her phone in her pocket and followed Hagen out the door. She'd respond to the text after talking to Serena.

"Mom! There's a package!"

As she locked the door, Hagen said, "It has my name on it." He opened the bag and pulled out a package of batteries, dropping the bag to the porch.

Mira picked it up and found a note inside. "'Hagen,'" she read aloud, smiling at Matt's careful print and the thoughtful note. "'I thought you might need a few extra batteries for the robot. Remember to be careful when you open the battery compartment. The latch can be tricky. Have fun at camp. Matt.'"

"Guy stuff, Mom. Matt says part of being a man is always being prepared."

Hagen shoved the batteries in his backpack and climbed

into the car while Mira tried to fit her ever-expanding heart back inside her chest.

She drove over to the Bayside Resort office thinking about yesterday. She'd heard Matt doling out life lessons in small enough doses for Hagen to listen to each and every one, but that didn't mean her son would retain them. She was glad to see that the excitement of the robot hadn't superseded the lessons. And even more touched that Matt cared enough about Hagen's happiness to have dropped off the batteries. She imagined most guys who had just started dating a woman would have focused on her—and most fathers wouldn't have thought that far ahead.

Dean was working in the gardens in front of the office when they arrived. He raised a hand above his eyes, shielding his tanned face from the sun's bright rays. His hair was cropped so short, that together with his broad, muscular frame, it made him look like a marine.

"Hey, little buddy," he said to Hagen as he darted by.

"Hi, Dean!" Hagen ran up the steps toward the office door. "I made a robot and Mom has a boyfriend."

Mira stopped cold as he disappeared into the building.

"You look like that's news to *you*." Dean rose to his feet, wiping his hands on a rag he'd had stuffed in his back pocket.

"*New* to me maybe but not news. I'm wondering how he put the pieces of the puzzle together. We never even kissed around him, but he did have his arm around me yesterday."

"Kids are perceptive. I remember when my mom introduced me to her new 'friends.' I knew every damn time they were making their way into her bedroom. I was twelve. I'm sure Hagen's not putting those pieces together yet, but he's a smart kid."

"You can say that again." Mira mentally planned out the

talk they'd have on the way to camp.

"So…Matt Lacroux? I wondered when you guys would turn your occasional dates into something more."

"Occasional dates?"

Dean squinted against the bright sun. "I don't know what you call them, but I think taking Hagen out counts as a date. Every time the guy's in town he makes a point of seeing you. That's a good thing. And I heard he brought you gloxinias, which shows he's a man who knows what he's doing."

Thinking of last night, she agreed. Matt definitely *knew what he was doing.* "How did you hear about the flowers? He just brought them yesterday."

"Lizzie, up at P-Town Petals. I picked up a few things this morning and she mentioned it. You know how tight she is with Matt's sister."

She'd forgotten that Sky's best friend owned a flower shop. "I guess Hagen figuring it out is a blessing in disguise. I'd rather he heard about it from me than anyone else. Is Serena inside?"

"Yeah, she, Drake, and Rick were going head-to-head when I got here."

"Someone's got to keep them in line." She drew in a deep breath, hoping she missed the three of them going at it.

"Hey, Mira?"

She pulled the door open and glanced over her shoulder at Dean. "Yeah?"

"I don't want to make something out of nothing, but you know what gloxinias stand for, don't you?"

She shook her head.

"Love at first sight."

Her jaw gaped, but before she could even begin to process that information, Serena called to her.

"Mira, thank God you're here."

Mira stepped inside. Drake glanced up from where he was peering over Serena's shoulder at the computer monitor. She saw Hagen through the open door to Drake's office, playing with the toy cars they kept for him.

"Mornin'," Drake said.

"Sis," Rick grumbled, staring at Drake. He stood in front of the desk, arms crossed, his jaw working overtime.

"Hi." *Love at first sight?* How would Matt know that? It couldn't have been why he chose them. Dismissing the idea that he knew what the flowers signified, she focused on the mounting tension in the room. "What's going on?"

Serena gave Mira a deadpan stare. "We need a surf instructor, and Thing One and Thing Two are trying to decide who to hire. It seems to be a battle of wills."

"Seriously?" Mira asked. "Just pick a good-looking guy. That's all the girls care about anyway."

"See?" Rick huffed. "Hot guy, hot girl. Winning situation on all accounts."

"We have a reputation to build," Drake reminded them. "We don't want to be known as a sex resort. 'Come to Bayside and Get Laid' won't get us very far."

"Works for Club Med," Rick said with a laugh. "What are you going to do? Hire Tony Black, a world-renowned surfer, to teach a couple of kids on vacation? We're not building competitors. We're teaching the basics, offering a fun vacation, which should include lots of eye candy."

"Tony? Now, there's a thought," Drake answered.

"I have to get Hagen to camp so I can get to work. Can I just ask Serena a quick question? I swear it's so stressful getting caught between you two. I don't know how she stands it."

"You got me this job, remember?" Serena said with a smirk. She patted Drake's six-pack abs and winked at Rick. "Besides, this is nothing. Child's play. In the end, I'll get to choose who we hire. They just don't know it yet."

Rick scoffed. Drake remained silent.

"Is your offer to babysit still open?" Mira asked.

"Absofrigginglutely. When?"

"This weekend."

"Yes. Definitely," Serena said. "Want me to keep him over-night?"

"No. Just a few hours. Maybe put him to bed? I'm not really sure."

"Going out with Matt?" Rick asked a little less gruffly.

"Yes." Rick had wanted to kill Larry when he'd found out he was married, and it had taken Drake stepping in to get him to realize it would do no good to hurt the guy. He'd always been extra protective of Mira and Hagen. To this day she still couldn't be sure Rick wasn't secretly behind the check that came in the mail shortly after Hagen was born.

Rick's eyes shot to Hagen. "You know Matt's only here temporarily, right?"

"Yes, but how do *you* know that?"

Serena raised her hand and winced. "Sorry. I might have said something."

Mira rolled her eyes.

"Wait, did you say this weekend?" Drake asked. "Rick and I are supposed to take Hagen camping. We promised him last month, remember? Or did you and Matt want to make plans with him instead?"

"I think she'd like to make plans with Matt instead," Serena said under her breath.

"TMI, Serena." Rick patted Mira's shoulder supportively as he passed and went into Drake's office. He ruffled Hagen's hair and crouched beside him, saying something Mira couldn't hear.

"I forgot the no-mom-allowed camping trip was this weekend. Yes, of course he can still go. Sorry, Serena. Can I take a rain check?" Her fingers itched to text Matt and tell him they had a weekend alone to look forward to.

"Absolutely. Anytime."

"Thanks. I'll remind Hagen today. It'll be all he thinks about until you leave."

And a weekend alone with Matt will be all I'll think about until you leave, too.

MATT GOT UP early and spent hours researching and writing on the deck of the cottage, his two favorite aspects of his teaching position. Even in the short time since he'd left Princeton—including the two weeks of research and writing he'd done in New Jersey before coming to the Cape—he already felt a huge weight lift from his shoulders. There was no one to block his progress, no red tape to wade through.

In addition to feeling free of administrative restraints, he'd forgotten how nice it was to wake up to something other than the sounds of the city and to breathe air that tasted of the sea. He'd even forgotten what it was like to have breakfast with friends and family, as he had this morning on Pete's deck. It was such a simple thing, and it felt like a luxury. Back home, his mornings consisted of a quick cup of coffee in a to-go cup, dealing with student issues, and sitting in the oppressive office he'd worked so hard to obtain. It was only eleven thirty and he'd already gotten more work done on his book than he could have by midnight if he were still teaching. His only distractions were thoughts of a weekend alone with Mira, which was the best distraction of all, the warm sun's rays on his skin, and the sounds of his niece and the other kids playing down at the pool. Even Kurt Remington, a bestselling thriller author who was once so set in his ways he had a hard time pulling away from his computer for more than a few minutes, had been down at the pool.

Matt hadn't been sure he could leave teaching behind and just write. But he was quickly learning that writing a book was very different from writing a research paper. There was no *just* about it. It was as exhilarating as it was challenging and offered an entirely different type of intellectual stimulation. And best of all, he had time with Mira and Hagen.

At around noon, Matt walked into his father's hardware store, and the sound of Mira's voice brought a smile to his lips.

"It'll pay for itself in productivity time alone," Mira said as she came out of the back room.

His father grumbled something Matt couldn't make out.

"Matt," his father and Mira said in unison.

Matt kissed Mira's cheek. "Hi, sunshine. I thought I'd treat you to lunch. That is, if my father can spare you."

"You're in town for a few days and you already scooped up the prettiest single woman around?" His father embraced him. "And here I thought you came to visit *me*."

"I want to visit with you, too, Pop. How about if I come by the house after you close tonight?" He wanted to see Mira this evening, too, but as much as he'd like to insert himself into her life, he didn't want to smother her.

"Sounds good to me," his father answered. "We close at

seven."

"I know. I'll come by around seven thirty. I take it you don't mind if I treat Mira to lunch?"

"It's about time you took this young lady out on a proper date. All those willy-nilly visits were driving me crazy." His father smiled. "Please, get her out of here. She's talking nonsense anyway."

Mira shook her head and grabbed her purse from beneath the counter. "You are a stubborn man, Neil Lacroux."

"You sound like my late wife," his father said.

No wonder I like her so much. Matt took Mira's hand. "No more willy-nilly, Pop. You've got my word."

"For the next three months, anyway," his father grumbled.

Not for the first time since he'd accepted the book deal and taken the sabbatical, the thought of getting close to Mira and then leaving again made Matt's gut knot up. When Mira had texted him earlier, they'd made plans to take Hagen shopping for his camping trip Wednesday evening, and he was even looking forward to doing that.

"Get out of here." Neil waved them toward the door. "Maybe she can convince you it's time to come home for good."

Matt's father had always supported his love of academics, and he knew he was just busting his chops now, though he knew how badly his father missed him and how much he wished one of his children would take over the store.

Matt held the door open for Mira. "I thought we'd go to the Sunbird Café."

Once they stepped outside, he gathered her in his arms and kissed her properly—slow and deep, with all the emotions that had been building up since the last time they'd kissed.

"Wow," she said breathlessly. "Will I ever get used to those kisses?"

"Not if I can help it." He took in her jade-green tank dress, which set off the green flecks in her eyes and fit snugly across her hips and breasts. "You look gorgeous, baby. I bet tons of guys come into the store just to get an eyeful of you."

"I wish." She laughed.

"Hey," he teased as they walked up the street toward the main road.

"I don't mean it like *that*. But more customers would be a good thing. Most of the people who come in these days only come in to chat with your dad. They love the familiarity and the feel of the family-owned shop, but if I had a dollar for everyone who came in and asked a hundred questions only to then say, 'Thanks for your help. I'll get it when I go into Hyannis to the Home Depot. Gotta watch my pennies!' I'd be rich."

They turned onto the main road and headed toward the café.

"You mentioned the other night that it was hard to compete. What's the problem? The cost of inventory?" His father had bought the building more than thirty years ago, and he knew he no longer carried a mortgage on the property.

She nodded. "The big chain stores get volume discounts that we just can't compete with, and people can usually get what they want online for around the same price. We have very little online presence, and unfortunately, we also need to update our inventory and accounting system to save on administrative time. We spend countless hours doing inventory when we could put that time into something else, like customer outreach. I know the cost of advertising is prohibitive, but we need it to stay in people's minds as more than a store an old friend owns."

As they made their way into the eclectic café, Mira described the challenges his father's store was facing, and Matt realized they were some of the very issues he was writing about. They ordered at the counter and found a quiet table by the windows.

"I won't bore you with all the details, but the book I'm writing focuses on the economic impact the Internet and societal changes have on small businesses. It's much deeper than that, of course, looking at the effect the changes have on familial and employer-employee dynamics, and other psychological aspects and how they trickle down and impact future economics. But my father's business is a prime example."

She speared a forkful of lettuce from her salad and said, "It's fixable."

"You've been thinking about it?" Of course she had. She was brilliant.

"A lot, actually. I love working for your father, and I've gotten to know the community through working with him. Working there has become a big part of my life. I know that sounds silly, but there's something wonderful about helping a pregnant woman to baby proof her house, and then a few months later, to help her get what she needs to put together a baby gate. And when the elementary school had their annual go-cart-building contest, all the dads and their kids came in for supplies. Half of them didn't buy them there, but they came in to show us what they were building because the fathers knew your dad when they were building their own go-carts twenty years ago."

"I remember building mine with my father." Matt smiled with the memory. "My father really got into those things. He's aware, then, of the trouble the business is in?"

"Yes, but he's in denial. I know all those valued customers would love to see him compete with the bigger stores. Nobody wants to drive thirty or forty minutes to get hardware. And if his business goes under…"

"You'll need to start over." It was hard enough for a single mother to make ends meet, but the thought of her finding another place to work that allowed her the hours and flexibility she needed to work around Hagen's schedule had to be stressful.

"Yes, but also, your dad takes so much pride in the business, and Pete told me about his drinking after you lost your mother."

"That was a difficult time for all of us," Matt said solemnly. "Luckily Pete was here to get him help."

"Yes. Then you understand why I'm thinking about all of this. It's one thing to retire and sell a business, but to retire because the business failed? After all these years?" Her eyes glassed over and she looked away. "I can't even allow myself to think about it, or how it might set him back. Your father is such a proud man."

She squinted, making those cute freckles across her nose dance. "Oh gosh. Do you think he would mind me talking about this? I just realized he might not want me to share it with anyone."

He reached across the table and held her hand. His father was a proud man, and he had a feeling he wouldn't want any of them knowing the business was in trouble. But that was an even bigger reason for Matt to know what was going on, so he could try to help.

"I don't want to put you in an uncomfortable position, so don't tell me anything specific about the company finances. But I'd love to hear your thoughts on how to fix the issues."

Maybe together they could figure out how to save his father's business *and* save the job Mira loved.

CHAPTER TEN

MIRA HAD BEEN working on the idea of an East Coast co-op for small businesses similar to Lacroux Hardware for months. Talking to someone who understood finances and economics, and how co-ops functioned, was beyond fulfilling. Accounting and economics weren't exactly exciting subjects, but Matt listened intently and seemed not only impressed with her ideas, but he had solid suggestions that made financial sense.

After lunch they held hands on the way back to the store. Mira was on a high, not only from Matt's surprise visit, but from their stimulating conversation and the way he was looking at her, like everything she said was important.

"I've already compiled a list of a dozen businesses, complete with the owners' contact information and a few other important details. I've also structured a business plan and done some research on central warehouse locations," she explained. "I know it's jumping the gun, especially since your dad isn't exactly receptive to the idea. But this is what I went to school for. It's a solid plan, Matt. I've researched similar co-ops, and if we could get buy-in from five or six companies we could make our initial investment back within two years. From then on out, he'd be making a profit."

He stopped walking and placed his hands on her hips. "It is a very well thought out plan, and you're clearly passionate about wanting it to work. Maybe I can persuade him to at least talk about it."

"Really? He's put his heart and soul into that business. He tells me stories about your mom coming into the store with you guys when you were little and I feel like those memories are alive in the store. When he talks about Hunter following him down the aisles when he was just a boy, or you sitting behind the counter reading for hours when you were growing up— which reminds me of Hagen, by the way—I can practically see it all playing out."

He folded his arms around her and pressed his lips to hers. *Mm.* She wanted to stay right there for the rest of the day.

"Me too, sunshine. Just hearing about it makes me happy."

"Did you know that I occasionally bring Hagen to work with me? Not often, but sometimes when he has a day off from school, your dad will suggest that I bring him in, and Hagen will spend the whole day following him around. They take inventory together, and your dad tells him what certain tools are for. It's nice for all of us. He's like a surrogate grandfather, and selfishly, I don't want Hagen to lose that connection."

"You've made a world of difference in my father's life. We've all noticed it. He's happier than he's been in years, despite his not wanting to talk about making changes to the business. That's our fault, not yours. He wants the business to stay in the family." He kissed her again. "Nobody wants to see you lose that connection. Maybe together we can make sure neither of you will ever have to."

He glanced over her shoulder, and his brows drew together. His entire body seemed to stand at attention. "Call nine-one-one."

He ran across the street. Mira dug out her phone and hurried across the street to where Matt was crouched beside a woman who was lying on the ground, her body convulsing uncontrollably. Spittle gathered in her mouth. Matt carefully rolled her onto her side and placed one hand behind her back, the other beneath her face to protect it from the concrete. Mira's pulse was racing, fear and empathy consuming her.

"Nine-one-one, Mira, *please*. She's having a seizure."

Mira nervously placed the call as Matt calmly and carefully took care of the woman. The woman lost control of her bladder, and Matt continued protecting her head and keeping her on her side, explaining to Mira that he was keeping her from choking. Despite the crowd gathering around them, Matt was completely focused on the woman lying on the sidewalk, her body still jerking violently.

"She's okay," he said to no one in particular, his eyes never leaving the woman. "She's having a seizure."

What seemed like an hour later, but in reality was probably thirty seconds, the woman's body stilled, and Matt brushed her hair from her cheeks, keeping her on her side. "She's okay," he said, breathing deeply. "She's in the postictal phase. Nothing to be afraid of. It's just a deep sleep. She'll be out of it soon." He shrugged off his shirt and placed it over her wet pants.

Sirens neared, and Matt glanced up at Mira. His serious dark eyes brightened a little as a small smile curved his lips. "Good job, sunshine. There isn't much you can do when this happens but make sure the person doesn't choke and keep them from harming themselves."

As the woman came to, Matt held her, talking softly, reassuring her with kind words and complete and total focus. Once the ambulance arrived, he explained what had happened, and Mira heard him say he didn't notice a medical alert bracelet or necklace. She wouldn't have even thought to look for one. In fact, she'd have had no idea what to do, while it seemed second nature to Matt. He had reacted instantly and wasn't the least bit frazzled.

He came to her side and tucked her beneath his arm. "You're shaking." He turned her toward him and held her against his bare chest. "It's okay. Seizures can be frightening for everyone."

"How did you know what to do?" She was shaking like a leaf, and felt ridiculous because she wasn't the woman who had experienced the seizure or the man who'd helped her. But the scene had been terrifying. What if Matt hadn't been there? What if the woman had choked, or cracked her skull on the sidewalk during her seizure?

"I've taken basic lifesaving courses." He placed his hands on her cheeks and searched her eyes. "You should sit down for a minute."

He was a pillar of strength, a caring, generous man with a heart of gold that extended well beyond her and Hagen. And even if only for a few months, she was so glad he was *hers*.

MATT ARRIVED AT his childhood home at seven thirty on the dot with all the fixings for a grilled steak dinner, his father's favorite, and, he hoped, a solid distraction for himself. He drew in a deep breath as he mounted the porch steps and entered the house. The worn wooden floors creaked beneath the area rug in the entranceway.

Even though his mother had been gone for several years, he still expected to hear her call out, "Matty? Is that you, honey?"

He still expected to see his father pull her into a quick kiss as she walked by his favorite recliner, where he'd be working his way through a crossword puzzle.

He still expected the life he had grown up with, the life he had counted on, to be intact.

"Matty?" his father called out, and just like that Matt's mind shifted to the present.

Mom's gone. Dad's not drunk.

I'm home.

"Right here, Pop. I brought dinner."

His father stepped out from the den down the hall with his reading glasses on the bridge of his nose and a crossword puzzle in hand. A welcome sight after his bout with alcohol. His father looked good. He'd long ago lost the belly he'd developed from drinking, and though he had a little more silver in his brown hair, he looked healthy.

"Bring it into the kitchen." He motioned to Matt to follow him.

Matt paused when he passed his mother's sewing room. He still had memories of her glancing up from behind her sewing machine, a warm smile always in place. *You should learn to sew, Matty. You never know when you'll need to fix something.* Matt never needed to be offered the chance to learn more than once. He'd taken her up on it, and by the time he was twelve he could sew better than most moms in the neighborhood. The familiar ache of missing her filled his chest. He cleared his throat to push the emotions back down and followed his father into the kitchen.

"I figured we'd grill out back." He began unpacking the bag and his father pulled out the cutting board and meat tenderizer. Or, as his father called it, the take-your-frustrations-out-on-the-steak mallet.

"I knew you would. The grill is ready." His father un-wrapped the steak and used the mallet to tenderize it as Matt prepared a salad. "So you finally came to your senses with Mira?"

"It was never a matter of coming to my senses. She's a single mom. I couldn't exactly go out with her for a day here and there. That wouldn't have been fair to her or Hagen." He pushed the bowl of salad to the side and leaned against the counter. "I've got three months."

"And then?"

"And then I'll figure it out." They worked in silence for a few minutes. Matt sliced potatoes, thick, the way his father liked them, brushed them with olive oil and seasonings, and laid them on aluminum foil, then he brought the sides of the foil together, leaving air around the potatoes, like a shiny sac, and folded them together. He put them in the oven and headed outside to grill.

"How's the boat coming along?" Matt asked after they set the steaks on the grill and settled into the chairs on the deck. He and Pete were refinishing a sailboat. His father had taught Pete to refinish boats when he was just a boy, the same way he'd helped each of his five children find their niche. There was always an endless supply of books available for Matt, and trips to the library that were like trips to the candy store for other kids. He'd taught Grayson and Hunter to work with metal, and he'd turned a shed into an art studio for Sky. Now, as he listened to his father tell him about the work he and Pete were doing on the boat, he realized he wanted to do those things for his own children. These thoughts didn't surprise him, as he'd been thinking about family more and more over the past year or two. But the yearning was stronger now. And he wanted to do those things with Hagen.

"We'll probably finish it up in a month or so," his father said.

Thinking of Hagen, Matt said, "Hagen wants to build a boat, and I told him we'd start with a raft. Would you like to build it with us? I could sure use your help."

His father's eyes narrowed and his lips curved up in a smile that told Matt he knew what he was up to. "You don't need help with anything. You could build a raft when you were thirteen without anyone's help."

Matt laughed and got up to flip the steaks. "Fine, you got me. I miss you. I want to build a raft with Hagen, and I want to spend time with you. Is that a crime?"

His dad joined him by the grill. "I'd like that, Matty. That boy is sharp as a tack, isn't he?"

"He is. We built a robot last weekend."

"I know. Mira told me. That's where the boy gets his smarts, you know. She's a bright woman. Pushy as all hell, but—" He laughed and patted Matt on the back. "You know I like that in a person."

"You must. You raised five stubborn children."

They joked about what it was like when Matt and his siblings were growing up, and they reminisced about his mother, easing some of the deep-seated pain of her absence. When dinner was ready, they ate out on the patio, and Matt eased into a conversation about the hardware store.

"How are things at the store, Pop?"

His father waved a dismissive hand. "No sense in getting all wrapped up in that."

"I don't want to get *all wrapped up* in anything." *Besides*

Mira. "I'm just wondering how business is going."

His father pushed to his feet and carried his plate into the kitchen. Matt gathered the other dishes and followed him in. He wasn't about to let him get off that easy.

"Come on, Dad. Please talk to me."

With a heavy sigh, his father turned to face him, his features lined with regret. "You only call me Dad when you are being serious. Let's not get serious, Matt. The business isn't going to stay in the family, so what's the use of pouring my energy into it? I want to retire in a year or two. Hell, I'd like to retire now, spend more time with Bea and you guys. But I've got to keep the business going long enough to get Mira through her CPA exam."

Hearing his father refer to Mira as if she were his daughter should have surprised him, but it didn't. He'd seen the picture of Hagen above his father's desk at the store. No one besides family had *ever* been pinned to that wall. That was more telling than any words could ever be. But he was surprised that his father knew about Mira's plans to take the CPA exam.

"You know about that?"

"Of course I know about that. She's too smart not to try to do better for herself. The way I figure it, when she passes the exam, she'll get another job, and I'll close up shop. Pretty simple."

There was nothing *simple* about his father closing the business he'd worked his whole life to create. "You worked hard to make Lacroux Hardware mean something to this community, and to our family. Even if none of us want to spend eight hours a day there, that doesn't mean we want to see it fail. Is that what you want? To close the business as if it never existed?"

His father shook his head and shrugged. "Matty, I built the

business to leave something to my children. You know that. And it's not surprising that you all went out in the world and found your own paths. That's what your mother and I wanted for you. It's what we encouraged each of you to do. The store is an outdated dream. A dream that had legs and gave us a comfortable life. But time has passed, and its legs aren't what they used to be. It served its purpose, and it's not going to stay in the family, so it's time to think about letting it go."

Matt didn't know if it was because of Mira or his father, or because he was in a nostalgic frame of mind and thinking about a future with both, but when the words "What if I'm not ready to?" left his lips, he didn't try to fight them.

"Then I'd say that makes no sense. You've got a career at Princeton and a big book deal, promises of a lecture circuit. What would you want with the business?"

"I'm not sure I'd disagree with you, Pop, but would you be opposed to me and Mira taking steps to see if there's a way to make the business more competitive? You never know. Maybe it will stay in the family after all."

His father crossed his arms, a Lacroux habit when confronted with a situation they didn't want to deal with. He lowered his chin, and Matt knew he was weighing his answer.

"It won't cost you a penny," Matt assured him. "Let us do a little research, talk to a few people, and see if there are any viable solutions."

"She's talking about new computers and an accounting system, Matt." He lifted his hand and rubbed his finger and thumb together, indicating a pricey endeavor.

"Talking and buying are two different things." Matt moved to the sink and began washing the dishes. "She's thinking of a co-op, where you and other small-business owners work together and form a business so—"

"Form a business? Why would I want another business when the one I have is already in trouble?" He grabbed a dish towel and began drying the dishes.

"Because there are plenty of small businesses just like yours out there. Mira has a list of a dozen other family-owned hardware stores already, and they're probably struggling just like yours is. In order to compete, you have to be creative. Working together, you can all reap the benefits of bulk buying and passing on larger discounts to your customers."

His father set the plate he was drying down and shook his head. "Running another business to save this one? I don't know, Matt. I'm getting closer to retirement every day. I don't have the energy to run another business."

"No, but Mira does." He paused, letting the idea sink in.

It might not be fair, throwing Mira into the mix, but the more Matt thought about it, the more he didn't want his father's business to perish. He was proud of what his father had built, and always had been, even if his aspirations had led him in a different direction. But now that he was back on the Cape, he couldn't imagine walking through Orleans and not seeing his father's store. Matt had seen fierce determination in Mira's eyes, had heard excitement in her voice as she'd outlined her business plan for the co-op. Technically, Mira wasn't family, but it was clear how much she adored his father and liked working at the store—*He's like a surrogate grandfather, and selfishly, I don't want Hagen to lose that connection.*

"Mira is invested in the business and the community. She's like family. I know you feel that way. Why hold on to the business just to let it—and her—go? Why not let us try to save it? To build it into something more, something she can dig her fingers into and make you proud of?" He paused again, allowing his father time to think about the scenario he'd just laid out. "If you won't consider it for yourself, consider it for her."

His father wiped his hands on the towel. He leaned his palms on the counter and his chin fell to his chest. "Mira," he whispered.

"You're here for only a few months, Matt. If you break her heart, she might leave the business anyway."

And if I don't, your dream of keeping it in the family just might come true.

CHAPTER ELEVEN

WEDNESDAY EVENING MATT picked up Mira and Hagen to go shopping for camping supplies, looking dangerously handsome in a short-sleeved white linen button-down and khaki shorts.

"Matt!" Hagen ran to the door, and Matt crouched to hug him, melting a little more of Mira's heart.

"How's it going, big guy?"

"Good! I brought my robot to camp and my friends loved it. My teacher said I'm going to make a great scientist one day."

"You'll be great at whatever you want to be when you grow up." He pulled a Princeton baseball cap from behind his back and put it on Hagen's head. "To keep ticks out of your hair while you're camping."

Hagen beamed at Mira. "Look, Mom!"

"That's a pretty sharp-looking hat."

"Hello there, gorgeous." He leaned in for a kiss on the cheek, and his masculine scent consumed her. "I'd have brought you one, but I thought you'd rather have this." He handed her a small envelope and held a finger up to his lips, then glanced at Hagen, who was going up on his toes to look at his new hat in the hallway mirror.

"What have you done?" She opened the envelope and read the handwritten note. *Sunshine, I would be honored if you'd join me on Nantucket for a weekend of pampering and relaxation. I promise to bring you home sexually sated (if you'd like) and rejuvenated for another week of mommying. Yours, M.*

Her hand covered her heart. She opened her mouth to thank him, but all that came out was, "Matt…?"

"Too presumptive?" He wrapped a hand around her waist and whispered, "We don't have to fool around. I just want to be with you."

She shook her head and pressed her lips together in an effort to calm her rampant emotions. "It's not that. It's just so *romantic*. Nantucket? I've never been there."

"I'm ready to go!" Hagen dashed out the front door with his robot under his arm.

"On our way," Matt called after him, then he gazed into Mira's eyes and said, "We'll leave Friday after you finish working. You deserve romance, and I want to be the man who gives it to you."

"I want that, too." It was a small admission, but it felt enormous, because she meant it in *every* possible way.

Mira's head was in the clouds the whole way down to Hyannis, where they enjoyed dinner at a waterfront restaurant. Hagen, refusing to take off his special hat, fed the seabirds pieces of bread, while Matt and Mira took pictures and snuck kisses. Mira made a mental list of what she needed for the weekend—sexy lingerie, condoms. *Ohmygod. Condoms.* She pondered the Nair hidden in her bathroom. Matt didn't seem to care about what he'd felt *down there* the other night, but they'd been so hot and bothered, maybe he just hadn't noticed.

"I talked to my father, and I think it's safe to start working on the co-op," Matt said quietly.

She was glad he inherently understood that some topics

weren't meant for Hagen's ears. She had a much harder time keeping her excitement over the prospect of the co-op contained. "He agreed?"

Matt wiggled his hand, indicating *not so much*. "But he's getting there. He won't fight us on it. I think we can move forward."

"Really?" She felt her eyes widen. "Matt, this is *huge*," she said in a hushed whisper. "But I'd like to talk to him about it, just to be sure. I would hate for him to think I was doing anything without his approval."

"Absolutely."

On the way to the mall, Mira began making another mental list—for the co-op. Could this day get *any* better?

They held hands walking into the mall, and when Hagen noticed, he moved around Mira to Matt's other side and took his hand. "You're Mom's boyfriend," he said matter-of-factly.

Oh yeah, the day just got miles better.

Matt glanced at Mira, and she knew he was looking for approval to confirm Hagen's comment. "We had a talk about us." She leaned closer and whispered, "I hope that's okay."

Matt draped an arm over her shoulder and kissed her temple. "Anything you do is okay." He smiled down at Hagen. "How do you feel about that, little man?"

Hagen shrugged. "Good. But I wish you weren't going back to New Jersey."

Matt bristled. Mira had wrestled with telling Hagen the truth about Matt being in town temporarily. When she weighed the pros and cons, she felt it was better to prepare Hagen for Matt's return to New Jersey than to let him build false hope. When he'd pushed about whether that would mean Matt would no longer be her boyfriend, she'd finally alluded to a long-distance relationship. She'd waited, dreamed, hoped, and fantasized about being with Matt for too long to even allow herself to consider anything less.

"I'm not sure if I'm going back or not, but I'm glad you feel good about me and your mom," Matt finally said. "Because I enjoy spending time with both of you."

"But you aren't my boyfriend," Hagen said. "You're my friend."

"Right." He arched a brow at Mira.

"He wanted roles, so I gave them to him."

"Friends are good," Matt said, then quieter and for her ears only, "*for now.*"

She tried to pretend her mind wasn't racing with that open-ended comment as they shopped in the outdoors store. Matt filled a basket with a first aid kit, bug spray, a battery-operated lantern, a utility tool that had no knife but a fork and spoon that folded up to fit in Hagen's palm, and a compass.

"All right, little man. Time to find the sleeping bags." He took Hagen's hand, and Mira touched his arm.

"Drake has sleeping bags, and I'm sure he has all the other stuff, too. I usually just send him with a new pair of pajamas and a few little toys or books to keep him busy."

Matt's brows knitted. "Every boy needs his own camping gear. Would you mind if I bought him a sleeping bag? I don't want to step on your toes."

Hagen blinked serious baby blues at Matt and tugged on his hand. "Tell her it's *guy stuff.*"

Mira could see she was outnumbered, and she wasn't sure how she felt about that. Flattered, for sure, but she didn't want Matt to think he needed to spoil Hagen. She also didn't want Hagen, who wasn't a needy child, to think he had to have new things for every outing. One look at her son and boyfriend's hopeful expressions and she relented.

"Okay, but this doesn't mean every time you have an outing you need this much new stuff."

"I know," Matt and Hagen said in unison, which made her laugh.

They arrived back at her cottage later that evening with new pajamas, a sleeping bag, and a host of camping paraphernalia that Mira's man and boy considered *essentials*. Matt and Hagen spent the next hour meticulously going through each item, removing tags, discussing proper usage, and then packing the lot into Hagen's camping backpack.

When they tucked Hagen into bed, he insisted he wear his hat, but Matt convinced him to hang it on the bedpost so it didn't become misshapen. His robot sat in the middle of his desk, next to his book about building robots. Mira was glad Matt had given them extra batteries, because he'd been playing with it every free minute and had already gone through the first set.

She stood in the doorway listening as the two of them discussed the raft-building information Hagen had learned from studying the website. Matt listened intently and complimented him on his research skills. *Research*, that was exactly what her son loved. She hadn't been able to pinpoint it until now.

"How would you feel about Mr. Lacroux helping us build the raft?"

"Mr. Neil?" Hagen asked. "I'd like that."

Matt ruffled his hair. "Yeah, Mr. Neil."

Hagen threw his arms around Matt's neck. "It's going to be the greatest raft *ever*." He settled back onto his pillow, and Matt smoothed the covers. "Matt?"

"Yeah, buddy?"

"Do you think I'm a nerd?"

Mira stepped into the room with her heart in her throat. Hagen had been teased in the past about being a nerd, but she hadn't heard anything like that since he started attending camp.

Matt eyed Mira, who shrugged one shoulder and narrowed her eyes, indicating she didn't know where this was heading, but please tread carefully.

"Why do you ask?"

"No reason." Hagen grabbed his teddy bear from the side of the bed and hugged it.

"Hagen, honey, is someone at camp teasing you?" Mira asked.

"No," he said on the tail of a yawn.

"Do *you* think you're a nerd?" Matt asked.

Hagen shrugged and turned on his side, obviously done with this conversation. Matt leaned down and whispered something in Hagen's ear, and Hagen hugged him again.

Matt squeezed her hand on the way out of the bedroom. Mira said good night to Hagen, hoping and praying he wasn't being teased again and wondering what Matt had said to earn that extra hug.

"I love you, sweet boy." She pulled the door partially closed on her way out of his bedroom and struggled to retract her mommy claws.

MATT PACED THE deck thinking about Hagen and rubbing the tension from the back of his neck. Mira joined him a few minutes later with worry swimming in her eyes. He gathered her in his arms and swallowed his frustration, knowing it would only further upset her.

"Are you okay?" He brushed her hair from her shoulder and kissed her softly.

"I wish I could say yes, but he's been teased before, and I thought we'd moved past it. I'll talk to the camp counselor tomorrow and see if she's noticed anything."

"I'll go with you."

She drew back, surprise replacing her worry. "You don't have to do that, Matt. It's kid stuff."

"It's *Hagen* stuff, and I don't mind. I want to be there."

He lowered himself down to the lounge chair, stretching out his long legs, and pulled her down beside him. She snuggled in, her fingers playing lightly over his chest. They lay like that for a long while, listening to the waves lapping at the shore and feeling the breeze wash over their skin.

Sometime later, after the initial shock of worry over Hagen's question subsided and Matt felt Mira's body relax against him, he gently rolled her onto her back and gazed down at her beautiful, troubled face.

"Am I coming on too strong?"

"I don't know. I'm used to taking care of Hagen myself, and suddenly you're ready to step up and protect him."

"And you," slipped out before he could school his thoughts, but now that it was out there, he wasn't about to deny it. "I care about you both, Mira. All these months I've liked you from afar. You're the only woman I've thought about since last summer. The only woman I've wanted, and now I can finally show you and Hagen how much I care."

The truth only made her expression more troubled.

"Talk to me, sunshine. What's wrong?"

"You talk like you're here forever, and we both know you're not. You're only here for a few months, and every day that time gets shorter. I have to protect Hagen's feelings. He's already getting all wrapped up in you. I can't prepare him for how he'll feel when you leave. He'll be devastated."

The truth was a bitter pill to swallow. "And you? How will you feel if I go back?"

"I'm an adult. I don't matter," she said without an ounce of regret, and that made him ache, because she mattered a hell of a lot.

"Your feelings do matter, just like mine do, and Hagen's. We're all important, even though Hagen takes precedence, as he should. I don't know what will happen in three months. It's only been a few days, but I'm learning as much about myself as I am about what it's like to live outside of the academic world. I'd forgotten so many simple things, like how great it is to spend time with you and Hagen without worrying about leaving in the morning and not seeing you for weeks on end. And how it feels to take the time to not just eat a real breakfast, but to sit down at a table with my brother and my niece and our friends and visit. Things I let go for too long."

"And...?"

"And I don't know," he said honestly. It was all happening so fast. "I can't make any promises, but I have wanted to spend time with you and Hagen—real time, not just an hour here or there—for almost a year, and we finally have a chance to do it. I don't want to blow off what we feel when we're together. It's too good. It feels too right. I want to explore it, to see what happens and how it naturally progresses."

He forced himself to say what he knew he had to, even though he didn't want to risk hearing an answer he wasn't ready to accept. "If that's too big of a risk for you, or for Hagen, I'll understand, but it won't stop me from trying. I'm done pretending I'm not dying to spend hours, days, weeks with you and to hold you naked in my arms." He brushed his lips over hers and she arched beneath him with a look of longing and a hint of worry. "You tell me, sunshine. What do you want?"

Her hand circled his neck and her head rose off the chair. "You, Matt. I want you."

Mira's admission unearthed an avalanche of emotions, made worse by the eagerness of her kisses. Her soft, warm hands moved beneath his shirt, up and over his back. He struggled to keep himself in check as he delved into the recesses of her mouth, telling himself that kisses were all he could take tonight. With Hagen sleeping just inside the house, he didn't want to test their control, because he knew it was a losing battle. But she was writhing against him, making sweet, wanton noises, and before he knew what was happening, he was cupping her breast, and the feel of her taut nipple slashed through his control. He sucked her lower lip into his mouth and gave it a gentle tug, earning a moan so inviting he moved his hands south, holding her hips as he ground against her center. Her head tipped back, eyes closed. She was a vision of beauty, flushed with need.

He lowered his mouth to her neck, kissing and sucking as they fell into sync, creating a scintillating rhythm with their hips. Her legs wrapped around his waist, squeezing him, making him ache for more. Not since he was a teenager had he dry humped with such passion, but when he gripped her ass, holding her at a better angle, she felt *incredible*.

Her fingers curled into his flesh, and he claimed her mouth once again, taking her in a wild, rough kiss that had them both moaning, clawing, *begging* for more. Her thighs tightened around him and her breathing became ragged. He pushed his hands beneath her panties, seeking her damp heat. She lifted her hips, guiding his fingers exactly where she wanted them.

"Don't stop," she panted out.

He rocked his hard length against her swollen, sensitive nerves and pushed his fingers inside her. Her head tipped back with a long, greedy moan. She was so into this, so into *him*, he never wanted to stop. She was so hot, so eager and willing, making all his senses rise to the surface.

She clung to his arms, panting out his name. "*Matt. Matt. Matt.*"

He wanted to slide down her body and feast on her, but there would be no easy way to cover *that* if Hagen woke up. His desires would have to wait, but her fluttering eyelids and erratic breathing told him she was on the cusp of release.

"Look at me, baby."

Her eyes bored into him, begging him to take her over the edge. The prolonged anticipation of having her was almost unbearable. A few strokes of her hand on his cock and he'd lose it. Gritting his teeth against the image of her delicate hands wrapped around his cock, he thrust his hips harder, creating intense friction that brought him right up to the brink as he teased the secret spot inside her and took her in a torturously slow kiss that he knew would wreak havoc with her senses. She moaned and mewed, moving with him so perfectly his thoughts careened away. He deepened the kiss, feeling her sex swell around his fingers, and just as he'd hoped, her hips bucked, her thighs tensed, and she cried out into their kiss. Her body pulsed, his heart soared, and their mouths made sweet, frantic love through the very last of her climax.

"Ohmygod." Her head fell back as she gulped in air.

He kissed her cheeks, her chin, her forehead, and finally, her lips. Her body trembled as he rolled to her side and gathered her close.

"You're really good at that and I'm utterly embarrassed."

"Embarrassed?" He kissed her again. "Nonsense."

"Oh please. How many girlfriends sent you home...*unfinished*?"

She pressed her lips to his and palmed him through his shorts. He stifled a groan and closed his eyes for a beat. When she pushed her fingers into his shorts and teased over the head of his cock, he gently took hold of her wrist and moved it away.

"I won't *be* unfinished if you continue doing that." He kissed the rosy flush on each cheek and couldn't resist also kissing the spray of freckles on the bridge of her nose. "We'll have time alone this weekend. I'm not in a rush, and pleasuring you is enough for me for now."

A sleepy smile crawled across her face. "Most guys *take*. You *give*."

"Don't count on that, baby. When I get you alone, there'll be taking going on for sure." He lay with her in his arms until her eyelids grew heavy. "Come on, let's get you inside. I need to wash up. Then I'll get out of here so you can get some rest." He helped her up, and they headed back into the house. After washing up, Matt checked the lock on the back door and found Mira peeking into Hagen's bedroom.

"Do you want me to come with you tomorrow when you take Hagen to camp?" he whispered.

"You have your own work to do."

"I can work around it." He followed her to the front door and drew her against him. "I know you're fully capable of handling this, but you don't have to handle it alone, and I promised Hagen that if someone was bothering him, I'd make sure it stopped."

"Is that what you whispered to him?"

"Yes. I wanted him to get a good night's sleep, and knowing he's got both of us looking after him should help."

"Matt, you can't make promises like that. You can't guarantee that you'll stop someone else from doing something."

"The hell I can't," he said more calmly than he felt. "No one is going to get away with making Hagen feel bad. Not while I'm around."

"Wow. You don't have to go all badass on me." She ran her fingers over the patch of skin revealed by his open collar. "But seriously, you can say you'll try to stop it, but you can't promise. He'll take it literally."

"I want him to take it literally. When I make a promise, I keep it. If he can't count on the adults who care about him to protect him, who can he count on?"

She seemed to mull that over, and he realized if he hadn't been coming on too strong before, he was now.

"I'm sorry. I'll be more careful with what I say from now on. If you'd rather I didn't go, I won't. I just hate the idea of anyone making him feel bad."

"Selfishly," she said quietly, "it would be nice to have you with me because I would get more time with you, but at the same time, it feels silly to have you go. It's a conversation with a counselor, not a deposition, and you have enough on your plate alrea—"

Her words were smothered by his kiss. She was so cute and so willing to put herself last in every situation—when all he wanted was to put her first. Where she belonged.

"What time do we take him to camp?"

CHAPTER TWELVE

"THIS IS ALL too fast, right?" Mira said quietly into the phone Thursday morning. Serena didn't answer, and Mira feared she'd lost the call. "Serena?"

"I'm here. I'm just cutting off my left arm to see if it leads to being you."

Mira heard the smile in her friend's voice.

"What is *wrong* with you? You practically named your vibrator after this guy, and now that he's basically being handed to you on a silver platter with a note that says 'Prince Charming is here,' you're worried about going too fast?"

Mira sighed heavily. "But I have Hagen to think about."

"Exactly, and Rick asked him what he thought of Matt yesterday morning and he said he wished he lived here all the time. Wake up, *sunshine*. Stop borrowing trouble."

"I'm not borrowing trouble. I've been a single mom for a long time. It's weird to suddenly have someone other than you or my brothers want to step in and help."

"I know," Serena said thoughtfully. "You're like those do-it-yourself guys who insist on fixing everything themselves, only they're plugging holes with toilet paper while you use concrete. Let him in, Mira. What's the worst that can happen? Hagen will stop being teased by some punk kid, you'll have a few weeks of great sex—by the way, we are going to talk about the sex—and then you'll go back to your battery-operated friend with new memories. You'll see each other every few weeks, and maybe one day it'll lead to more. I don't see how you or Hagen are losing out on anything."

"But *Hagen?*" She was concerned about her son, but she was beginning to wonder if she was using him as an excuse to keep a little space between her and Matt so *she* didn't get too attached.

"I just answered that. This is about you. You don't want a knight in shining armor anymore. It scares the shit out of you, and don't even try to deny it. You're afraid that after you spent all these years building a solid life for you and Hagen, someone—or more specifically, super-sexy, super-smart, secret savior *Matt*—will upend it."

Mira rolled her eyes. "I hate that you know me so well. I shouldn't have told you what I heard about all that secret savior stuff. It's not as worrisome as I thought. He helped a woman having a seizure when we went to lunch, and he was amazing. Like a true EMT."

"Even more of a reason to let him in. He'll always keep you and Hagen safe, and even though you don't realize it, you could use that comfort in your life."

Everything Serena said made sense, but Mira was still nervous. She wished there was a guidebook to help her know how *not* to mess up her son's life.

"Now, tell me, worried mommy, have you played naughty coed yet?"

MATT AND MIRA spoke with the head counselor of Hagen's summer camp. Nora was a friendly blonde with an *I've got*

everything under control vibe, an athletic figure, and serious green eyes, all of which Mira assumed she needed to manage a children's day camp.

"And Hagen hasn't given you any indication of who might be teasing him?" Nora asked.

"No," Mira answered. "He hasn't specifically said that anyone was teasing him. He asked if we thought he was a nerd, and the question came out of the blue, which to me is a red flag."

Matt squeezed her shoulder supportively. He'd agreed to let her do the talking, and she could see by the tightness of his jaw that he was struggling to hold back his thoughts.

"Then it could be that he's just worried about it," Nora suggested. "When you enrolled Hagen, you mentioned that he was teased during the school year, and we're all keeping our eyes open for any hints of that type of behavior. When he brought his robot in the other day all the kids seemed intrigued, so I'd be surprised if someone was teasing him. But they are children, and you never know what goes through their heads. We'll keep a closer eye on him."

"Okay. Thank you. Please let us know if you notice anything." Mira turned to leave, and Matt's hand slid down her arm to her hand, keeping her there.

"One more thing," he said to Nora. "Is there any time when the kids pair up away from the group? When they use the restroom or take walks?"

Mira hadn't even thought to ask. She was glad he did. She had to admit that it was nice to have his support. Otherwise she'd just silently agonize over it. At least now she had someone to talk to. She'd tried to talk to her brothers and Serena about it before, but all of them—even Serena—had reacted so strongly it had scared her into silence. She didn't want anyone going into the school—or camp—ready for a fight. Their intentions were good, but Hagen would pay the price of such actions in a hundred little ways that Mira didn't want to think about.

"Well, sure," Nora answered. "We use the buddy system, so they have someone with them at all times. As you said, if we're doing an activity across the field, we'll send them in pairs to the bathroom. But they don't always have the same partner."

Matt shifted serious eyes over Nora's shoulder at the children playing in the distance. His dark eyes then swept over the grounds and landed softly on Nora once again. "Thank you for your help, and please keep us in the loop if you notice anything."

"I hate this," Mira confided on the way back to the car. "When they haven't seen anything and Hagen isn't clear about why he asked the question in the first place, I'm left wondering what I'm missing."

Matt put an arm around her waist as they crossed the parking lot and pulled her against his side. The possessive touch sparked a hum of desire low in her belly.

"But you're not left to wonder on your own," he said in a low voice. "Together we'll get to the bottom of this."

How did he know exactly what to say to make the woman in her and the mommy in her want to kneel at his feet? He kissed her neck, sending shivers down her spine. His hand moved along her hip as his talented mouth distracted her from her thoughts, placing kiss after wonderful kiss along her neck. Thank goodness they'd parked at the far end of the lot. They were almost to the car and out of sight from the camp. But then again, she knew Matt was fully aware of their surroundings. He was always careful.

She felt sneaky and naughty and it was such a rush, she

wanted more of it. More of *him*. She'd never been like that, not even when she was first dating and everything was new.

He guided her around the car, blocking them from the rest of the lot, and trapped her between the cold metal and his hard body. She felt every hard inch of his arousal and loved knowing she had that effect on him. He lowered his mouth to her neck again, and good Lord, he knew exactly where to kiss her to make her knees weaken. When he drew back, his riveting stare turned her to liquid fire. She pushed her fingers into the waist of his jeans and held on for dear life to keep from puddling at his feet. His lips curved up in a toe-curling grin.

"You make me want to jump in the backseat and skip work." Her confession came fast and breathless.

"You make me want to take you back to my bed and skip *everything* else until we have to come back and pick up Hagen," he whispered, and then he kissed her—*hard*.

His mouth was hot, wet velvet, and she wanted it all over her—on her neck, her breasts, between her legs where heat pooled and need swelled. His hands moved over her hips to her ass, and he held her as he had last night, deliciously, perfectly, enticingly *tight*. His hips ground sensually against her, and he groaned into their kiss. The raw need of that sound shattered what little restraint she had. Her knee rode up his thigh and his hand moved beneath her skirt.

"Oh *God*," she whispered as his hand pushed beneath her panties and his fingertips found her wet heat. "Matt," she panted out. *Oh God. There. Oh. Yes. There!*

He claimed her in another kiss, touching her with deft precision. She wanted him *inside* her. *Now.*

"Matt," she pleaded.

He pushed his fingers inside her and she lost it. She bit

down on his shoulder to silence her cries as her inner muscles clenched around his magical fingers over and over again. She heard a keening sound and realized it was coming from her. She was so far gone. Her body tingled and burned, swelled and throbbed. She needed more of him. The unexpected orgasm was a gift from the gods, but it wasn't nearly enough.

"What time do you have to be at work?" he asked against her neck.

Work? Oh right. Work. Um... "Nine thirty."

He withdrew his fingers and she gasped with the loss. He dragged her to the passenger side of the car, threw open the door, and nudged her inside. He ducked in and kissed her hard. "It's only five after eight."

MATT SPED THROUGH every green light on the way to the cottage. The stars were aligning in his and Mira's favor. *Thank fucking God*, because Mira was palming him through his pants as he drove and he was on the verge of losing it.

They scrambled out of the car and ran like horny teenagers to the back door, kissing and groping along the way. Stumbling up the back steps, Matt trapped her against the door and kissed her deeply as he fumbled with the keys.

"Hurry," she pleaded.

He shoved the key in the lock and pushed the door open, pulling her inside with him. And then his mouth and hands were on her. They tore at each other's clothes. Her dress and his shirt sailed to the floor in a heap. He made quick work of stripping off his pants and fumbled with the front clasp on her bra. When it finally sprang free, he let out a loud groan at the sight of her in nothing more than a pair of pink lace panties.

"Christ, sunshine. I'm going to devour you."

He filled his palms with her perfect breasts and sucked one taut peak as he teased her other nipple with his fingers, earning a needy whimper. She tugged at his briefs, and he grabbed her hands and pressed them against the door, taking her in another passionate kiss.

"I need to taste you." Tearing off her panties, his eyes raked over her sweet curves, her smooth, silky skin, and the sexy tuft of curls hiding his next meal.

Her cheeks flushed, and she moved her hands over her stomach.

He pushed out of his briefs and laced his fingers with hers. "None of that, baby. You're mine. *All* of you. I want to see, and taste, and touch every luscious inch."

He rocked against her mound. Her eyelids grew seductively heavy, and her breathing quickened. When he angled his hips, pressing the root of his cock against all that sweet, wet heat, they both moaned.

"You feel so good," he said against her mouth. "I bet you'll taste like heaven."

He kissed her roughly, unable to slow his greed, and moved down her body, kissing each breast, laving his tongue over her nipples. She writhed and moaned, clawing at his skin as he blazed a path down the center of her body. He kissed the smooth expanse of skin above her damp curls, breathing in her feminine scent, and grazed his teeth over her inner thighs, coaxing her legs open wider. He pressed a kiss to the cleft of her swollen sex and slicked his tongue along her wetness, taking his first taste of her sweet desire. The pit of his stomach ached with his need for more of her. He gripped her hips and brought his mouth to her again, licking and sucking and plunging his tongue deep inside her. She rocked against his mouth, fisting her hands in his hair and holding him against her.

"Yes. There," she pleaded. "Oh Lord. *There.*"

He couldn't get enough of her. Using the door for leverage, he grabbed her firm, round ass and lifted, guiding her legs over his shoulders and angling her slick heat so he could take more of her. He sucked her clit into his mouth, licked a path to her center, then repeated the sublime rhythm until her breathing quickened and her thighs tightened around his head. He covered her sex with his mouth and thrust his tongue in deep. She cried out so loud it echoed off the walls. He stayed with her, licking and sucking, fucking her with his tongue through the very last quiver.

She fell limply back against the door, and he gathered her into his arms and kissed her hard and deep, until the taste of her arousal covered both their tongues.

"Gorgeous," he said between kisses. "Delicious." He grabbed her ass and held tight. "*Mine.*"

He carried her into the bedroom and laid her on the center of the bed. Her skin was flushed, her eyes so full of emotion he felt himself disappearing into them as he came down over her. Her legs opened for him, inviting him in. His mouth covered hers hungrily. He loved the feel of her smooth thighs cradling him, her juices coating the head of his cock. *Aw hell.*

"Condom," he said between kisses, and retrieved one from the bedside table.

He tore it open with his teeth and quickly sheathed his thick length. She watched with wide eyes and licked her lips. Holy hell she was so beautiful, so feminine, and yet he could see the fierce temptress in her eyes. The desire to be wicked and naughty, which they didn't have time for now, was overwhelming. But soon he'd give her wicked. He'd give her naughty. He'd give her anything her big, sexy heart desired.

Perched above her, he paused, taking in her gorgeous features, the trusting, wanting look in her eyes. In these few quiet seconds he realized she was shaking. He kissed her softly.

"Baby, what is it?"

She shook her head. "I'm okay."

"*Okay* is not good enough. Do you want to stop?" Stopping was the last thing he wanted to do, but there was nothing he wouldn't do for Mira.

"No!" She wrapped her arms around him. "I'm just nervous. It's been a long time."

"For me, too," he admitted. "I haven't been with another woman since I met you."

Her brows knitted, and a small smile curved her lips. "Really? That's almost a year."

"Yes, *really.*"

"No wonder your hands are so strong." Laughter burst from her lips. "Sorry. I can't help it. I'm nervous, and I have you beat. I haven't done this since I got pregnant with Hagen, so go slow, because I may have closed back up by now." She laughed again, which made him laugh, too.

"That's not exactly a bad thing." He kissed her softly. "No battery-operated boyfriend?"

Her cheeks flamed.

"Ah, now the truth comes out. That makes you even hotter."

She closed her eyes and he ran a finger down her cheek. "Open your eyes, sunshine."

When she did, she looked adorably embarrassed and excruciatingly sexy.

"I would have been surprised if you didn't," he reassured her. He laced their fingers together and moved them beside her head. "Now I know you're not opposed to playing around in the bedroom."

He waggled his brows to ease her embarrassment, but when he gazed into her eyes, the passion he saw sent teasing out the door. He lowered his mouth to hers, and she rose up to meet him, her legs circling his waist so naturally, so eagerly, as he pushed into her tight heat, the immense pleasure stole the air from his lungs. He filled her completely, like their bodies were made for each other. He'd been dreaming of this very second for so long, but nothing—*nothing*—compared to burying himself deep inside the woman he adored while she gazed up from beneath him. He slowed their kiss to focus on the incredible pleasure.

"I've waited so long to be with you. I'd have waited forever." His admission came honestly and easily, and the sweet sigh that escaped her lips told him she was right there with him.

Their mouths came together hard and urgent, mirroring their bodies as they fell into sync. She made sexy little noises, and her nails carved memories of this moment into his back as they rocked and thrust, pouring months of anticipation into their lovemaking. He slid his hands beneath her ass, lifting and angling, allowing him to take her deeper. Their bodies grew slick with sweat as they loved their way through the passion, clawing and pleading, chasing the rainbow. Heat streaked along Matt's limbs, bloomed in his chest like wildfire, and stroked between his legs, coaxing him to the verge of release. He held on to Mira's shoulders, driving in deeper, harder, time and time again. Her soft curves pressed against him, and her tight body engulfed his hard length. There was no way he'd last much longer. Her body shifted, guiding his efforts so he stroked over that magical spot that made her gasp, and her head tipped back.

"That's it, baby." He sealed his mouth over the base of her neck, the way he'd learned would get her there.

"Oh God, *yessss*," she cried out.

He slowed their pace, wanting to draw out her pleasure, withdrawing slowly, only to tighten his grip and drive in with all his might, repeating the tease until she finally cried out his name. As she clawed at his flesh, her inner muscles convulsed. A wave of passion crashed over him, sucking him under, drowning him in pleasure until the world spun away and the only thought he could hold on to was *Mira, Mira, Mira.*

CHAPTER THIRTEEN

MIRA WONDERED HOW she'd made it through the workday Thursday without anyone pointing at her and saying, "Hey! You look all sexed up!" It was a ridiculous thought, but she'd sworn the scent of sex and Matt had permeated her skin, wafting around her like the soft scent of perfume even after they showered. She also felt more alive than she had in years, and when she looked in the mirror, the radiant afterglow of their lovemaking shone in her cheeks and gleamed in her eyes. She'd chickened out about talking to Neil, waiting instead until Friday, and having almost as hard of a time. When she finally got up the courage to speak to him about the co-op, she half expected him to call her out on the fact that Matt had driven her to work the day before *and* she'd arrived exactly at nine thirty. She was usually at least half an hour early, as she made a point of being today.

She drew in a deep breath and headed for his office. He was hunkered down over the desk working on the inventory ledger. She hoped Matt was right about Neil not fighting them on looking into the co-op idea.

"Neil?"

He cocked his head, his cheeks lifting with his kind smile. Most people aged from year to year, but Mira swore he'd gotten younger in the past year, more relaxed at least.

"Do you have a second to talk?" Her pulse was racing, but she couldn't tell if it was because of their impending conversation or the tryst she'd had with Matt.

"Of course." He waved to the chair beside his desk and leaned back.

She settled into the chair, telling herself to stop being silly about Matt. They were adults, and people expected them to have sex. Maybe not frantic, rush-to-beat-the-clock sex, but still…

"Was Hagen excited about his camping trip?" Neil asked.

He was always asking after Hagen, who had left earlier in the afternoon with her brothers. "Yes. He's excited to use his new equipment. Drake called when they picked him up from camp, and Hagen told him that they should call day camp, 'play time,' because they don't do any real camping."

"He's a smart cookie."

"He is." Talking about her son eased her nerves. "Matt said you were okay with us checking into the co-op idea?"

His smile widened so unexpectedly, she didn't know what to make of it. "Did he?"

"Um…" *Didn't he?* "Yes?"

Neil laughed. "My son doesn't waste any time, does he?"

Oh God! You could tell we had sex yesterday!

When she didn't respond right away—because she couldn't get past that thought—he said, "Out of all my children, he comes across as the most patient, doesn't he?"

Now she was thoroughly confused. What exactly were they talking about?

"He's very patient," she agreed, growing increasingly more nervous.

"*Usually.* But once he makes his mind up about something,

patience isn't his strong suit. I suppose that's how Bea and I raised our children—to follow their hearts *and* their heads and not to let anything stand in their way. Matty's finally figured it out."

"I'm sorry, but are we still talking about the co-op?"

The slow shake of his head made hers spin. "The co-op. The book deal he's taken on. Coming home. You and Hagen. Isn't it all in part of the same picture?"

The book deal? She and Hagen were part of the book deal picture? No, the book deal was Matt's fallback position. He really wanted the position of dean, and when he'd realized he couldn't have it, he'd decided to take door number two.

I'm door number two.

That went down hard, battling with Matt's confession from earlier that morning. *I've waited so long to be with you. I'd have waited forever.* Could he have meant waited for sex with her? Just sex? That didn't sit right in her mind or her heart.

"I don't know about all that," she finally managed. "But I know he wants to help with the co-op, to try to save the business you've worked so hard to build."

"Yes. Yes, he suddenly does, doesn't he?" Neil said with a sagacious smile.

Suddenly? She was reading too much into all of this, she was sure of it. But Neil hadn't been inclined to even talk about this topic before, and now he was, which made her wonder if he was...*matchmaking?* Rooting for them as a couple? No, surely not. He must have simply come to his senses after talking to Matt and realized how much was at stake if he left the business as it currently stood.

"So, you've changed your mind, then?" she asked cautiously.

"I think it's worth exploring. We can figure out how far to

take it as things progress."

Yesterday's mind-blowing sex had definitely rattled her brain, because she was interpreting every word out of his mouth as having to do with her and Matt. The bell on the door jingled, and Mira was thankful for the distraction.

"Thanks, Neil. I'm excited to see where we end up." She pushed from the chair and she was so flummoxed that in her head what she'd said also sounded like she was talking about her and Matt. "With the co-op, I mean," she clarified.

She turned to leave and smacked into Matt's chest.

"Hey there," Matt said, wrapping his arm around her waist.

"Sorry," she said quickly. Her insides were melting and trying to flee at once. She *never* got flustered, but between the thoughts about being door number two, the weird conversation with his father, and the feel and now-familiar scent of Matt waking up all of her hormones, she was a hot mess.

Matt gave her a quick kiss and said, "Don't be."

His father smiled as her skin burned off her bones. She was sure it would slough off her body any second.

"We were just talking about the co-op," his father said as he patted Matt on the back.

"It's a great idea," Matt said. "Isn't it?"

"The best one I've heard in years," Neil said as he headed into the store.

Mira realized Neil hadn't asked her any questions, like how the co-op might work, or what companies she was thinking of looking into as potential business partners. Maybe he'd been talking about her and Matt after all.

MATT HAD THOUGHT long and hard over where to take Mira for the weekend before finally settling on his cottage in Nantucket. He'd thought about taking her to Boston, but he knew Hagen wanted to see a library there, and he wouldn't feel right going without him. He also didn't want to go too far in case Hagen needed them to return at the spur of the moment, but he wanted to take her someplace special and memorable. He hadn't spent much time at his cottage, and he'd never been with a woman on Nantucket, making it the perfect weekend getaway to begin building memories with Mira.

The ferry ride was fun, and passed too quickly. When they arrived at his quaint water-view cottage, Matt paid the driver and hitched the bags over his shoulder. The look of sheer bliss and appreciation on Mira's face as she took in the quaint cottage told him he'd made the right decision. An abundance of pink and white roses climbed over the white picket fence, up the sides of the house, and along an arbor surrounding the front porch. Splashes of weathered cedar shingles and white trim peeked through the mass of pretty blooms and lush greenery.

"This is gorgeous," Mira said as they followed the seashell walkway up to the front door. "How did you manage to rent this on such short notice? I would think the entire island would be booked all summer long."

He draped an arm over her shoulder as they walked to the side of the house and took in the view of the water. A sandy path cut through a deep expanse of dune grass separating the cottage from the private beach. Just beyond, the water glistened like glass. Boats decorated the water, and for the first time since Matt had bought the cottage, he wondered what it might be like to spend more time here. They were walking distance from town, but Matt had phoned ahead and purchased two bikes, which he'd had delivered and stored in his shed in case Mira wanted to explore the outer reaches of the island.

"The owner doesn't rent it out."

She squinted up at him. The setting sun reflected in her eyes, bringing out vibrant specks of green and gold around her pupils. "Then how'd you manage to get it?"

"It's mine, sunshine."

Surprise registered in her expression.

"I bought it as an investment, but never got around to renting it out."

"You *own* this?" She glanced around the property with awe as he unlocked and opened the door. "Why are you renting a cottage at Seaside if you have all *this* at your disposal?"

He smiled at the wonder in her eyes and set the bags inside, then joined her in the yard and wrapped his arms around her waist. "Don't you know? Haven't I been clear?"

Confusion riddled her brow.

"It's okay. I didn't really know either. Not until Friday night."

"What...?"

"I thought I came back to the Cape to reconnect with my family and to see what might come of us, but I was wrong." He pressed a hand to her cheek and kissed her softly. "Friday night I realized that I came back to the Cape to see what would come of us. Connecting with my family was a bonus."

"But we're door number two," Mira said absently.

"Door number two? Baby, what are you talking about?"

"You said you realized you wouldn't ever get the job you wanted, so you chose door number two."

"Oh no, baby. That was about work, not about you. You're not door number *anything*."

She hooked a finger into the waistband of his slacks. "So, what are you saying?"

"I'm saying that I've spent almost a year falling for you from miles away and trying to stay on the *friendly* side of our texts because I couldn't take the chance of messing up your life. But I know now, without a doubt, that the main reason I came back to the Cape was to see if we could make things work. Everything else was secondary."

CHAPTER FOURTEEN

MIRA KEPT WAITING to be plucked from the romantic rabbit hole she'd fallen down. She and Matt enjoyed a scrumptious dinner at a lovely French restaurant in the center of town and made their way outside. They meandered through the center of town, where bulbous streetlights cast halos of gold over brick-paved sidewalks. Couples walked hand in hand, children devoured ice-cream cones, and dogs trotted happily beside their owners. Bicycles lined the empty cobblestone streets, and the din of carefree summer nights filled the air. Nantucket wasn't so different from the small towns on the Cape, with old-fashioned-looking storefronts, wide sidewalks, and a nautical theme. But somehow, being here alone with Matt made it seem like they were a lifetime away. It felt *magical.*

"Are you sure we shouldn't call and check on Hagen?" Matt asked for the third time since they'd arrived on the island.

"Yes, I'm sure," she said, missing her little man. "If he needs me, my brothers will call. When he was younger I'd call and check on him when he stayed overnight with them or with Serena, and it made him *remember* that he missed me. It's like he gets so caught up in having fun he forgets I exist for a while."

"And that doesn't bother you?"

"It did," she answered softly. "But then my mother reminded me that this was what being a parent was all about, raising our children to be independent. Selfishly, I'd like to hear his voice, but that's for me, not him. He's out having a blast, doing boy things."

"*Guy* things," he said with a coy smile. "You're a wonderful mother, sunshine. I can't imagine it's easy."

Matt tucked her snugly against his side as they walked toward the water, talking about intimate topics they hadn't ventured into before crossing the friends-to-lovers line.

"Nothing's easy, but with parenthood there are more wonderful times than hard times. I wouldn't change my decision for anything."

She told him about the many sleepless nights and zombie-like days she'd endured when Hagen was a baby and how she'd napped when he did. They talked about how her mother had stayed with her for the first week after Hagen was born, and how much her brothers and Serena helped her since.

"Do you want more children?" he asked.

"Yes, someday," she answered honestly. "You?"

He nodded. "Definitely."

She wasn't a woman with a checklist, like some single women out there. But if she were, being with a man who wanted a family would be on the top of the list, alongside reliable, loyal, loving, and trustworthy.

Mira learned about how Matt's father used to take him on weekly trips to the library and they'd hunt down book sales all summer long.

"Hagen would love that," she said.

"Then let's make a point of doing it. There's no reason he should miss out on the things he would love." He stopped walking and tipped her chin up with his finger, bringing her mouth in line with his.

Standing beneath the black velvet sky, Mira smiled up at the man she was falling harder for every minute they spent together.

"Come to Boston with me next weekend. I have to do some research, and Hagen would love spending hours in the library. It's on your road-trip list."

"Both of us?" Her heartbeat quickened at the prospect.

"Of course. We'll rent a two-bedroom suite. You and Hagen can stay in one room and I'll stay in the other. It'll be our next adventure."

"You wouldn't mind staying in a separate bedroom?" In the dating realm, she had *baggage*, a term she hated when used in reference to her son, but a term that was tossed around like a volleyball just the same. During all of his visits, Matt had never tried to push Hagen out of the picture. He never made her feel like her son was an inconvenience, just as he wasn't now.

Our next adventure.

She'd spent so long trying not to think about Matt as a prospective boyfriend that she was still getting used to the idea that they had become a couple. A couple that might have a *next* adventure.

He pressed his lips to hers. With a thoughtful, loving—yes, *loving*—gaze that made her heart soar, he said, "I will do whatever it takes to be with you and Hagen. I'd get my own hotel room, but selfishly, I'd like to be more involved with bedtime, morning...*family* time. That's why I suggested a suite."

The dreamy sigh that escaped her lips came straight from her ovaries. *Family time.* Surely he was just using it as a loose term for daily activities that seemed typical for couples with children, but it tweaked all of her heartstrings. She knew she needed to be careful with Hagen's heart—and her own—since

Matt was supposed to return to Princeton, but she didn't want to be careful. Especially not when her heart was pushing careful as far away as possible. Serena was right. Even if they went back to seeing each other every few weeks, what were she and Hagen losing out on? This time together was too good to pass up.

"Okay," she answered. "We'd love to."

They walked toward the water, talking about the trip and how excited Hagen would be. A quartet was playing by the wharf, and Matt swept Mira into his arms and began dancing.

"I never knew you liked to dance so much," she said, laughing as he twirled her around.

"I don't, but I'll take any excuse to have you in my arms." He kissed her then, long and slow, and oh so sensually, tightening his grip when her knees weakened.

"You make me want so many things," he whispered in her ear as they swayed to the romantic melody. "You, Hagen, time with both of you. *This.* You make me want to stay."

Oh, how she wanted to believe him, to take those words and make them come true, but she knew better. "You can't say things like that to me," she said softly, holding him a little tighter.

"But it's true, baby. Why wouldn't I want you to know how I feel?" He spoke directly into her ear, holding her securely against him, as if he never wanted to let go.

"Because it makes me want what can't be, and I have to be careful, for Hagen's sake."

"You have to be careful for your sake too, sunshine." He pressed his lips to her cheek. They were warm, soft, and reassuring. "But it's true," he whispered in her ear. "It's true and I want you to hear it. You have me, Mira. Even if I go back to New Jersey, there'll only be you. We'll figure it out. But for now, for these next several weeks, *be* with me. Please, let go of your fears and *be* with me."

Questions raced through her mind about *how* they might figure it out. The thought of a long-distance relationship was too painful to linger on, and the idea of moving away from her family and friends after she and Hagen had finally gotten on stable ground was unsettling. But she would never in a million years ask Matt to give up the very things he'd worked his whole life to achieve. She closed her eyes, allowing herself to soak in his impossible hopes, and pretend, just for a few moments, that they could one day come true.

He gazed into her eyes and said, "*Be* with me, Mira."

The worries lingering in her mind were no match for her heart, which was so full of Matt, she didn't know how to be any other way.

"I already am."

BY THE TIME they headed back to the cottage, the streets were nearly empty, and the closer they got to Matt's private stretch of beach, the more it felt like they had the whole island to themselves. They'd talked about so many things—Mira's plan to address the co-op, Hagen's comment about being a nerd, her brothers, his family, his writing. When they reached his cottage, he knew her even more intimately than he had only hours earlier, and it wasn't nearly intimately enough. They grabbed blankets and pillows and spread them out on the beach, stretching out beside each other.

Mira's hair tumbled over her chest in luxurious soft waves. She wore the pretty pink dress she'd worn the day he'd met her at Grayson's engagement party. It gathered over the tops of her thighs. His heart swelled with memories of that afternoon. He'd felt the world shift around him then, but he never could have anticipated how deeply she'd affect him in the coming months.

"Aren't you worried about your pillows getting all sandy?"

He tucked her hair behind her ear so he could see her face more clearly. "Not at all. You live within the confines of mommyhood every day, and until recently I've lived within my academic walls. This weekend we have no rules, no walls. Only each other. This is a private beach, and I intend to take full advantage of our privacy. Sandy pillows and all."

"God, where did you come from? I've never met a man like you."

He kissed her tenderly. "I've never been this man until now. Until *you*."

She laughed softly, and the sweet sound floated around them. "I feel like we've been dating for months."

"We kind of have, sunshine. When I think about how many things led to my decision to take this sabbatical, it seems like most led back to you. All those times you sent me texts telling me that you'd had fun at a bonfire or barbecue with your family or our friends, or sharing something Hagen did or said. Or those torturous texts that said, 'Wish you could have been there.' I realize now that each and every text fed into my decision to finally take the sabbatical and give this—us—a real shot."

He'd been back for only a week, and he was already wondering how he'd ever return to teaching full-time and living hours away from Mira and Hagen—and his family. Morning coffee with Pete had become a habit that he looked forward to, and this week he'd see Grayson and Hunter and their fiancées,

Parker and Jana. Time was slipping away too quickly, and he wished he had three more days for every one that passed.

"I wonder if you'd have taken time off sooner if I'd sent you the texts I really wanted to send." She turned a sultry gaze on him.

Matt ran his fingers along her cheek, and she smiled. He loved her smile. He loved her face, her body, her brain, her son. How did he go from having all of his emotions in check back in New Jersey to the explosion that took place inside him every time they were together? He was usually methodical and careful about decisions, but being with Mira woke up a part of him he'd never known existed.

"Tell me about those texts I never received," he urged.

Her cheeks flushed, and she licked her lips nervously. She was so damn cute he couldn't resist sweeping his arm around her and tugging her against him. God, she felt good. Warm, soft, and perfectly matched to every inch of him.

"Tell you?" she asked shyly. "I can't *tell* you."

"Yes, you can, sunshine. You can tell me anything because you trust me." He shifted her gently onto her back and gazed into her lust-filled eyes. He slid his knee over her legs and pressed his hand to her cheek. "Tell me everything you held back."

"Matt," she whispered, and trapped her lower lip between her teeth.

He freed that trapped lip with his teeth, sucking it into his mouth.

"I want to hear you say it. Did you want to text dirty things to me?" He knew he was pushing her past her comfort zone, but he wanted that, too. He wanted her trust, her words, her *heart*.

"Did you want to offer an invitation?" He kissed her softly.

"To tell me you missed me and you wished I was in your bed at night?"

Her lips parted and her long eyelashes fluttered, searching his eyes as if they held all the answers. He was working on that and hoped one day soon they would.

Waves rolled up the shore, and a gentle breeze whisked over their skin. Matt slid his hand along Mira's outer thigh. She breathed harder, and when his fingers touched the edge of her panties, she sucked in a sharp breath.

"Tell me what dirty thoughts you withheld while we were apart," he coaxed.

"I wanted *you* to flirt with *me*."

Hearing her voice her desires, even something as simple as wanting him to *flirt* with her, opened a door that Matt had a feeling held much darker desires.

"You want to hear how I fantasized about you?" he asked, hoping she'd say yes, because he wanted to see just how much the sultry single mom had been holding back.

She nodded, her eyes widening with anticipation, darkening with lust.

He squeezed her thigh. "How I wished I'd have stayed longer so we could get to know each other more intimately? How on the long drive home to New Jersey I thought about having these gorgeous long legs wrapped around my hips as I loved you so deeply you felt me the next day?"

"Yes," she whispered anxiously. Her fingers fisted in the blanket.

"How I imagined you in your sexy lingerie, lying in the center of my bed, watching as I drew your panties down slowly. With my teeth." He paused, letting the visual take hold. "How I wanted to tease you until you begged for every hard inch of me?"

Her body began to tremble, and he slid his hand up over her ribs and palmed her breast, teasing over her pert nipple as he spoke. "Should I tell you how I wanted to suck on your beautiful breasts until heat consumed you and you felt it between your legs? Or maybe how I'd like to bury my mouth between your legs and devour you until I knew your taste by heart and you were so swollen you *ached* for me to make love to you?"

She whimpered, and he slid the strap of her dress down, freeing her breast. Her eyes held his as he lowered his mouth and slicked his tongue over her taut nipple. She closed her eyes, and he stopped. Her eyes flew open.

"That's it, sunshine. Watch me love you."

He brought his hand to her breast again and traced slow circles around the rosy bud with his tongue. She arched up, pulling his head down, but he resisted her efforts, wanting to bring her right up to the edge, until she was dripping with desire.

"Maybe you wanted to hear how I envisioned you on all fours on my bed as I took you from behind, holding on to your hair just tight enough that you felt every tug between your legs," he said brazenly, testing the depth of her naughtiness.

Her eyes widened again. "I've never…"

"Don't worry, baby. We won't do anything you don't want. And I promise, we *will* do everything your little heart desires. Are those the types of texts you wished for?"

"Yes." Her voice was shaky, her skin flushed.

He righted her dress and bra, and confusion washed over her beautiful face. He moved his hand beneath her dress, stroking her through her damp panties.

She closed her eyes again and his hand stilled. "Open, baby." Her eyes fluttered open. "That's it."

"More, Matt. Tell me more."

He couldn't suppress the wicked grin lifting his lips. He pulled off her panties less than gently, fisted the silk and lace in his hand as he brought them to his nose and inhaled deeply. Her jaw dropped open.

"Your scent is intoxicating," he said, and dropped her panties beside her. He brushed his hand over her pubic hair, and she sucked in another sharp breath. He covered her mound with his palm, his fingers brushing lightly over her wetness. Her legs spread wider, and she rocked against his hand, her eyes imploring him to continue describing his fantasies.

"Do you know how many nights I lay awake imagining what it would feel like to touch you here?" He stroked his thumb over her clit, and she trapped her lower lip again. He slid one finger between her wet folds, moving from front to back in a slow rhythm, feeling her breathing quicken, her hips rock, her arousal grow even slicker with need.

Her eyelashes fluttered, and he dipped the tip of his finger inside her, moving in and out, though not going deep. She whimpered, and the sound tore through him, electrifying him from the inside out.

"How many nights I thought about what you would look like when you came apart beneath me? On my tongue? On my hands?" He felt her sex clench, and he cupped his fingers over her, stilling his movements, reveling in the pulsing sensations against his flesh.

"You're so sexy right now, sunshine." He withdrew his hand from between her legs and she gasped. "Sit up for me, baby."

He helped her sit up and lifted her dress over her head. She crossed her hands over her chest, her eyes darting nervously over the dark, deserted beach.

"We're alone. I'd never share you with anyone else." He took off his shirt and rose to his feet to strip off his pants. Naked, he knelt beside her and stroked his hard length. She licked her lips, and it took all his will not to push his cock between them, but he had other plans. He wanted to see her surrender to him completely, to strip away all of her inhibitions.

He gathered her close and gently lowered her to her back. He lifted her head and slid a pillow beneath it. Then he took one of the extra blankets and tucked it beside her for warmth. She reached for it, and he placed his hand over hers.

"I'll warm you up, baby. Trust me."

Her hand fell beside her. He reached for the other pillow. "Raise your hips for me." She did, and he centered the pillow beneath them. "Perfect."

CHAPTER FIFTEEN

MIRA WAS SHAKING all over, from the breeze, from nerves, from the fact that she was lying naked on a beach while Matt visually devoured her, like he was deciding where to start. She'd never been spoken to so dirty before, and she freaking loved it.

Matt stretched out beside her, his erection resting temptingly against her hip as he ran a single finger slowly from her neck to her belly button, over her pubic hair, to the cleft of her sex. Her body shuddered beneath the intimate touch, and when he followed that path back up, she thought she might combust. Her nipples tightened, her sex clenched, and her mouth went bone dry. He followed the same trail south again, only this time he covered her sex with his hand. His long fingers rested over her wetness as he took her in a rough, intrusive kiss that went on and on, every second stealing more of her ability to think. When his thumb began circling her clit in slow, precise movements, she couldn't contain the greedy pleas that escaped her lungs. His long fingers slid up and down the center of her sex, teasing and taunting as he devoured her mouth, shattering any and all thoughts.

His mouth moved to her jaw, then the base of her neck. She loved when he kissed her there. Sparks ignited under her skin, in the air around them, beneath his mouth as he grazed his teeth over her nipple, sending exquisite pain straight to her core. Her sex clenched against his fingers, and he groaned.

"My girl likes it a little rough." His voice was sinfully deep.

While she was reveling in *my girl*, he dipped a single thick finger inside her.

"Oh *God, yes.*" She arched off the pillow, and he continued teasing her, pushing his finger in and out with lethal accuracy while his thumb applied the perfect amount of pressure to all those sensitive nerves at the tip of her sex.

He sucked her nipple so hard she cried out, and he stopped.

"Too much?" Regret laced his words.

"No, I just...I never...No. It's good." Holy crap, it was *so* good.

He lowered his mouth to her breast again, and she felt him close his smile around it. He sucked and teased and bit—*Oh God, yes!* He sucked again, laving the tender spots with his tongue, then bit down at the same time he thrust his fingers into her.

"Oh *God. Yes. So* good." She had no hopes of quelling the stream of praise coming from her lips. "Incredible. *There.* There. Oh God. *Bite.* Yes. *Ohgodohgod.*"

Her eyes slammed shut as he withdrew his fingers and stroked between her wet lips. Her sex throbbed. She arched and rocked her hips, but he wouldn't delve inside her body.

"Tell me what you need, baby." His eyes burned through her, begging for her words.

She couldn't do it. She couldn't say what she wanted. His mouth crashed down over hers in a kiss so demanding it took her right up to the edge of release. She could barely breathe. Her toes curled under, and her fingers dug into the blankets. She was so close she could feel it, see it in the periphery of her being. He slowed the kiss, meeting her tongue with long, slow strokes. She panted into his mouth, the orgasm ebbing, and it was then she realized he knew *exactly* what he was doing.

"Please, Matt. I need you inside me," she begged.

He thrust his fingers between her legs. Her senses reeled, her thoughts shattered, and she cried out his name. He took her in another possessive kiss as her body quaked and quivered. Her hips bucked off the pillow, and he eased the kiss while moving his fingers quicker, taking her back up to the peak again. When she finally came down from the peak, her limbs were weak, her breathing shallow. He moved his mouth to her breast again, and in seconds she was on the verge of another explosive orgasm— and then he was gone. Moving lower, between her legs, replacing his fingers with his mouth, and—*oh God*—she lost it again, coming so hard her whole body felt like one taut muscle.

He moved up her body in one swift effort, his balls brushing against her sex. Her nerves were so raw she knew she'd come again if he applied any amount of friction.

Matt kissed her tenderly. The taste and scent of her arousal was everywhere.

"Taste that, baby?" He smiled down at her. "So good. From now on, when you kiss me, I want you to think about my mouth between your legs. I want you to remember how good it felt to come on my tongue."

Hearing him use that language turned her on even more. How would she ever kiss him again and not think of those very things?

He reared up on his knees, dragged his fingers along her sex, making her entire body thrum, and wrapped his glistening fingers around his cock. He stroked himself with one hand and moved beside her, stretching his long, hard body out on his side, and placed *her* hand between her legs.

"Make yourself come for me," he coaxed.

She froze. She'd never done that with anyone watching before.

"Come on, baby," he urged, still fisting his cock. "We're going to do a lot more than this. There's no room for embarrassment."

Oh, how she liked that promise, but she still wasn't sure she could touch herself in front of him. "But I want to make love to you," she said shyly.

"Don't worry. We're nowhere near done." He took her hand in his and together they brought her to the edge of another orgasm.

He released her hand. "Keep going. I want you to feel free with me."

She closed her eyes and continued touching herself.

"Eyes open, baby."

She groaned, too deep into the next orgasm to resist, and her eyes dropped to his big hand around his shaft, sliding up to the head, over the top, and back down again in a quick, repetitive rhythm. A bead formed at the tip, mesmerizing her as it glistened in the light of the moon.

"Faster, baby," he said urgently.

She hadn't realized she'd slowed her efforts. She closed her eyes again.

"Eyes on me," he said in a heated tone.

"It makes me want you more." The confession burst from her lips.

"Good." He lowered his mouth to hers, taking her in a fierce, demanding kiss.

Then his hand was on hers, moving with her, pushing her fingers inside her body alongside his. It was so taboo, so erotic, that she didn't want to stop—not when she came so hard she could barely breathe. Not when he continued the pressure, the probing. She clutched his hair with her free hand, holding his mouth to hers as together they gave a repeat performance. She'd never come so many times, so hard, in her life. It was addicting, and as she came down from another orgasm, he turned on the blanket, bringing his mouth to her sex.

"Oh, *Matt*," she cried as he sucked her clit to the point of titillating pain and pleasure. She rocked against his mouth, and when she opened her eyes, his cock was right there beside her, that alluring, glistening bead weeping for her. She wrapped her fingers around him and he groaned against her sex. It vibrated through her core, and when she finally got her mouth on him, she moaned loudly, hoping to create the same enticing vibration for him. She took him to the back of her throat, humming aggressively around his cock.

"Holy hell, baby," he said, sliding his fingers in and out of her sex, giving her unrelenting pleasure. "You're going to make me come if you keep doing that."

She hummed louder, rocking her hips to the same beat as she sucked him off. She clawed at his side as her orgasm consumed her, moaning continuously, trying to bring him the same explosive pleasure. He tried to pull out of her mouth, but she had a tight hold, and she wanted *all* of him. The first hot jet slid down her throat, the next clogged it, but she didn't back off. She forced herself to take everything he had, just as he was doing for her. And the gratification of knowing she gave him as much pleasure as he gave her was so immense, it brought tears to her eyes.

Matt moved beside her and gathered her in his arms, kissing her so thoroughly, the taste of him mixed with the taste of her and literally became one.

When their mouths parted, his hand slid down her belly to her oversensitive sex again. She didn't know if she could keep up. He was like a sex machine, and her body felt limp and sated. His fingers teased over her flesh, and her senses reeled.

Oh yeah, she could do this.

"Now, my sweet girl," he whispered into her ear, sending a shiver down her spine. "Turn over and let me love you into tomorrow."

He reached for his pants and retrieved a condom, quickly rolling it on.

Turn over? She worried as she turned onto her stomach.

"God you're gorgeous. Don't worry, baby. I'm not going to do anything you don't want to."

Don't *want* to? She had no idea if there was *anything* she didn't want to do with him.

His strong hands moved over her skin, rubbing her arms, her shoulders, her upper back and then following the line of her spine south. She closed her eyes as he moved between her legs, his hands running up and down her hips, his mouth leaving a trail of hot kisses at the base of her spine. The pillow remained beneath her hips, angling her ass up, and when he spread her cheeks and ran his tongue along the crease, she fisted her hands in the blanket. Never had she felt anything so exquisite. His tongue slid lower, to her sex. She pressed her hips back, wanting that talented tongue deep inside her. He pushed a hand beneath her and found the other elicit spot as he loved her with his mouth, sending her body into the throes of another orgasm.

As she came down from the peak, he aligned the head of his cock with her entrance and gathered her hair over one shoulder, placing tender kisses along her skin. "I told you I wouldn't do anything you didn't want."

"I know you wouldn't." He felt incredible, all those hard muscles pressing down on her back, his hips planted firm against her ass.

"When you want to do more, we will."

She knew they would, and now she understood what Serena meant when she said with the right guy she'd go *there*.

Matt laced his fingers with hers and said, "I want to make love to you face-to-face, but this will feel good for you. Let's just play for a minute."

That made her wonder what she'd been missing out on for all these years. She'd never been very creative when it came to sex. Missionary position was all she'd done. He entered her, moving over that magical spot with renewed pressure. The angle was perfect, the friction intense. *Holy mother of all things orgasmic.* It felt out of this world. Who would have thought a pillow and lying on her stomach could make this much of a difference? He sealed his mouth over the back of her neck and pushed his hands beneath her, squeezing her nipples. A rush of sensations engulfed her, and when he began moving at a slow, sensual pace, it was all she could do to remember to breathe.

"That's it, baby. Feel it? That's *us*." One of his hands moved south, taking up residence between her legs, while the other continued teasing her nipple.

"Are you"—she tried to get her brain to focus—"really a professor of *sex*?"

He laughed and kissed her cheek. "Only with you, baby. Christ, sunshine, I need to see you."

She turned over, and as their bodies came back together, he kissed her again, deeply, thoroughly. The kind of kiss she wanted to keep her warm on cold winter nights.

"I've never felt anything like this," he confessed. "I can't get enough of you. I need to see your face when we make love. I need this connection."

As their bodies came together, the passion swimming in his eyes and the feel of him loving her coalesced, and she knew in that moment it didn't matter if they'd been together a week, a month, a year, or ten. She was falling in love with Matt Lacroux, and she had been for a very long time.

Chapter Sixteen

AFTER MAKING LOVE on the beach last night, Mira had fallen asleep nestled safely in Matt's arms on his king-sized bed. Matt lay awake for a long time, thinking about how quickly he'd become accustomed to a life outside of the classroom. A life where his top priorities were governed by what he wanted and not red tape and boxes that needed to be checked off. It was midafternoon, the sun was shining, and Matt felt happier than he had been in years. He looked down at his shorts and flip-flops.

I might never wear socks again.

It was a silly thought, but a thought he never would have had before taking this sabbatical. He glanced at Mira, leafing through a book a few feet from him in an eclectic bookstore in town. She looked beautiful in a sexy green tank top that set off her hazel eyes and a pair of white shorts. How was it possible that she looked more radiant every day?

She glanced up, and a shy smile curved her lips. When he'd woken up with Mira in his arms, it had taken all of his willpower to let her sleep in rather than waking her up to satisfy his own ravenous desires. Luckily, she'd woken up shortly after with the same insatiable appetite for him. Making love with her was heavenly, made even better by her willingness to trust him and explore her naughty side, which he loved as much as her sweet and her maternal sides. They made love before breakfast and again before showering and throwing on bathing suits beneath their clothes, and taking off on bikes to explore the island. They checked out an art gallery, a handmade clothing store, and a jewelry store, where Mira practically drooled over a canary diamond ring. They had lunch by the water, and for the last hour they'd been perusing this cozy bookstore, which smelled like apples and cinnamon. He'd known how well he and Mira would get along, but he hadn't realized how effortlessly their lives would come together.

"What's that look?" she asked quietly.

He closed the distance between them, aware of her quickening breaths and the darkening of her gorgeous eyes. Sliding a hand around her waist, he whispered directly in her ear—because he loved the way she held her breath every time he did.

"Thinking about how hard I'm falling for you."

She nibbled on the corner of her mouth and gazed up at him with a sultry, slightly shy gaze that made his insides soften and his outside harden.

"Matt," she said dreamily, and went up on her toes to kiss him. "This is all wonderful, but it scares me a little."

"I know it does. I told you I'm considering my options. With the dean position out of the picture, and the research and writing fulfilling that academic craving I know I'll always have, I don't miss teaching."

Worry lines crept across her forehead. "I'm not asking you to stop teaching."

He pressed a kiss to those lines, hoping to ease them. "I know you aren't. You never would. I've been growing tired of teaching for quite some time. It's the research and writing that holds my interest, and even that is hampered by administration.

Sunshine, so much has changed for me these last few years. Watching my siblings fall in love and manage to be happy both professionally and personally has opened my eyes to the things I always wanted but put off to 'one day.' I'm in my thirties. One day has come, and I'm still churning the academic wheel. When my father began talking about retiring, I realized that I haven't been around in a meaningful way since I was eighteen. I don't want to miss out on being part of his life anymore. Or part of my brothers' or Sky's life. Or Bea's. And then I met you and Hagen..."

He slid a hand to the nape of her neck, gazing into her hopeful and worried eyes. "And I haven't been able to stop thinking about you ever since. I know you're scared to let yourself fall for me, or to let Hagen become reliant on me, because my future is up in the air, but I'm going to prove to you that I'm worth the risk. You can't deny what's between us, sunshine. It's too strong."

"But how will we...?"

"Figure it out? We have to trust that we'll both know what the right thing to do is when we get to that point." When she smiled, he pressed his lips to hers. "Let's pay for these books and go parasailing."

Her eyes nearly bugged out of her head. "Parasailing?"

He carried the books to the register and paid while they discussed the idea.

"I might be afraid of heights," Mira said nervously.

"Might be?"

"I've never tested the theory, but there's a possibility."

He hugged her to him as they left the bookstore. "You'll have me by your side. Come on, sunshine. I've only got a few weeks to convince you that you can trust me. What better way than from high above shark-filled waters?"

"I CAN'T DO this." Mira clung to the grips of the parasail for dear life. "The scariest thing I've ever done was give birth, and that was in the safety of a hospital bed!"

Matt patted her thigh. "NASA came up with this idea as part of their survival training for pilots who had to eject from their aircraft over the water. It's safe."

The instructor, a burly guy who looked like he ate sharks for breakfast and had spent the trip out telling them about his GoPro videos, explained that they'd take off and land on the special parasailing boat. He said they could take a dip in the water if they'd like. Swimming near shore was one thing, but now that Matt had planted the idea of sharks in her mind, there was no way she was dipping even a single toe in it.

She gazed into the dark sea surrounding the boat. "Unless you fall and get eaten in these shark-filled waters."

"I was kidding. There are probably only a couple in there."

"Matt!" She swatted him, and he leaned over and planted a loud kiss on her lips.

"Are you ready?" the instructor asked.

Great. She was going to fall from the sky and get eaten by sharks and this guy would probably film it with his GoPro and make millions from a highly monetized YouTube video.

Matt gave the instructor a thumbs-up and the boat began to move.

"I get the idea of living in a safe little world where you control everything around you. I've done it my whole life, just like you have since you've had Hagen. It's time for us to see what we're missing."

"You have not! You're a secret savior." She said this casually, but at some point, when they weren't about to be flown like a kite above shark-infested waters, she wanted to delve deeper into that side of him and see what it was all about.

He laughed.

The wind kissed her face as the boat picked up speed and the cables began to tug into place. As they lifted from their seated position and her toes left the safety of the boat, she realized what Matt had said.

"You haven't done this before?" she hollered.

Matt smiled and wrapped his hand around hers, which was still clinging for dear life to the grip. "No, but I trust we can get through anything together."

"That's *not* how you earn a woman's trust!" She white-knuckled the grips as they sailed into the air and the sleepy little town, and the sea around it, came into view. It was a spectacular sight.

Matt pointed out their cottage and the streets where they'd ridden their bikes, but Mira was busy watching him. The wind whipped his hair away from his face, accentuating his striking features, which had taken on a golden tan over the balmy afternoon. His tank top looked sprayed on over all those hard planes of muscles she'd gotten to know so intimately last night. When Matt turned to face her again, his eyes warmed, even against the whipping wind.

"Okay, sunshine?"

It was all she could do to nod. Waking up in his arms, making love with him, was an entirely new experience. He didn't just love her physical body; he reached deep into her soul, caressing her heart with tender, careful hands, making her feel safe and special. He was breaking down her barriers one moment at a time. She never stood a chance against the passionate, loving man who was looking at her like she'd created life itself.

"We should bring Hagen," he said, and her heart skipped.

She bit back her initial reaction of, *Hell no! It's way too scary for him.* He grabbed her chin and pulled her into a long, sensual kiss, bringing all of her senses tingling to life anew. She got lost in his unforgiving mouth, the feel of his strong, warm hand sliding to the back of her head as he deepened the kiss, and the wind whipping over her skin. And just like that, her fear drifted away.

CHAPTER SEVENTEEN

RELAXED DIDN'T BEGIN to touch the feelings floating through Mira. The sunny afternoon had given way to a warm, clear summer evening. She and Matt had biked all over the island, seen the beaches and lighthouse, the historic homes, and everything in between. When they'd come back to the cottage, they'd opened the front and back doors, and the evening breeze filled the cozy space. It was only six, and they decided to have a late dinner after taking some time to relax. She checked her messages, of which she had only two. One from Drake telling her that Hagen was doing fine and teaching him and Rick how to use a compass, and one from Serena, who wanted to know if Mira had given in and used Nair. She quickly sent off a text to Drake—*Thank you! Give him extra kisses from me. I'll see you Sunday afternoon*—and Serena—*No! And he hasn't complained.*

She stretched out on the couch and closed her eyes, thinking about the incredible day they'd had.

Matt came out of the bedroom a few minutes later wearing nothing but a towel and a pair of black-framed glasses. Her jaw dropped open. Her naughty-professor-slash-coed fantasy sprang to life in vivid color.

He chuckled, rounding the couch.

"If you changed your mind about calling Hagen, we should probably do it now."

"No need. Drake texted and said he's having a great time and showing them how to use his compass." She couldn't take her eyes off of him as he reached for her hand and lifted her to her feet.

"Glasses," she whispered. How could glasses make him even hotter? "Holy moly. Where have you been hiding those?" She pressed her hands to his chest, feeling his pecs jump beneath her palms.

"My contacts were bugging me." He swept an arm around her waist, pulling her against his now tented towel.

"Were your clothes bugging you, too?"

His low laugh rivaled the seduction in his eyes. "I promised you pampering." He kissed her tenderly, then led her into the expansive bathroom, where candles burned on every surface. The oversized tub was filled with bubbles. The window was open, bringing a cool edge to the heat simmering between them.

Matt lifted her shirt over her head and laid it on the sink, then helped her out of the rest of her clothes, kissing her skin as it was revealed. He kissed her shoulders, the swell of her breasts, and when he removed her panties, he sank to his knees and pressed a single kiss to each thigh and to the curls above her sex. She was no longer embarrassed or felt the need to cover up. Matt seemed to appreciate her curves. Heck, he appreciated everything about her; there was no *seemed to* about it.

He took off his towel and set it beside the tub and stood before her naked, his eager arousal grazing her stomach. He was every professorial fantasy she'd conjured up since the day she met him, only better.

"Do you wear those glasses in class?"

"Sometimes. Why?" He gathered her hair over one shoulder and helped her into the tub. She expected him to climb in behind her, but he sat across from her and gently guided her legs around his so she was nestled between his knees and their bodies were only a few inches apart.

"Do you…? Have you…?" She was embarrassed for even thinking the crazy thought that was in her head, but his glasses made him look *very* professorial, sparking memories of friends who had slept with their professors.

He set his glasses beside the tub and wet a washcloth, lathering it up with heavenly smelling body wash. "What, sunshine?"

"Have you played 'naughty professor' with any students?" She bit her lip, feeling ridiculous for asking.

"Only a few," he said as he brought the washcloth to her shoulder and gently washed her arm.

"Only a *few*?" Her stomach sank. "Isn't that against the school's policy or something?"

He lifted her chin and shook his head. "Do I seem like the kind of guy who would sleep with a student?"

She let out a relieved breath. "You can't do that to me. I think you just shaved ten years off my life."

He wrapped his arms around her. "The girls who try to seduce their professors have 'daddy issues' written all over them. I'm attracted to *women*, not *girls*, Mira. Give me some credit." He drew back with an intense look in his eyes. "And give yourself a little credit, too. Would you spend the weekend with a guy you *thought* would do that?"

"No, but…" She picked up his glasses and shook them. "I blame these. You looked so hot in them that my mind went lots of places it shouldn't."

He smiled, but his eyes remained serious as he lovingly washed her sides and belly.

"Does that mean you think I have daddy issues because I

want to play naughty professor with you?" She had to ask.

He smiled and kissed her shoulder with a seductive look in his eyes. "You're not my student. There's a world of difference." His expression turned serious again, and as he spoke, he ran the washcloth over her breastbone and around her breasts, making her thoughts hard to pin down. "It's a wonder you trust anyone after what Hagen's father pulled."

He lifted his eyes to hers, moving that washcloth down the center of her body, then detouring over her thigh. She watched his hand, hoping it might slip between her legs.

"Is that also why you haven't been dating?" he asked.

It took her a minute to get her lustful brain to process his question. She knew they'd talk more about this subject at some point, but she hadn't been anticipating it now, and it took her off guard. She wrapped her hands around his legs, needing something to anchor her.

"Partially." This was not going to be easy, but she wanted to be honest with him, and somehow baring her soul in the bathtub, where neither had anything to hide behind, made it a little easier. "I think it's always in the back of my head that guys lie." She knew how harsh that sounded and added, "I'm sure women lie, too. I don't mean that we're perfect, but *of course* my experience affected me. And the few dates I went on proved to me how different my life is from a single woman's. Most guys have no idea what it takes to raise a child. They think a child's like a puppy. Put them in a crate for a while and they'll get used to it."

She paused, taking in his serious expression and the thoughtful way he was touching her now, his hands holding her around her waist. He'd become her anchor, knowing exactly what she'd needed. *Again.*

"I think the reason I let myself move so quickly with you is that I feel like we've been heading toward this for almost a year. That's a really long time, and I know your family and friends, and I've had months to get to know you and trust you."

He took her hands in his and gazed into her eyes. "I will always be honest with you. That's one thing you can count on."

She nodded, believing him with her whole heart, and her next words came surprisingly easily. "I don't like to admit it, but it *was* hard, trying to juggle a new baby and work and *life*. Before your father hired me, the companies I worked for weren't very accommodating when it came to time off for Hagen, and with kids you never know when they're going to get sick. We'd moved a few times based on babysitters and jobs. Our lives are finally stable, and if something happens to me, my family is there for Hagen."

"You've done a good job with him," Matt reassured her, picking up the washcloth and running it along her back, bringing their bodies even closer together. "He seems very grounded and happy."

"Thank you. My biggest fear is that I'll somehow screw him up. The prospect of letting a man into my life is still scary, because in the end, my decisions affect Hagen's life. You mentioned daddy issues, and I'm not sure he won't have them, once he learns the truth."

MATT HAD BEEN thinking about that himself, and about Hagen's comment about being a nerd. That issue was far from closed in his mind. But Mira was telling him she needed to keep some boundaries and he knew he had to be careful how strongly he voiced his concerns.

He washed her tenderly, placing kisses along her wet skin.

"I don't think all children who grow up with only one parent have issues. Hagen has a strong support system in place."

"That's true, and I hope it's enough. I lost my dad when I was twelve, as you know, and that was hard. But I think it's different, because I know how much he loved me before he died."

"Yes, it's different, but every situation is different. I wasn't ready to lose my mother as an adult. But losing a parent and being treated as if you don't exist to that parent are totally different. Maybe, when the time comes, when Hagen is older and inevitably learns the truth, you can get him into counseling, so he has a safe place to deal with it."

"That's already on my list. I'll protect him from the truth as long as I can, but there'll come a time when he's filling out medical papers or just curious, when he'll need to be told. I don't look forward to it."

Matt wrapped his arms around her and held her, wanting to promise he'd help her when the time came, but he sensed that wasn't what she needed to hear, so instead he said, "He's lucky to have you."

When the water cooled, he dried her with a thick towel, blew out the candles, and led her into the bedroom. He knew she wasn't used to all the physical activity they'd done today, and he'd planned a nice relaxing evening of pampering his lovely girlfriend.

He took the towel from around her and she climbed onto the bed on all fours, moving like a seductive kitten across the mattress. Gone was the shy girl of last night. She looked over her shoulder, her hair tumbling over one eye, and he nearly forwent the pampering he'd planned, but he didn't want her to miss out on being cherished like she deserved to be.

"Lie down on your stomach, beautiful."

She followed his request, looking utterly gorgeous sprawled out on the blankets, her hair streaming away from her face in soft waves, her sweet curves on display. She closed her eyes and he retrieved the body lotion from the bedside table and straddled her hips. Pouring the lotion into his hands, he brought them to her shoulders and began kneading what little tension she had.

"That feels *so* good."

"*You* feel so good, baby." He massaged her shoulders, down her arms, then worked his way back up each limb again.

"My arms feel like wet noodles."

"Good. Relax, sunshine. You never have a chance to put yourself first, so tonight is all about you."

"Matt?"

"Mm-hm?" He focused on the back of her neck, rubbing all the places he knew she carried tension.

"Why haven't you been dating?"

He moved lower, carefully massaging her upper back. He smiled as he answered, because he knew how cheesy the truth sounded. "Because I met you, and you weren't in New Jersey with me."

She craned her neck and gave him a look of disbelief.

"It's the truth." Once she settled onto the pillow again, he said, "I've never been the type of guy who could sleep with a woman without caring about her. I know that makes me sound either like a liar or a fool, but I am who I am." His hands glided over her sides, massaging all the way down to her hips.

"But *look* at you," she said, eyes still closed.

He came down over her back and kissed her cheek. "Baby, look at you. There's no difference, except you had Hagen to look after."

She opened her eyes, and he shifted so he was lying beside her. "But you're a *guy*."

He pressed his erection against her hip. "I'm fully aware of that fact. But that doesn't mean I'm an animal who can't control myself. I had a healthy sex life. I wasn't a saint, but once I met you, you were the only woman I wanted."

She smiled and touched his cheek. "But you couldn't have known we'd end up like this."

He brought her fingers to his lips and kissed them. "I didn't, but my heart wanted you. I was busy with research projects and students and trying to figure out what I wanted to do with my life. When they offered me the book deal, I took it as a sign. And here we are."

"All that time?" she asked with wide eyes.

"It's amazing what the mind and body are capable of." He kissed her again and resumed massaging her back. She snuggled into the blankets with a sweet smile on her lips.

He worked his way down her spine, easing the tension from her muscles. Kissing the dimples just above her rear, he reminded himself this was pampering, not foreplay, though his body had other ideas. He kneaded her rear, biting back a groan.

"Mm. Feels *so* good," she repeated.

He parted her thighs and moved between them, massaging each leg from the back of her knee upward to the very tip of her hamstrings. She rocked against the mattress, moaning softly, *erotically*. He ground his teeth to keep himself in check. His hands moved over her inner thighs, grazing her wet center. She inhaled sharply, and he clenched his teeth harder, fighting a losing battle for control. Moving south, he massaged her calves, and finally her feet, which earned another sensual moan.

"Turn over, baby."

She rolled onto her back, looking so relaxed and beautiful his heart swelled. She licked her lips, her long lashes fluttering above eyes heavy with desire. Matt poured lotion into his hands and caressed the front of her legs. When he reached the apex of her thighs, her breathing quickened. He brushed his thumbs over her glistening sex, dying to delve inside, and she let out a long, needful moan.

"Christ," he said under his breath. This was not supposed to be about sex. He forced his hands down to her hips, pressing his fingers deep and kneading every last ounce of tension from them. His hands traveled up her ribs, beneath her breasts, and he lowered his mouth and pressed a kiss to one rosy nipple.

"Matt," she whispered urgently, eyes still closed. She curled her fingers around the sheets. "Touch me."

He filled his hands with her beautiful, full breasts, fighting the urge to take them in his mouth, and pressed a kiss to her other tight nub. She whimpered, her whole body arching up for more.

"This isn't supposed to be about sex, baby." He forced himself to move away from her gorgeous breasts and massaged her shoulders and arms. When he'd massaged every inch of her, including each individual finger and toe, he made his way back up her body. She was trembling, her breathing shallow. And as he massaged her thighs, her sex visibly clenched.

"Please, Matt. *Make it* about sex."

He pressed a kiss to her inner thigh, inhaling the intoxicating scent of her arousal—his new favorite drug.

"*Please*, touch me."

The plea in her voice seared through his will and drew his mouth to her sex. He slicked his tongue up the center of her swollen, wet flesh.

"Oh God, *yes.*"

He dragged his tongue along her sex again, and her legs opened wider, accommodating his broad shoulders. He loved her with his mouth, feeling her sex pulse and twitch and drinking in the sweetness of her desires. Her hands pushed into his hair, holding him as he pleasured her. Her legs became rigid, and sexy noises streamed from her lips. He knew she was about to come, and he wanted to be right there with her. In one swift move he grabbed a condom from the bedside table, sheathed himself so fast he should win a gold medal, and imprisoned her hands beneath his on the mattress, driving his hard length into her.

She cried out, and a stream of sexy pleas flew from her lips. "Yes! Harder! Oh God, Matt. *Yessssss.*"

Her inner muscles squeezed him like a vise. All that tight heat was sheer perfection. He released her hands, gathering her body against his to take her deeper. Her fingernails clawed down his back, dragging him under as tides of passion crashed over them. The real world spun away, and all that was left was the two of them and a flood tide of sheer, unadulterated love.

ONE HOUR, ONE shared shower, and several delicious kisses later, Mira stood on the deck gazing out at the water. Down the beach she saw twinkling lights. She squinted, trying to make out what it might be. The screen door opened behind her and she drew in a deep breath, her pulse quickening in anticipation of

Matt's touch. She'd already come to expect the feel of his warm lips, hard and insistent against her skin, when he greeted her.

His arms circled her waist, and he pressed a tender kiss beside her ear. "Are you ready to go to dinner?"

"Mm-hm. Look down there." She pointed to lights dancing in the distance. "What is that?"

Matt slipped an arm around her waist, and as they stepped off the deck and onto the sand, she rested her head against his shoulder. He looked like a model in a pair of dark linen pants that tied at the waist, a white cotton shirt stretched tight across his broad chest, and those sexy glasses that made her stomach go ten types of crazy.

"Maybe we should go see what's going on down there," Matt suggested. He took her hand and led her toward the front of the house.

"But I thought we were going to see—" She swallowed her words at the sight of a horse-drawn carriage parked out front. A man dressed in black slacks and a white button-down shirt stood beside two impressive white horses at the front of the wooden carriage.

Matt placed a hand on her lower back. "I don't think your dreams of being romanced by Mr. Right were immature. I think you simply had them too early."

Her eyes burned with tears of happiness. "It's…Oh, Matt." She threw her arms around his neck and kissed him. "I can't believe you did this. How? When? I was with you the whole day."

He lifted one shoulder in a coy shrug. "When there's a will…"

Matt gave the driver his phone and had him take a picture of them in front of the carriage. *To remember our adventure.* As if she would ever forget this magical moment.

The driver set a wooden stool on the ground, and Matt held Mira's hand as she climbed into the carriage, where she found a bouquet of gloxinias waiting for her. *Love at first sight.*

"Happy Saturday night, sunshine." He draped an arm over her as the driver took his seat in the front of the carriage and the horses led them down the cobblestone street.

She hugged Matt again, listening to the *clippity-clop* of the horses compete with the loud beat of her heart. "Thank you. You didn't have to go to all this trouble. I'm glad you did, but just being with you is enough for me."

"We'll have plenty of time to just be together without any bells or whistles. But you've missed out on a lot while focusing on being a mommy. We've got catching up to do, and I'm going to make sure you never miss out on anything again."

As the horses led them through the streets they'd ridden their bikes on earlier in the day, and some they'd somehow missed, Mira felt like she was living in a fairy tale. But fairy tales weren't real, and Matt was very, very real. *And you haven't been with another woman since we met.* She couldn't stop thinking about that. She didn't know men pined after women. She thought it was just something she read about in romance novels. Her mother often told her that good things came to those who waited, but she hadn't exactly been waiting for Matt. He'd been off-limits in her mind. A man whose life and lifestyle were too far away from her own.

Maybe her mother had it wrong. Maybe good things came to those who got screwed over by cheating exes.

"We have to bring Hagen here," Matt said casually. "He'd love that little bookstore, and parasailing, and you know the minute he sees a horse-drawn carriage he'll want to build one."

She loved that Hagen was never far from his mind.

The carriage brought them to the edge of the beach where they'd seen the dancing lights. A shiny silver canopy draped in sparkling lights shimmered in the breeze above a table set for two. A waiter in full black-tie attire stood at the ready with a white cloth draped over his sleeve. Candles danced inside red vases, positioned around the canopy in the shape of a heart. Mira had never seen anything so elegant in all her life.

The driver stepped out and set the stool on the ground. Then he reached up and helped her out of the carriage. She clung to the lovely bouquet as Matt thanked the driver, and she saw him slip him something, which she assumed was a tip.

"You set up the dancing lights, too?" She probably shouldn't be surprised, but she felt like a breathless girl of eighteen again.

"Let's go find out." Matt knelt beside her, smiling as he slipped off her sandals, removed his shoes, and set them off to the side.

He hugged her closer as they stepped onto the cool sand. Maybe she *had* been hoping for Mr. Right too soon.

CHAPTER EIGHTEEN

MIRA WATCHED THE island fade in the distance as the ferry carried them swiftly back toward the Cape. Sunday had come too fast. She didn't want their weekend to end. The thought came with a touch of motherly guilt. She and Matt sat by the railing with the midmorning sun shining down on them and the salty air kissing their newly bronzed skin. She closed her eyes and rested against Matt's side, making a mental list of the things she'd have to do when she got home—*check Hagen for ticks, laundry, prepare my spiel about the co-op*—nixing her daydreams and the motherly guilt that accompanied them. It wasn't like she'd dumped her son with a stranger to go away for a sexcapade. Hagen was probably having a great time with his uncles, and her life would go back to normal in a few hours. Thinking of all the things she had to do, she wondered when she was going to fit in the phone calls to the companies. The best time to reach any business owner was when the companies opened before they had time to get busy, but she'd be driving Hagen to camp at that time. She imagined leaving messages that would never be returned. Maybe she could call on her lunch hour, but what were the chances of business owners being available during lunchtime?

Matt kissed her temple, pulling her from her thoughts. "Ready to be a mommy again?"

She smiled, wondering if it would make her an awful mother to admit she wished they had one more day alone. "I'm always ready to be a mommy, but I want more time with you."

"I'm not going anywhere." He kissed her softly. "I like my writing schedule of getting up early and hammering out a few hours of research, sometimes seeing you for lunch, and being with you and Hagen in the evenings."

She quieted her hopeful thoughts, knowing he was referring to the remainder of his sabbatical, not his entire future, which made her heart hurt a little.

"I meant now. Selfishly, I want another day alone with you."

"Me too, sunshine. Don't worry, when there's a will…We'll find time alone. What else is going on in that pretty head of yours?"

She shrugged. "Just work stuff."

"Thinking about the co-op?"

"Yeah. I want to start calling companies tomorrow." She explained her dilemma about timing.

"That's easy to fix. I'll take Hagen to camp tomorrow while you make the calls. That'll give me more time with him. Maybe he'll open up about why he asked about being a nerd."

He kissed her again. He was always kissing her, and she loved it.

"But you just said you like to do research in the mornings."

"That's the great thing I'm discovering about being a real writer instead of a teacher who *also* writes papers. There's no one to report to. I make my own schedule, and tomorrow I'll drive Hagen to camp and work a little later."

"Matt, I don't want you to feel like I'm using you as a babysitter, or—"

He silenced her with another wonderful kiss. Maybe she should always ramble around him.

"I don't feel that way," he assured her. "I offered, and I'm totally okay with you *using me* as a boyfriend. There's a big difference between a babysitter and a boyfriend. Boyfriends and parents don't babysit. They take care of children they care about."

She tried to swallow past the emotions clogging her throat. Most people had no idea there was a distinction. "You can't possibly know how much it means to me to hear that."

"You can't possibly know how much it means to me that you're letting me into Hagen's life."

They sat in comfortable silence as the Cape came into view. Mira got up to go to the ladies' room, and Matt went with her, a protective hand securely in place on her lower back. She hadn't needed to be taken care of or walked to the bathroom since she was a little girl, but Serena was right again. She took comfort knowing Matt cared enough to do the little things she didn't *think* she needed.

As they approached the ladies' room they passed a couple in a heated argument. They were whispering, but there was no mistaking their tones. Mira raised a brow to Matt, as if to say, *Glad that's not us,* but it was lost on her overprotective man. His hand tightened around her, his eyes never leaving the angry couple. Mira didn't know what he was so worried about. Couples fought. It was part of life. And it wasn't like the guy looked like a derelict or the type of man who would fly off the handle. He looked like he'd walked off the golf course in a pair of nice khakis and a polo shirt. Although, after taking a second look, Mira noticed the woman slowly stepping backward.

"Go on into the ladies' room, sunshine. I'll be right here

when you come out," Matt said, nudging her toward the entrance.

She went into the ladies' room imagining him standing with his arms crossed like a bodyguard waiting for her to come out. She pushed open a stall and heard a shriek. Mira ran out of the ladies' room, and her heart lodged in her throat. Matt held the arguing man prisoner against the wall with one hand on his throat. His other hand was stretched out behind him, a barrier between the man and the woman, who was now crying.

The veins in Matt's neck and arms bulged like pregnant snakes. His narrow-eyed stare was lethal as he seethed through gritted teeth, "You lay a hand on one man, woman, or child and I will make sure you can *never* do it again." He seemed oblivious to the gasping of the crowd gathering around them.

"Fuck you, asshole," the guy snapped. His eyes shifted to the woman with a stare that made Mira's blood run cold, but it was the bruises appearing on the woman's arm that had her sidling up to the frightened woman and putting her arm around her.

"Shut. Your. Mouth," Matt said too calmly. The restraint in his voice told Mira he was acting that way for the sake of the spectators. "The authorities will take care of you, but one more foul word out of your mouth and you won't be able to tell your side of the story."

Mira focused on the trembling woman beside her. "Are you okay? What happened?"

"I don't"—she sobbed—"know. We had a blind date, and I..." She shook her head and swiped at her tears.

Mira embraced her, telling her it was okay and watching Matt with awe and concern as the authorities broke through the crowd and took over.

By the time the authorities released Matt, the ferry had docked. Matt's arm circled her waist as they walked to the car.

"Sorry, sunshine," he said casually. "Are you okay?"

"Me? Matt, you just put yourself in danger for a stranger. What if that guy had hurt you?"

He smiled down at her. "Then I'd say my years of self-defense training were pretty worthless."

She was as turned on by his badass manliness as she was concerned. He could have been hurt. And then her mommy brain kicked in again. "I'm serious, Matt."

"So am I," he said casually.

"What if Hagen had been there?"

"I would have had you take him into the restroom with you."

"That's it? You would have still put yourself in danger? I've heard the rumors about you saving people like some kind of superhero, which is totally hot. And Parker told me that you looked like you'd been in a fight when she met you. Stepping into that situation on the boat was really dangerous."

They stopped beside his car, and he took both of her hands in his. His chin fell to his chest, and he closed his eyes for a second.

MATT'S FIRST INSTINCT was to brush off Mira's comments. He'd been getting away with brushing people off since college. Why should now be any different? He drew in a deep breath and opened his eyes. One look at the worry in Mira's eyes and his heart took a nosedive. She didn't deserve to be brushed off. *Everything* was different where she was concerned.

He'd asked for her trust, and she had the right to expect the same in return.

"I promised I would never lie to you," he said, "and I won't. But I'm not sure what you want to hear." He released her hands and paced. "That guy grabbed her so hard she screamed. Would you rather I pretended like it wasn't happening?"

"No, but…" She crossed her arms, a bevy of emotions passing over her face.

"But what? Do you want me to say that if Hagen were there I would have walked away? Because it would be a lie. I would make sure he was safe, just like I did with you. But I saw the telltale signs in that guy's posture, the danger lurking in his eyes. That woman was backing up before he even touched her. Clearly she was scared."

"I know, but—"

"But it's not our problem?"

"No. That's not what I meant."

Misdirected anger coiled deep in his gut, anger over not being there all those years ago to help his friend. He raked his hands through his hair, struggling to suppress the ugly emotions coursing through him. He took a few deep breaths and forced a calmer tone.

"Mira, I'm not a guy who can say 'It's not my problem' and walk away, and I know you wouldn't want me to. I'm sure it was scary for you to see that, and I'm sorry, but I can't lie to you and pretend I wouldn't do it again. But that doesn't mean I'd put you or Hagen in danger. If I didn't think I could handle a situation I'd back off."

"Would you?" Her tone was so serious he stopped to think before answering.

"Maybe not," he said honestly.

She rolled her eyes, and he stepped closer, his love for her pushing the anger out of the way.

"It's just not that simple. There's *history* there." *And it's held securely in place with enough guilt to keep me going forever.*

Her gaze softened and she touched the center of his chest. She smiled so sweetly it felt like an embrace.

"I shared my history with you," she said. "Will you share yours with me?"

CHAPTER NINETEEN

MATT MULLED OVER where to begin as he and Mira drove back to her house so they'd be there when Hagen arrived. It was one thing to admit what he'd done to Pete, who had his back no matter what. He knew that admitting the truth to Mira wouldn't be nearly as hard as seeing the look in Mira's eyes when it finally sank in. When she realized what his selfish drive to succeed in school had cost another woman.

"Do you mind if we sit out back?" he asked as he carried her bags to her bedroom.

"No, that's fine."

They sat on the steps to the deck with their feet in the sand, and she looked at him with a mix of awe and concern.

"What you did took courage, and now that we're not right in the thick of it, I'm crushing on you even harder. Let's face it. Who wouldn't want a boyfriend who wasn't afraid of, well, anything? But I have to think about Hagen and the examples we set for him. I don't want him thinking he should step into situations he can't handle. Plus, I worry about you."

She pressed her hands to his cheeks and kissed him. "I just found you. I don't want to lose you because some jerk pulls a knife or something. I need to understand this."

Matt stole another kiss before trying to explain. "First of all, nothing's going to happen to me. Second of all, don't you think if Hagen ever witnessed something like that, I'd immediately explain to him why I did it and define boundaries so he didn't think it was okay to step into something he couldn't handle?"

She wrinkled her nose and smiled again. "I know you would."

He couldn't resist kissing her right on the bridge of her nose, where all those adorable freckles danced.

"Mira, what I'm going to tell you might change how you feel about me."

"I doubt it," she said easily.

We're about to find out. "When I was in school I had one focus—graduating at the top of my class. I knew I wanted to teach at Princeton, and in order to do that, I had to surpass everyone else. My brothers will tell you I lived and breathed schoolwork, while they lived and breathed life, women…"

"So, you're saying that you had a limited social life?" She looked perplexed, as she should, since she was waiting for a clear answer and he was trying to give her the full picture, as if it might make a difference.

Nothing would make a difference.

"I guess you could say that. My social life came *after* my studies. I dated and went out with friends, but neither was my priority." He wrung his hands together, thinking about those stressful years when he'd pushed himself past reasonable limits. "I had plans to meet a friend one night. Cindy Feutra." He hadn't said her name in so long it brought a chill to his skin. "We were supposed to go to a party together, but I lost track of time, studying until three in the morning, and I never showed up."

He shifted his eyes away, remembering the shock of hearing what had happened the next morning when he'd sought her out to apologize for not meeting her. "Cindy was attacked that night on her way back to her dorm."

His throat tightened, and when Mira touched his arm, he forced himself to meet her gaze. The empathy he saw there nearly slayed him.

"That poor girl."

"Yes." His voice cracked with emotion. He waited for her to say something more, to get angry or disgusted and place blame where it clearly belonged. His muscles tensed in preparation of accepting his due, but she simply squeezed his forearm, her gaze remaining warm and caring.

He didn't know what he'd done to deserve her, but he thanked his lucky stars just the same and told her the rest of the story. "When I went looking for her to apologize the next morning, she was gone. She'd been taken to the hospital that night, and news had spread throughout the campus by morning. She never returned to school. I tried for weeks to reach her, but she didn't return my calls."

"And you blame yourself," Mira said softly.

"Of course I do. If I had met her when I was supposed to, that wouldn't have happened. I never would have let her walk home alone."

"But you can't know what would have *actually* happened," Mira pointed out.

"You're right. The only thing that matters is what *did* happen."

"Oh, Matt. I get it, I really do, but sometimes having a big heart makes life much harder than it needs to be. Did they catch the guy who did it?"

Matt shrugged. "There were rumors, but as far as I know, no one was ever arrested."

"So ever since that night you've been stepping in and help-ing people when they're in trouble, as some kind of self-inflicted penance?"

"Pretty much. Making up for the mistake I can never take back. And trust me, I understand all the psych stuff behind it. It's not like I don't fully comprehend why I do it. Although my brothers will tell you that I went out of my way to help people even before that, which was true. It just wasn't fueled by the same fire."

"So…are the rumors true? Do you go out *looking* for people to save?"

He could deny it, not reveal exactly how deep those demons ran, and she'd never know. But he didn't want there to be any secrets between them. That was something his mother had drilled into his head as he was growing up, just as she'd drilled into his head that following his heart was the key to a happy life. Matt was beginning to understand that in a much bigger way than he ever had.

"I used to," he admitted cautiously, watching her process his words. "I've helped a lot of people." He had no idea how many people he'd helped over the years, because he hadn't been mentally ticking off a debt. It had simply become a way of life.

"Why did you stop?"

"Stop?"

"You said you *used to* go looking for people to help. Why did you stop?"

He smiled. Finally an easy question. "It wasn't a cognitive process. I realized the other day that since I've been home, since you and I started going out, things changed. I'm no longer restless and unsettled like I always was. I don't have that urge to chase ghosts."

Her thin brows slanted in a frown. "Does that mean you think me and Hagen need saving?"

"No, sunshine. You and Hagen don't need saving. I care about you both, and part of caring is protecting, but it's not saving." Her lips curved up, and the worry seemed to drift from her expression. He moved closer, needing the connection as he revealed his truest secrets.

"My *life* has changed. When I was teaching, I rarely had time for anything else, which is one of the reasons I'm seriously considering giving it up. Helping others was probably also my way of filling a void that I was trying to ignore. And after we met that void became harder and harder to ignore. I wanted *you*, and I worried about you and Hagen, but I had to continually bury those feelings because you were here and I was hours away." He paused briefly.

"I'm not going out looking for those situations anymore because that void has been filled in a normal, natural way by being here for you and Hagen, and probably also by reconnecting with my family and being here for them."

She squeezed his hand. "Good, because I don't think we need saving either, but we love having you in our lives. Have you thought about tracking down Cindy to apologize and try to gain some closure?"

"I've thought about it many times, but it might do more harm than good for her, and she's the one who's important in that scenario. And, Mira, closure won't change my behavior. This is who I am. I won't turn my back on someone in need, but I promise you I will never do anything that puts you or Hagen in jeopardy. If this is a problem for you, then you have a decision to make, sunshine. Either you can deal with a guy like me, or you can't. It's best we figure that out sooner rather than later."

The front door opened and Hagen ran through the house. "Mom!"

Matt and Mira rose and ascended the steps just as Hagen flew through the back door with a big smile and leaped into Mira's waiting arms.

"We had the best time!" Hagen said as Mira kissed his cheek. Pushing from his mother's arms, Hagen hugged Matt. "I showed them how to use the compass and led a hike through the woods! Are you staying for dinner? Uncle Drake and Uncle Rick taught me how to cook over a fire, and I want to cook for you and Mom."

"That's your mom's decision, little man." Matt looked at Mira.

Her eyes brimmed with unmistakable tenderness and passion. "My decision is"—she paused for a prolonged moment, and in the silence, in the love in her eyes and the warmth emanating from her, her answer to his earlier question became clear—"*absolutely*. Matt can stay as long as he'd like."

CHAPTER TWENTY

FALLING BACK INTO mommy mode was easy, work mode, not so much. Thoughts of her love-filled weekend with Matt clouded Mira's thoughts. When Matt showed up to take Hagen to camp Monday morning, the sparks she'd come to expect when they were together flew, but they were carried by much deeper emotions than just a few days earlier. They'd shared so much of themselves, the line between where her life ended and his began blurred, and she liked it. A lot.

Forcing herself to take advantage of the quiet time Matt afforded her by driving Hagen to camp, she set to work calling the companies she hoped to interest in the co-op. The first few calls garnered minor interest, but only after answering questions that made her feel like a felon or a scam artist—*How did you get my name? What makes you think our business needs help?* This was not being received as the promising endeavor she'd hoped it would.

As she gathered her things to leave for work, her phone rang, and Matt's picture flashed on the screen. Just seeing his image made her pulse quicken.

"The eagle has landed," Matt said in a mysterious voice.

Mira laughed. "Thank you so much. Was Hagen okay?"

"He was great. We had a blast. We talked about the raft we're going to build, and if it's okay with you, we thought we could start a week from Saturday. I figured it might take a few weeks to get your arms around the co-op stuff, and I didn't want to put any pressure on you."

Tumble, tumble, tumble.

She was tumbling head over heels for this incredibly caring man. "Sure. That's perfect."

"Great. I'll let Pete and my dad know. Let's make a day of it. Bring your suit, and you and Jenna can hang out on the beach while we do guy stuff."

Guy stuff. Why did she love that so much? *Because it's his and Hagen's thing.*

"Sounds like a sly way for you to see me in my bathing suit again."

"Sunshine, I'll take all I can get of seeing you—clothed, naked, scantily clad."

She felt herself blushing. "Mm. Sounds good to me."

"I'd take this further, but I'm pulling up to Seaside and don't need to be caught with tented pants."

"No, we wouldn't want that," she said with a giggle as she carried her things out to the car.

"I almost forgot. Apparently there's a field trip at Hagen's camp Thursday."

"Yeah, to the playhouse. I filled out all the forms. Do they need something else?"

"No, but Hagen asked if I would chaperone."

As Mira started her car, she thought maybe she'd heard him wrong. "He asked *you* to chaperone?"

"Yup. Is that okay?"

"Do you *want* to chaperone?" Mira had chaperoned school trips so many times in the past, her nerves were on edge just thinking about watching over all those excited children.

"Why not? I haven't seen *The Wizard of Oz* in years, and Hagen promised to make sure I didn't get scared when the flying monkeys came on stage. How can I pass that up?"

It warmed her heart thinking about Matt wanting to do this for Hagen and that Hagen had made that promise. He liked to take care of the people he cared about just like Matt.

"What about your writing? I don't want you to feel like you have to do it just because he asked."

"Mira, I want to, and my writing is fine. This morning I wrote for two hours before driving Hagen, and I'll write for another few hours after we get off the phone. Rest assured, I don't feel like I *have* to do anything. I've waited months to be able to do these things. Now, stop worrying and tell me about your calls."

As she drove to work, she told him about her morning. "All the research I did just made me look like a scam artist who wants to take their money."

"Because they don't know you. I get it. It's like when I first began receiving emails from publishers. They were just faceless sales pitches. You need a personal connection."

"A personal connection? But how? What made you decide which publishers to call back?"

"That was an easy decision. One of the emails was less of a sales pitch. It asked if we could sit down over lunch and talk. It was a no-brainer after that. He was a living, breathing person. That's it, Mira. That's what you need."

"How can I do that? I work full-time and have Hagen. I can't exactly take the time to visit a dozen businesses."

"No, but you said you had three out of nine companies who requested more information, and you only need six, right? Isn't that what you said?"

"Depending on the investments from each, five or six, yes." She parked behind the hardware store. "Are you thinking I should keep trying to garner interest, and then go visit the businesses who request more information? Two of the three are in Boston and the other is in New York."

"Exactly, sunshine. You wanted to take a trip down the East Coast. Why not mix business and pleasure?"

"I want to take the road trip as a vacation with Hagen. There's no way I can meet business owners with a six-year-old in tow, and I can't leave him for a week."

"You've got me now, and a little boy who wants to see a few special libraries. We'll all go. I'll watch Hagen while you meet with them. It can't take more than a few hours at most with each. Then we'll hit the libraries. It'll be fun. We might not be able to see all of the locations you and Hagen planned, but I'll make sure he has a great time."

"Are you kidding? Even if I get five or six people to agree to meet with me, that could take a week or more with driving time."

"So we'll fly if we have to."

"I can't afford that." She cut the engine and sank back in her seat. "This is too much, Matt. I don't think I can make it happen."

"But I can, and it's my father's store you're trying to save."

"Matt..." Could she let him do this? It was a lot of money and time. "What about your writing? You said you needed to go into Boston next weekend for research. I can't keep you from that. Besides, how can you get anything done if we're traveling? You only have a few weeks before you have to go back."

"I have *several* weeks, and I'll make the time to write in the mornings before Hagen's awake, or after he goes to sleep at night. And I'll put off the research in Boston until we take the trip."

"But I can't leave your father without help for that long."

"You won't need to. My father built that store for his family. It's about time we stepped up and helped him out. I'll take care of it. If we work together, we *can* do this. Can you handle making more calls if I drive Hagen into camp for the next few days?"

Between her excitement over taking this project to the next level and Matt's selfless offer, she could barely think.

"What do you say, sunshine? Want to go on a road trip with your two favorite men?"

"More than you can imagine."

MATT HEADED OVER to Pete's yard, where he and Caden were unloading pieces of a swing set from Pete's truck. Joey barked and trotted over. She jumped up, putting her paws on Matt's thighs, and he loved her up.

"Hey, Matt," Caden said. "You two catch up. Pete, I'm going to run inside and grab a drink. You two want anything?"

"No. I'm good, thanks," Matt answered.

"No, thanks. Down, Joey," Pete said, and the pup dropped to all fours. "Sorry about that. I was going to text you. You up for a baseball game with me and the guys Tuesday night?"

"I haven't been to a game in ages. Yeah, I'm in. Should I ask Mira and Hagen?"

"Not this time. Just Hagen, if that's okay? We're doing a daddy-child outing. We do it every few weeks. It gives the girls a break, and we get time with our kids. Win-win."

"Sounds good. I'll ask Mira, but count me and Hagen in."

"Will do. What's going on with you? How was Nantucket?"

"We had a great time, but I need a favor. Remember what I told you Mira said about Dad's store?"

"Yeah." Pete reached down and petted Joey, who was whimpering for attention.

Matt knelt beside her and let her lick his entire face.

"You're such a pushover," Pete teased.

"Look who's talking." Matt told him about his and Mira's plan for the co-op. "I need everyone to pitch in and watch the store while we're gone. I'll talk to Grayson, Hunter, and Sky. Can you help for a day or two?"

"What are you thinking? A week? Ten days?"

"A week on the outside, I think." Matt rose to his feet as Jenna came out of the cottage with Bea, and Joey ran to greet them.

"Unca Matt!" Bea toddled over in a pretty blue sundress.

"Hi, beautiful." He lifted her into his arms, kissing her pudgy cheeks.

Pete smiled. "She loves having you around, you know."

"Yeah. I love being around." Matt met Pete's serious gaze. "What do you say? Think you can help out while we're gone?"

"Where are you going?" Jenna asked as she came to his side wearing a similar dress to Bea's and matching flip-flops.

Pete explained what was going on.

"They'll do it. Don't you worry, because if they can't, the girls and I will." Jenna waggled her brows. "Things are looking serious, huh?" She went up on her toes and pulled Matt's shirt, tugging him down so she could speak in his ear. "If you break her heart, Pete will kill you."

Matt glanced at Pete, who shrugged and said, "She's probably right. She's been a saving grace for Dad. He treats her like another daughter."

He gave Bea one last kiss, then handed her to Pete. "She's a saving grace for me, too."

After talking with Pete, Matt called Grayson at Grunter's, who put him on speakerphone so Hunter could take part in the conversation.

"Hey, bro," Hunter said. "I hear you and Mira have become inseparable. It took you long enough."

Matt laughed, because he'd been telling himself it was about damn time, too.

"We're happy for you," Grayson said.

"Thanks. I appreciate that." He explained what was going on with the co-op and asked if they'd be willing to help out.

"Sure. Parker and I are back until the wedding, so I can definitely make the time," Grayson answered.

"I'm in," Hunter offered. "But let me get this straight. You took a sabbatical to write, and instead you're spending weekends on Nantucket screwing your brains out, and—"

Hunter's voice faded, and Matt heard a scuffle but couldn't make out what they were saying. He grinned, knowing Grayson was giving Hunter hell for his crass remark.

"Christ, Gray!" Hunter hollered. Then there was more scuffling.

"Tell him," Grayson said sternly. Then they both laughed.

"The idiot sucker punched me," Hunter snapped.

Good times. Matt snickered.

"Sorry, Matt," Hunter relented. "You know what I meant. You're putting writing second to a relationship. That's a huge deal for you."

"Why didn't you say that the first time?" Grayson asked

with a serious tone.

"Jesus, Gray," Hunter said. "Screwing his brains out is a *good* thing."

The conversation circled back to covering the store, and by the time Matt hung up and called Sky, he was grinning like a fool. He'd missed his brothers far more than he'd ever let himself realize.

He explained to Sky where he and Mira were relationship-wise, because that's what she cared about most, and *then* told her about their plans.

"Are you kidding?" Sky squealed. "Of course I'll pitch in. Whatever you need. Cree can fill in for me here, so you guys figure out a schedule, and I'll be there." Cree was her newest employee.

"Thanks, Sky."

"I'll call the girls. Mira's going to need help. She can't possibly get everything she'll need for these meetings done by herself."

"She's got me," Matt reminded her, though he was thrilled to hear his sister wanted to rally the troops for Mira.

"Yeah, but you're not *us*. The girls and I planned the whole triple wedding. Well, with the help of Lizzie and her friend Brandy for flowers and catering, of course. We can whip up whatever Mira needs so she's prepared." Sky filled Matt in on every detail of what they'd planned for her upcoming nuptials. "My only wish is that Mom could be here to see us all walk down the aisle."

Matt's heart squeezed at the mention of their mother. He missed her, and he, too, wished she could be there to see his siblings get married. He realized that the guilt that had shadowed him ever since his mother's death had finally lifted, and he felt that was connected to being back home and reconnecting with his family.

"She'll be there," Matt assured her. "She's always watching."

CHAPTER TWENTY-ONE

TUESDAY EVENING MIRA sat at the table on her deck reviewing the list she'd made of materials to prepare for prospective co-op partners. Hagen had been thrilled to go to the baseball game with Matt and the others. Matt had invited Drake and Rick, which she was also happy about. She didn't want them to feel pushed out of Hagen's life because Matt was getting more involved in it.

True to his word, Matt had driven Hagen to camp the last two mornings, giving her time to try to garner interest in the co-op. Not that she was having much luck. Monday and Tuesday she'd gone through her entire list of potential companies and had found another six to call as well. None of them were interested, but she wasn't giving up. Matt had offered to continue driving Hagen until she secured enough interest to make the co-op work. There was no way she could get the research done to find other companies to call *and* prepare the materials she'd need if the meetings came to fruition. Luckily, Serena was coming over to help.

"Is my favorite mini-man off to do *guy stuff*?" Serena asked as she came around the side of the house carrying a bag in one hand and her laptop in the other.

"Yes, off and happy as a clam."

"I got him something today." She set her laptop and bag on

the table, withdrew a thin children's book, and plunked it down in front of Mira. "You told me they were going to build a Huckleberry Finn–style raft, so I got him a knockoff kid's book, *Hinkleberry Funn the Raft Builder*. And I brought *supplies* for us."

She pulled a bottle of wine, a box of crackers, and a container of assorted cheese slices from the bag.

"Hagen will be over the moon, and I am, too. Have I told you lately that I love you?" Mira asked, getting up to grab two wineglasses.

"I can stand to hear it again. Your brother is making me crazy," Serena called after her.

What else is new? She carried the wineglasses out to the deck. "Which brother?"

"That would be Drake. No, Rick. Okay, both." Serena tilted her head, listening to several car doors closing. "Who's that?"

"No idea. I'm not expecting anyone."

They stepped off the deck as Sky, Bella, Jenna, Amy, Leanna, Parker, Jana, and Jessica came around the side of the house, each carrying a colorful beach bag and wearing sundresses over bathing suits, like they'd just come from the beach, even though it was six o'clock.

"I think we need more wine," Serena said quietly.

"There she is!" Jenna said when she spotted them. "We came to help with the co-op stuff. Seaside girls at your service!"

"Really? All of you?" Mira was overwhelmed. "How did you even know I needed help?"

The girls came around to the deck and began unloading their bags—laptops, towels, wine, plastic cups, paper plates, a big bag of M&M's, and two tubes of cookie dough covered the middle of the table.

"Matt said you were working on the materials for your trip," Amy said, lining up the plastic cups with the two wineglasses. She struggled to open the wine bottle, and Bella took it from her hands.

Bella opened the wine and poured everyone a drink. "We're experts at all things presentation related, and weddings, too. The triple wedding is planned, catered, and ready to roll." She turned to Serena, who was taking in all the commotion with a glint of amusement in her eyes.

"I'm Bella, and you must be Serena, Mira's BFF that we've all heard about. You're so cute. Do you have a boyfriend?"

"Um…?" Serena raised her brows.

"Ignore her." Parker, Grayson's fiancée was a beautiful blond actress. Luckily, she didn't have a stuck-up bone in her body. She wore very little makeup and her hair was pinned up in a high ponytail. "Bella's the prankster of the group, and she's sworn off playing tricks on Theresa, the property manager of Seaside and the woman who's officiating our wedding ceremony, so Bella needs a project to keep her mind busy. Being a mom, running a work-study program for high schoolers, and hanging out with us just isn't enough for her. She's like Wonder Woman on Energizer batteries."

"In that case, *please* feel free to find me a worthy man," Serena said with complete seriousness. "I like them tall, dark, and well hung."

"Oh Lord. You are Bella's dream project." Jessica swung her long dark hair over one shoulder and sank down to a chair. She'd been a professional violinist before she and Jamie had their son, Dustin. Unlike busy Bella, Jessica was thrilled to devote all of her time to her family.

"I could hook you up with my brother Brock," Jana offered. "I have no idea about the well hung thing—and have no interest in knowing—but girls love him. He owns a boxing club in Eastham. He taught me to fight."

"You fight? Mira, where have you been hiding these amazing women?" Serena lifted her glass of wine and said, "To finding me a man. I might just have to start with Brock."

They toasted, and Mira introduced Serena to each of the girls. Then, as if the wind had shifted, everyone began opening their laptops and pulling out notebooks and pens and talking about the co-op.

Amy pointed a pen at Mira. "Tell us what you've got."

"Okay." Mira took a deep breath, exhaling slowly as she glanced around the table. "But first I just have to say thank you. I have been stressing out over how I was going to get everything done."

"No more stressing," Sky said. "It's bad for your aura, and with us around, you'll never have to stress again."

Mira had been friendly with the girls since she started working with Neil. Everyone associated with the Lacrouxs were like one big family. But each of them giving up their free evening to help her? She felt like she'd fallen into a sisterhood. *Sisterhood of the Traveling Helpers*, she mused.

She explained what she was thinking of presenting, and they all took notes. "Basically, I need everything, but I can get away with a professional-looking outline of the business plan, lists of warehouses, including prices, locations, and restrictions. I also need to formalize the projected return-on-investment financials. I've got the numbers, but I'll need to present different scenarios, like if we get five investors versus six, or four. I also think it would be wise to give them examples of other businesses who have successfully formed co-ops. Nothing speaks louder than proof that it works. I have my initial research notes, but they're not in a format that I can present to anyone." Her shoulders dropped in defeat. "There's a lot to do, and Matt and I think we should try to make the trip soon, so the people who are interested don't *lose* interest."

"Nail them down before they get off the couch," Parker said. "That's what they say in Hollywood."

Jana and Sky laughed.

"Not like that!" Parker insisted, which made everyone laugh. "You guys have sex on the brain."

"Look at our men," Bella said. "Look at *your* man. Do you blame us?"

Parker blushed. "I do adore my soon-to-be husband."

"Ladies," Leanna said loudly. "Less sex talk, more co-op talk."

They divvied up jobs and formed teams to work on each one. They were the most organized women Mira had ever worked with. When they were finished, Jenna set a list in the center of the table outlining what they'd discussed.

"Amy and Mira, you'll handle the financial documents. Sky, Leanna, and Bella will research warehouses in the areas we discussed. Parker and Serena will take care of formalizing the business plan you've already outlined, and Jana, Jessica, and I will formalize your research on co-ops and also find others to include in the report." Her eyes danced around the table. "Deadline? Does next Friday work?"

"Pfft." Amy waved her hand. "Easy-peasy."

"Absolutely. And I'll ask the business manager of my foundation for any tips he has, too." Parker had created a very successful children's foundation, and Mira knew her experience would be invaluable.

"Thank you all *so* much," Mira said. "You can't even begin to imagine how relieved I am to have help. I feel better already."

"Good!" Sky reached for the cookie dough and tore the package open. "Now give us the scoop on you and my brother."

"Wait, I thought we were going to skinny-dip," Amy said with a pouty face.

"Skinny-dip? Here?" Mira and Serena exchanged a wide-eyed glance. "We can't. Anyone could see us."

"Your beach isn't private?" Jessica asked. "I'm not stripping down on a public beach."

Jenna's hand shot up in the air. "To Parker's!"

"I've got the cookie dough!" Amy held the tubes over her head.

A flurry of packing began as food, towels, and computers were put away.

"Wait." Mira looked around the table in confusion. "Why are we going skinny-dipping?"

Parker flashed a mischievous smile. "Remember I told you about the initiation?"

"I thought that was a joke," Mira said, remembering the story Parker had told her about skinny-dipping for the first time in her life with the girls in the pond by Grayson's house.

"No joke, sweet cakes." Jenna winked. "You're a Seaside girl now by association. We were going to initiate you last summer, but then you and Matt looked like you were eventually going to hook up, so we thought we'd wait and do it all at once."

"Oh my God. I love you guys!" Serena said as she gathered her things. "Skinny-dipping! We haven't done that since we were kids!"

"Oh, so you have done this before?" Jana asked. "I knew

Mira wasn't as goody-goody as she seemed." She held her hand up, and Mira halfheartedly high-fived her.

"But now I'm a *mother*," she pointed out. "It feels wrong to skinny-dip."

"*Please*. Five of us are mothers," Jenna pointed out. "Now go lock up so you can be a *fun* mother with us."

As Mira locked up the house and met them out front, excitement crept in. By the time they arrived at Grayson and Parker's house, it was dark out. Christmas, Parker's English mastiff, bounded out his doggy door and followed them through the woods to the pond. The girls took turns loving him up.

The other girls dropped their clothes as they walked along the pier, leaving a trail of sundresses and flip-flops. When they reached the end of the pier, they stripped naked, held hands, and jumped in, shrieking on the way down, sending Christmas into a barking, whining frenzy.

Serena and Mira shrieked from the dock as the girls' splashes soaked their clothes.

"Chipples!" Jenna yelled as she broke the surface. "Get ready for chilly nipples!"

One by one the girls' heads popped out of the water and a plethora of shouts ensued. "*Brr! Freezing! Hurry! Get in! Good thing we're not guys. Our dingies would disappear!*"

They all laughed.

"Come on!" Serena stripped off her clothes. "Hurry up! It's cold."

Mira glanced at her best friend's hairless body as she stripped out of her clothes, lulled by the excitement of the group. "You really do use Nair!"

Serena rolled her eyes. "You never know when the right guy

will come along. Now, hurry up!"

"You have to hold hands! It's tradition!" Bella yelled.

Mira pushed aside the embarrassment of standing naked on the dock and grabbed her best friend's hand.

"It's not tradition," Jenna snapped through chattering teeth.

"It is now," Amy said.

"Do I have to do something?" Mira asked. It was an *initiation* after all.

"You already did," Sky said. "You brought my brother home for the summer!"

"But what if we break up?" The words flew from Mira's lips out of fear of losing not just Matt, but all these glorious friends, too. "You'll hate me and you will have already initiated me. Isn't that against a rule or something?"

"Come on, silly girl," Parker said through chattering teeth. "Once Lacrouxs fall, they never look back."

"Trust the Lacroux way!" Sky urged. "Take a leap of faith."

A leap of faith. She remembered what Matt had said when she'd asked how they'd figure things out when he went back to Princeton after his sabbatical. *We have to trust that we'll both know what the right thing to do is when we get to that point.*

The girls in the water began chanting, "*Jump! Jump! Jump!*"

Mira had made one giant leap of faith in her life—when she'd had Hagen. She looked out over the bobbing heads of her smiling friends, feeling like she'd become part of another, bigger family.

Trust the Lacroux way! Take a leap of faith!

She'd never regretted her first leap of faith, and as she and Serena jumped off the pier and sliced through the chipple-inducing water, she thought of Matt and knew she wouldn't regret this one, either.

CHAPTER TWENTY-TWO

MIRA WAS SURE she'd been fueled by lust and adrenaline for the past two weeks. It was Saturday afternoon, and they'd come to Pete and Jenna's house to build Hagen's raft. She and Jenna were hanging out on the beach with Bea while the guys worked in the yard. It felt good to have some downtime after working day and night since they'd made the decision to push forward with the co-op, and she could hardly believe they'd pulled off the first step and were leaving tomorrow to meet with prospective partners.

Embarking on our next adventure.

The girls had come through with every little detail, giving her more support than she ever imagined possible. And just as Matt had promised, he'd driven Hagen to camp every morning for two weeks, giving her time to do the things she needed to in order to garner interest and prepare. She'd ended up making fifty-four calls instead of twelve, but it had paid off. She'd scheduled five meetings with six potential partners. Luckily, the two in Boston agreed to meet with her at the same time. Matt had made arrangements with his family to fill in for her at the store while they were gone, and Neil had surprised them both by agreeing to it all. She didn't know for sure, but she had a feeling that might have been because she and Matt were taking on this endeavor together. She knew how much Neil hoped

Matt would decide to stay on the Cape and run the hardware store. But she knew Matt had no interest in taking it over. His eyes sparked with excitement when he talked about how much he enjoyed the process of writing. She couldn't see him giving that up, regardless of how great a team they made—in the bedroom and out.

"They've been at this all morning," Jenna said. "Do you think Hagen will last?"

The raft was a much bigger endeavor than Mira had imagined. Matt had wanted Hagen to experience the entire project from start to finish, and had taken Hagen, along with Neil and Pete, to purchase the supplies earlier that morning. Her little man was eating up every second of being included in *guy stuff.*

"Definitely. He's as excited about the raft as he is about our trip. Thank you again, by the way. I couldn't have done it without all of you. I still can't believe all of Matt's siblings are going to help mind the store while we're gone. That's a huge relief."

"Everyone's excited about your trip and what it'll mean for Neil's store. He put his life into Lacroux Hardware, and until you came along, it looked like it might not last after he retired," Jenna said.

"I can't imagine his store not being there. He has such fond memories of his wife visiting him there, and all his kids as they were growing up. The store, and Neil, are also a huge part of the community. Guys come in who knew Neil when they were Hagen's age. I hope we can pull the co-op together. This trip will make it or break it."

"I bet you have it all planned. If it were me, I'd have an itinerary a mile long, with everything mapped out, from the moment our plane touched down until we set our heads on the pillow at night. Including a list of outfits and accessories for each outing." Jenna sighed. "That would be so fun."

"I've planned every detail of the meetings, but I'm so nervous about them I think I'll be lucky to get through them without passing out. If I had to plan a whole itinerary, I might lose my mind. Luckily, Hagen and Matt like to plan. We decided to drive, since it's only a couple hours between cities. I asked them not to overschedule our days because pressure will make me even more nervous, so they planned the library visits, chose the hotels, and made lists of what they wanted to see in each city. They were so cute looking at all the websites together and making lists, then whittling them down to a reasonable number of things to see. I swear those two are so alike it's mindboggling. We're starting in Boston, then working our way down to Rhode Island, Connecticut, and New York, and seeing three of the four libraries Hagen and I had on our list. I just hope I can pull this off. I've never done anything like this before."

Mira shielded her eyes from the blazing sun, watching the men working in the yard. Matt was shirtless, his muscles glistening with perspiration, flexing under the weight of the wood he carried over his shoulder. He patted Hagen's shoulder, and her son looked up from where he sat beside Neil, doing something on the ground. How could she ever have thought she could be careful with their hearts around the man who had owned them for so long?

"You'll do great," Jenna said.

Joey trotted toward them and plunked down beside Bea on a blanket. Bea giggled and the pup licked her cheek.

"And as for Matt?" Jenna added. "You're exactly what he needed. You and Hagen both are. Pete's been looking forward to today since Matt first mentioned it. It's been years since they've worked on a project together. I mean *years*. Up until this summer, Matt always spent summers teaching and working on his never-ending list of research papers. I swear that man's got more published papers than half the professors in his field combined."

"I'm glad he took this time off. I feel like we've been trying not to think about dating since Grayson and Parker's engagement party."

"I know. We *all* know." Jenna raised her brows. "He'd talked about taking time off before, but he never did it. And then you two met, and *wham*! He's here for the summer, and you two went to Nantucket, and you're leaving tomorrow for your big trip. It's all so exciting, and you have to know we're all pulling for you guys."

Mira couldn't stop smiling. "You make us sound like a horse race."

"It's a *love* race," Jenna said conspiratorially. "Heck, Pete had you two nailed as a couple that very first day. But Matt's the most careful of his siblings. Pete says he's like their mother in that way. Matt plans and thinks and *overthinks* like I match accessories to outfits." She wiggled her toes, showing Mira her pink nail polish, which matched her pink bathing suit and flip-flops. "Everything has to feel right before he'll make a move."

Thinking about the last time they made love, Mira smiled. Matt had this way of taking complete control but making every movement feel passionate and oh so good. He sure didn't have any trouble making a move, and everything felt more than right. It felt *perfect.*

"Matt and Hagen have become really close. That's got to make you feel good."

"You have no idea," Mira said. She and Serena had talked for an hour last night about how much had changed in just a few weeks. "I was afraid to let a man into Hagen's life, and Matt snuck under my radar in *every* way. One day we were friends and the next we were making out on my couch after Hagen was asleep. I've *never* done that before. *Ever.*"

"That's how you know it's real, when you do things you never thought you would."

"That's what Serena says, too." Mira smiled, thinking about their Nair, condom, and lube conversation. "I'm still worried about what will happen after his sabbatical is over."

"You could always go back to Princeton with him, couldn't you?" Jenna fidgeted with her bathing suit top, trying to keep her boobs from popping out as she bent to wipe more sand from Bea's face.

"We haven't talked about it. We agreed that we'd wait it out and see where we were when the time came, so I try not to think about it too much. I mean, realistically speaking, leaving the Cape would be hard. My brothers are a big part of Hagen's life, and I could never leave Neil high and dry. Especially if the co-op comes through. But the idea of a long-distance relationship would be hard, too. Especially now that Hagen's gotten so close to Matt. He's even confiding in him, which I admit, I'm slightly jealous of."

"Oh, I wasn't taking all that into consideration. It does sound complicated. No wonder you guys decided not to talk about it right now. Why get all stressed over something that's still several weeks away? And I hear you on the jealousy thing. My little muffin does that, and she's not even old enough to have big issues. But I know when she's a teenager she'll come to me, not Daddy, who will probably fit her for a chastity belt before then."

They laughed, but now Mira was thinking about Matt going back to Princeton. She reminded herself not to borrow trouble and once again pushed those uncomfortable thoughts aside. Then shoved them harder, making room for happier thoughts.

"I think being protective is a Lacroux trait. Matt's super protective of me and Hagen." Mira realized Matt had been that way since they'd first met. Even when they took Hagen to the park before they were dating, he kept an eagle eye on him. "I never thought I'd say this, but I'm glad he is. It's nice knowing he's watching out for us. And even though I'm a tiny bit jealous, I'm glad Hagen's opening up to him. Hagen had us both worried for a while when he asked if we thought he was a nerd."

"Oh no. Was he getting teased again?" Jenna asked.

"We thought so, but when Matt chaperoned Hagen's field trip last week, a little girl asked if she could sit next to Hagen, and Matt said she looked right into Hagen's eyes and said, 'I like nerdy boys best.'" Mira had been so relieved when Matt had texted and let her know, she'd actually teared up. "And when Matt asked Hagen if that was why he'd asked if he was a nerd, he said yes, because he *wanted* to be one."

"That's the cutest thing ever!" Jenna said.

"I know, but it's too soon," Mira said. "I'm nowhere near ready for that. Even the thought of giving up my time with my little boy for a girl who will inevitably break his heart is hard."

Jenna shared her first-love heartbreak story, and as Mira listened, watching Matt work side by side with Hagen, she realized she was smack-dab in the middle of her first true-love story. Second if she counted Hagen, but that was a whole different type of love.

MATT WATCHED HAGEN wind the rope and secure the bottom logs of the raft to the decking lying crosswise over top, just as he'd taught him. He'd never seen a child who paid such close attention to directions, or who had such a long attention span. It was midafternoon, and they'd been building the Huckleberry Finn–style raft for hours. Hagen had helped him choose the logs from a local lumberyard. When they'd gotten back to Pete's, Hagen had helped measure and mark them so Pete could cut them to equal lengths. Once that was done, they laid four logs across the grass about a foot apart, and Hagen took extra time to ensure the logs were equally spaced.

Hagen was a meticulous child, something Matt could relate to. Neil, like Matt, explained the reasoning behind every step. Matt took a nice stroll down memory lane, remembering the many projects he'd worked on over the years with his father. He'd been more interested in the research and preparation than the actual building, but Hagen seemed interested in both, and his father was soaking it all in. It warmed him to see Hagen working closely with his father and Pete.

Hagen worked carefully securing the decking logs. "How's that?" He held up the two ends of the rope. His eyes were shaded from the sun with his Princeton baseball hat.

"Perfect. I think you're a natural raft builder." Matt tied the ends together, while Pete cut another length of rope for Hagen.

Hagen's eyes filled with pride. "It's going to be the best raft ever. Just like Huck Finn's."

Pete handed him another piece of rope. "At this rate, maybe you will be able to build a boat after all."

"I might want to be a boat builder for real when I grow up."

Hagen sank down on his heels beside Matt and began winding the rope around the bottom log, then crossed the two pieces and wound it around the top log. "Is a boat builder a nerd?"

Neil draped an arm over Pete's shoulder, smiling down at Hagen. "Do me and Pete look like nerds?"

Hagen scrunched his face up, looking the two of them over.

Matt stifled a chuckle and rolled his own assessing gaze over his father and brother. They'd always been there for him, during good times and bad, and he'd missed them with a vengeance these past few years. He was getting used to feeling the emotions he'd refused to acknowledge for so long, and he found himself wanting to *feel* more of everything. He glanced toward the beach, where Mira and Jenna were playing with Bea and Joey, and his heart felt full. Nothing compared to this—being with family, being with Mira and Hagen, working alongside his brother and father.

Nothing.

Not teaching, not writing, not helping strangers.

Not a damn thing.

"Yes, I think you are nerds," Hagen determined, bringing Matt's mind back to the conversation. "That's good, because I want to be a nerd like Matt."

Pete laughed, and Neil shifted a surprised glanced at Matt, who was as shocked as his father. He knew Hagen wanted to be a nerd because a certain little girl with bouncy blond ponytails said she liked nerdy boys best, but to hear him say he wanted to be like Matt was overwhelming. It didn't matter that Hagen was another man's son and Matt had no claim over him. Every time they were together, Hagen, like his mother, stole another chunk of Matt's heart.

"Why do you want to be a nerd like Matt?" Pete asked,

smirking at Matt.

"Because my mom says smart boys are the best kind of boys, and she loves Matt. That means he's a smart man, and I think he's a nerd because he sometimes wears black glasses that everyone calls nerd glasses. And he likes to read, like me."

Matt's eyes shot to Hagen—who crouched beside the raft and began wrapping the rope around the wood again, as if he hadn't just turned Matt's world upside down.

"You know what that means, don't you?" Neil patted Hagen's shoulder, and when the little boy shook his head, he said, "It means your mommy is a very smart woman."

"Yup. That's why I'm so smart." Hagen went back to working on the raft.

Matt squinted against the sun, peering intently at Mira again and feeling Pete's and their father's eyes on him. *You love me?* Surely Hagen had misinterpreted something Mira had said or done.

He'd been holding back those three words for what felt like an interminable length of time, afraid to confess his feelings while his future was still up in the air. He didn't want to put pressure on Mira after she'd made it clear that she wanted to go slow and needed to be careful. They'd blown *slow* to smithereens.

We have to trust that we'll both know what the right thing to do is when we get to that point.

Was this *that* point?

CHAPTER TWENTY-THREE

THE ROCKY BAY floor felt familiar beneath Matt's feet, like an old friend greeting him as he and Pete carried the raft into chilly, chest-deep water. Behind them, their father carried Hagen, who was sporting a new blue life vest Matt had bought for him. Jenna and Bea stood at the water's edge with Mira, who held her phone, ready to take pictures of Hagen's big event. Her windswept hair framed her face, wayward strands whipping across her cheeks with the warm summer breeze. Her sun-kissed skin glistened in the late-afternoon sun. She bit her lower lip, holding his gaze and looking sexy as sin in a pale green bikini. The excitement and the heat he'd come to expect when they were together twinkled in her beautiful eyes as they lowered the wooden raft onto the surface of the water.

Everyone seemed to be holding their breath for what they'd deemed *Hagen Savage's First Rafting Adventure*. Hagen insisted he was going to write a book about it, and Matt was sure the determined child could do anything he put his mind to.

Matt knew the raft wouldn't sink, but that didn't stop adrenaline from pumping through his veins as the raft rose with the ripple of the bay's gentle waves. He saw Jenna nudge Mira and gesture to her phone.

Mira laughed and lifted her phone, pointing the camera at them, and said loudly, "I wasn't drooling." She slapped her hand over her mouth, and everyone laughed.

"Keep telling yourself that," Jenna teased.

"It floats!" Hagen yelled, pointing to the raft. "Look, Mom! It floats!"

"Of course it floats, baby," she said. "*You* built it."

"*We* built it!" Hagen corrected her. "The *guys*."

Behind her phone, Mira's smile appeared.

"Remember our raft battles?" Pete asked.

Memories of rafts and water fights sailed into Matt's mind. "How could I forget? You insisted on putting a sail on yours, which Hunter tried to climb and broke in half."

They both laughed.

"I remember the broken rafts and the wrestling that ensued after each of those battles," their father said.

"They wrestled?" Hagen asked.

"Like little monkeys." Neil laughed and handed Hagen to Matt. "Matt and his brothers were always getting into some kind of trouble. But not Sky. She was too busy doing her artwork."

They'd tied ropes to each corner of the raft so they could pull it through the water. Pete stood on the left side of the raft holding both ropes. When Neil settled Hagen in Matt's arms, he joined Pete, who handed his father one of the ropes.

Hagen's arms circled Matt's neck. "I wish I had brothers. I want to wrestle like a monkey."

Matt's gaze shifted to Mira. She lowered the phone with a look of longing in her eyes, and he felt it everywhere, as if her hands stroked over his skin. When she smiled, it drew him in, just as it did when she laughed, the feminine melody making his heart sing right along with it.

Oh yeah, he was at *that point* all right.

"Maybe someday you will," he said, his gaze never leaving the woman who owned his heart.

Mira's eyes widened, and for a quiet moment no one said a word, but Matt was sure everyone could feel his burgeoning love for her. He blew Mira a kiss, and it must have landed hard, because she blinked a few times and covered her heart with her hand.

Jenna said something to Mira and Mira's cheeks flushed, sending rivers of emotions rippling through him.

"Where's the captain of this raft?" Pete said loudly, jolting Matt's brain back in gear.

He placed Hagen in the middle of the raft, but Hagen clung to him.

"Are you sure it will hold me?" His tiny fingers pressed into the back of Matt's neck.

"Absolutely," Matt assured him, and peeled the little boy's fingers from around his neck. "You're a master raft builder, remember?"

Hagen nodded and nervously took hold of the rope handles they'd fashioned for him. Matt kept one hand on Hagen's back, walking beside the raft as Pete and Neil pulled it through the water.

"Look, Mom!" Hagen yelled, holding tightly to the ropes. "We're going! We're going, Matt! We did it. I'm like Huckleberry Finn!"

"You're better than Huckleberry Finn," Matt said, looking up at Mira again, who was walking along the water parallel to them with Joey trotting beside her. He assumed she was recording his big debut. "You're Hagen Savage!"

Hagen's first voyage was a great success, and lasted more than an hour and a half. The men got quite a workout, pulling the raft and towing it deeper at the command of their young captain. Afterward, they stowed the raft in Pete's boat shed for safekeeping and cooked dinner in a cool new steel hibachi Grayson had made for Pete and Jenna. They ate dinner on the beach and roasted marshmallows, which Hagen loved. Jenna, the marshmallow princess, had Pete show Hagen how to make golden brown marshmallows. Not golden, not brown. *Golden brown*, which Hagen agreed were perfectly delicious.

Long after Bea had given in to the call of slumber lying on her daddy's chest, as the moon rose high in the sky and the fire burned down to embers, Hagen fell asleep in the center of the blanket. Matt and Mira said their goodbyes, and Matt carried the sleeping boy to the car. He liked the familiar weight of him in his arms. Hagen didn't even stir when Matt buckled him into the backseat.

Matt reached for Mira, as he'd been dying to do all night. Bringing their bodies together as his mouth came down over hers, he took her in a series of slow, intoxicating kisses. Kissing Mira was a whole-body experience. His legs grounded them as heat bound them together and she melted against him. She tasted sweet and hot, and gloriously delicious.

"I've been dying to kiss you like that all day," he confessed, before taking her in a deeper, punishingly intense kiss that left no room for misinterpretation of what else he'd been dying to do to her once he got that hoodie and skimpy little erection-inducing bikini off of her.

"Take me home," she whispered against his lips.

MATT KEPT A hand on Mira's thigh as he drove home, his

thumb moving in slow, sensual circles. Every few minutes his fingers would dip between her thighs, not touching her sex, just hovering close enough to make her *want* him to. By the time they reached her cottage, she was hot, bothered, and so in love she wasn't sure she could contain the words.

Hagen didn't wake when Matt carried him into the house, or as Mira changed him into his pajamas. The little guy was completely tuckered out.

They pulled the door partially closed behind them and Mira took Matt's hand, leading him silently toward her bedroom. She closed the door and put a finger to her lips.

"You're sure?" he asked as he tugged her so close his erection pressed into her.

"God, yes."

He claimed her mouth, crushing her to him and making quick work of removing her hoodie and bikini, somehow never breaking their connection as he stepped out of his bathing suit. The heat of his body coursed down the entire length of hers, and they tumbled down to the bed. He tugged the covers over them.

"In case Hagen gets up. I'll listen for him, but I'm pretty sure my brain isn't going to be working in about seven seconds."

"Seven seconds is a very long time." She wiggled beneath him, aligning his thick cock to her entrance. She'd watched him all day, all those enticing muscles calling out to her, making her so wet she had to take a dip in the bay to mask her arousal. She ached for him to love her, physically and emotionally.

"You shouldn't be allowed to prance around in that skimpy bathing suit," he said, and took her in another toe-curling kiss. "I had to think of big, fat, hairy men to keep from sporting wood all day."

"I'm going to wear it every time I see you now." She nipped at his lip, and he nestled the head of his cock inside her entrance. "Mm. More."

He gazed down at her with the possessive, seductive look he got every time they made love, and suddenly his face blanched and he pulled back.

"*Condom*," he ground out. "I'm sorry. I—"

She pulled him back down to her. "I'm on the pill, so unless you're worried you might have a disease, I know I'm clean."

"No diseases, sunshine."

She lifted her hips, aligning their bodies once again. "Then kiss me."

She pulled his mouth to hers, drinking in his heat, his love, as she moved with him, accepting all of him, until they were as close as two people could be. Her sex clenched around him, their hearts hammered out the same frantic beat, and he drew away from the kiss.

"Come back," she pleaded.

"I need to see you," he said urgently.

Cradling her face in his hands, so much love gazed back at her it drew her heart from her lungs.

"I love you," she confessed, at the same time he said, "I love you so much."

She held her breath, watching a smile curve his beautiful mouth. The mouth that had just professed his love for her.

"I love you, sunshine. I love you and Hagen so much I can't imagine *not* loving you. I love when you smile, when you laugh, when you crinkle your nose. I love the way you worry about everything Hagen does, and how you feed his need for facts. I love how much you care about my father and how you cherish your family. I love your big heart and your brilliant mind and your insanely sexy body. I love how you look at me, the way you touch me."

Overcome with emotion, her voice lodged in her throat. It was all she could do to tighten her hold on his ass, where her hands had been resting.

"Especially when you touch me," he said with a spark of dark pleasure in his eyes. "I want more of you. More of these days with Hagen. More nights like this."

She'd waited so long to be here with him, to fully open her heart, to allow herself to let go of the protective walls she'd created around her life with Hagen. A tear slipped down her cheek, and he kissed it away.

"I love you, too," she managed, seconds before his mouth descended on hers, and they began to move. "But when you leave...?" *We'll go with you.*

"I'm not going to leave, baby. I'm building a life here. I've been away long enough. I want to see you and Hagen and my family. I want to be on the Cape. There's nothing left for me in Princeton. I've achieved everything I can there."

Her mind spun. He loved her and wanted to stay on the Cape. This was huge news. Bigger than huge. *Ginormous.* "But you could still get the job as dean, if not now, a few years from now."

He shook his head and kissed her softly. "That's an impossibility, and one I don't want to think about anymore."

As their mouths came together again, she felt all the pieces of her life shifting into place. The unanswered question of Matt's future no longer loomed over them like a thunderous cloud waiting for the air to shift. The air had shifted, and he was staying at the Cape.

And he loved them.

He loved them both.

She gazed up at him, needing to hear it again. "You're staying?"

"Yes, baby. I'm staying. Now let me kiss you and stop that beautiful brain of yours from spinning."

They made love carefully at first, as if their confessions had opened new doors and they wanted to walk through them together. His hands skimmed over her sides and hips, and her body conformed to his as it had so many times before, but this felt different, more powerful, as if this time they were branding each other.

"I love you, baby," he whispered, and kissed the corners of her mouth before taking her in another thrilling kiss.

As his thrusts grew stronger, driving his thick shaft deeper, filling more of her, the depth of his love electrified the surface of her skin, heated her blood, and became the very air she breathed. His hands pushed beneath her bottom, lifting and angling her hips so he could love her more thoroughly, until her entire world was filled with him.

"Mira," he panted out. "I love you, baby, and I want to say it a million times because it feels so good to finally set the words free."

She wanted to say it back, to tell him so many things—how much she loved him, how she'd been waiting to say the words, too, how his love for her son meant the world to her—but waves of ecstasy crashed through her, drowning her as she succumbed to the haven of their love.

CHAPTER TWENTY-FOUR

MIRA SAT IN an office in the back of Mr. Sag's Hardware Store in Boston Monday morning with her heart pounding so hard she was sure the men sitting across from her could hear it. Ken Sagner, the owner of Mr. Sag's, had a much larger office than Neil's, with a window view of the street behind the store and modern, comfortable furniture. While Neil had all sorts of family pictures posted on the wall with thumbtacks, their edges curling and yellowed, Ken's pictures were all nicely framed and featured him and an older man with the same dark brown hair and sharp blue eyes. His father, she assumed.

Mira fingered the edge of the file containing the documents she and the girls had prepared, hoping they were enough to get the job done. What if these men knew even more than she did about this subject? What if she'd miscalculated something?

She'd practiced her spiel so many times she could recite it in her sleep, yet here she sat, so nervous she was sure when she opened her mouth she'd babble incoherently.

She recalled what Matt had said before she'd left the two-bedroom suite at the hotel that morning. *These guys are probably just like my father, hoping this is the answer to their small-business prayers. You have the knowledge it takes to help them. Keep that in mind, and let your personality and your brilliance shine through, and maybe, just maybe, you'll get them to focus on business instead*

*of how hot you look in that sexy little skirt. Good luck, sunshine. I
love you. Now go blow them away.*

He'd told her he loved her a hundred times since the first
time, and still every time he said it, emotions bowled her over.
Although they hadn't verbalized a need to keep their confessions
from Hagen, she'd noticed that Matt, like her, had been careful
not to say he loved her in front of him. She knew that when the
time was right, the words would come, but as a mother, she
wondered if she should talk to Hagen about her feelings first, or
if that was unnecessary. A parenting manual would be a good
thing to have right about now.

She sat up a little straighter and looked across the table at
Ken and Martin Long, the owner of South Side Hardware.
Forget the parenting manual; she needed a sales manual. Ken
and Martin were *not* like Neil Lacroux. Ken was the son of
Arnold Sagner, who had built the business Ken was trying to
save. Martin was older, probably closer to fifty based on the gray
sprouting around his temples. Martin looked skeptical, which
she understood, even if she didn't like it. They were more like
Mira and Matt than Neil. Her mind drifted to Matt. He hadn't
tried to step in and take over this project, or take credit for any
part of it, though he was helping her every step of the way. He
was with her boat-loving son right this very second at the
Boston Tea Party Ships and Museum, where they had tickets
for the interactive exhibits and historical reenactment. He
hadn't seemed the least bit worried about being with Hagen
twenty-four-seven for the next several days, and Hagen had
been elated about it. Matt's whole family had pulled together to
make this happen. There was a lot riding on her to pull this off.

Mira opened her folder, clearing her throat to push the
surge of emotions down. She'd given birth and raised an

amazing little boy. She could handle Mr. Sharp Blue Eyes and Mr. Skeptical, even if they knew more than she did.

When there's a will…

"Thanks for meeting with me," she said confidently. "I think you're going to like what I have in mind."

LATER THAT AFTERNOON, after meeting Matt and Hagen at the hotel, changing her clothes, having lunch at a café, and listening to Hagen recount every moment of their day, Mira was still reeling from the meeting. She didn't want to go into too much detail in front of Hagen, so she briefly filled Matt in. She told him how nervous she'd been at the start of the meeting, and how, once she began presenting the information she'd worked so long and hard to prepare, her confidence had returned.

"It was as empowering as it was frightening," she admitted.

"The idea of a co-op is not an easy sell by any means," Matt said. "I'm so proud of you for taking it on."

"I hope at least one of those two men comes through."

When they arrived at the Boston Public Library, Hagen stood wide-eyed and jaw gaping on the front steps of the stately building. Mira's reaction wasn't much different, temporarily distracting her from her racing thoughts. The magnificent arched windows, triple-arched entrance flanked by wrought-iron lanterns, and granite carvings made for a visual feast of grandeur. The interior was no less impressive, with marble as far as the eye could see, murals that looked like they were painted by the gods, and vaulted ceilings with domes in the side bays. They'd seen it all online, but experiencing the stunning architecture in person was a thousand times better. Of course, once inside the actual library rooms, Hagen wanted to run his fingers along the spines of every book.

As they took it all in, Matt gave the six-year-old version of a history lesson on the twin lion sculptures by the main staircase, the murals, and a number of other facts that Hagen ate up and undoubtedly memorized to recount later in great detail.

Several hours later, Mira was still thinking about the meeting.

They walked beside a wall of elegant dark wooden shelves. When Hagen was distracted inspecting a row of books in the next aisle, Mira took advantage of his absence to talk with Matt about the meeting. "I'm pretty sure Ken was at least curious. Hopefully he will want in after he reviews all the data without me shoving it down his throat, but Martin was clearly on the fence. He's worried about going into business with people he doesn't know, of course. We all are, but it's the only way to make something like this work without selling out. I hope he comes around, but I'm not sure he will."

Matt kissed her cheek and whispered, "Do you have any idea how much I love you?"

Her heart skipped. She'd never tire of hearing those words from him.

He didn't wait for an answer. It was like he just couldn't hold back telling her, and that made her a little dizzy in the best possible way.

"You gave them both the same presentation," he reminded her. "They'll probably discuss it at great length, and if Ken wants in, he may help sway Martin. You can follow up in a day or two with a phone call. Remember, sunshine, he didn't know you at all before today. Give him time to digest and reflect on you and your presentation. I'm sure he'll come around, but if not, we'll see where we are after you've met with everyone at the end of the week."

Over the course of the afternoon she grew terrified that this wouldn't work and she'd let everyone down. How could Matt be so calm about it? He *never* seemed to get flustered. When she and Hagen had woken up that morning, Matt had already been writing for two hours, wearing those heart-stopping glasses. He hadn't given any indication of being annoyed when Hagen tore out of the bedroom and leaped into his lap, disturbing the little work time he had while they traveled. He'd simply pushed his laptop to the center of the table and fell into a conversation about "While Mommy's at her meeting..."

Like I would have.

Like a parent. The thought surprised her. Their lives had melded together in every way. They'd had dinners together every night for the last few weeks, saw friends together, put Hagen to bed together. They'd become a *family* as seamlessly as they'd become lovers.

She shifted her eyes to the library shelves, scanning the spines of the books to distract herself from the impact of that thought, but all she saw was Hagen in his pajamas sitting on Matt's lap at the table in the hotel and the smiles that brightened her little boy's *and* Matt's features. Her pulse quickened at the enormity of her emotions. Being in love was magical and wonderful, but a lifelong commitment was a whole other story. And what if the co-op didn't work and she let everyone down? Would it affect their relationship?

Her mind righted itself on that thought, forcing rational thoughts to the forefront and pushing her girlish dreams aside. She had a little boy's heart to protect, even if it already belonged to Matt, too.

"Aren't you worried that I might blow this?" she asked quietly, to keep Hagen from hearing.

"Not even a little. I have unwavering faith in us."

Was he talking about the co-op or their relationship? "But this is your family's legacy. What if we can't make the co-op work?"

"Then we'll try something else. I know how important this is to you, and now that I've finally got my head out of my a—" He glanced at Hagen, then back at Mira and lowered his voice. "On straight, I realize how important it is to me and the rest of my family. We'll make it happen. There's nothing we can't do. We're a team."

He glanced at Hagen again. "A team of two and a half."

He placed a hand on her lower back and reached for Hagen's hand as they headed into the hallway. "Ready for the Children's Library, buddy?"

Hagen nodded eagerly.

As much as she loved knowing he believed in her *and* in them, she felt like she was under a mountain of pressure. There was a good chance she wouldn't be able to pull off the co-op, even though she truly believed it was a smart business move. Ken and Martin might *both* decide they weren't interested. Maybe all six prospective partners would.

She glanced at Matt as he listened intently to Hagen telling him what books he wanted to find at the Children's Library, and her chest filled with love for both of them. She was wholly and completely in love with Matt, and she knew her little boy was right there with her.

They were a team of two and a half, and that just might be more powerful than any six people could ever be.

CHAPTER TWENTY-FIVE

MIRA BURST OUT of the bedroom of their New York hotel suite Friday afternoon after changing out of the professional outfit she'd worn to her last meeting and flopped onto the couch with a loud sigh, looking beautiful in a peach-colored top and sexy, summery skirt.

"It's finally over." She rested her head back against the cushions. "Five meetings in four cities over five days. I don't know *what* I was thinking. Don't ever let me do anything this crazy again."

She looked at Matt, and he wondered if she saw how much he adored her. Could she tell when she left the hotel each morning how proud he was of her for having the courage to take on such an enormous endeavor when she already had such a full life? She glanced at Hagen, sitting on the floor playing with his robot, and her expression warmed. The look of love that came over her when she looked at her brilliant boy was the most beautiful thing he'd ever seen. She met his gaze again, and he wondered if she realized that the way she was looking at him, like she was desperately in love, made his insides melt. Did she know he felt like the luckiest guy alive to have her and Hagen in his life?

He smiled and touched his toes to hers. "I guess I won't tell you about the road trip Hagen and I are planning for his

Christmas break from school."

"Do I have to talk people into going into business with strangers?"

"No," he answered. "But you might have to go on Space Mountain."

Her eyes filled with disbelief—and just as quickly, with excitement.

"And to the Animal Kingdom!" Hagen added with a wide grin.

"Animal Kingdom I can do, but Space Mountain? *Not* happening. I'd get too nervous." She mouthed, *Disney World?* to Matt, and he nodded. She shook her head, as if he were making promises he shouldn't, but the smile on her face told him she wasn't really upset.

"Remember how nervous you were when we went parasailing? And then you loved it. And in Boston, before your meeting? By the time you did the presentation in Connecticut, you said you only had minor butterflies. And this morning you were like a true New Yorker, full of guts and glory and ready to take on the world. There's nothing you can't do. You're a force of nature."

An incredibly enticing force of nature.

Mira's eyes shimmered with the spark of positivity he adored. "I *nailed* it today, too. I have a really good feeling about this last meeting. Rhode Island was rough, and Connecticut was iffy, but this one? I'm ninety-nine percent sure I got him hook, line, and sinker. Still, I *never, ever* want to do something this crazy again."

Hagen climbed onto her lap, and Matt sank down onto the sofa beside her.

"But it's been so fun!" Hagen exclaimed. "We got to see two

of the libraries on our list and we're seeing the third today. Matt said I could ride the carousel and see the castle, and we got tickets to see the *Lion King*. I *love* the apple!"

Hagen had been an excellent traveler. He was interested in everything, slept well in every hotel, and seemed to enjoy the time he and Matt spent alone as much as Matt did.

"The *Big Apple*, buddy." Matt pulled him onto his lap.

"That's a lot for one day." Mira patted Hagen's hand. "Are you sure you're not too tired?"

"I'm *not* tired," Hagen insisted. "This morning we went shopping and I didn't get tired, did I, Matt?"

"You sure didn't," he answered, hoping Hagen wasn't going to tell her where they'd gone shopping and ruin his surprise. "Are *you* too tired, sunshine? You've had the extra stress of being *on* this morning. Do you want to stay here and rest while Hagen and I head out to find the best pizza in the city and hit the library? We can come get you before we go to Central Park to see the carousel and Belvedere Castle. I'd like to take you guys to Times Square, too, but if it's too much we can skip it."

"No!" Hagen complained. "I want to see the square."

"I'm not about to miss a minute of the Big Apple with you or Hagen," Mira insisted. "I want to see Hagen's face when he finally sees the lions out front of the library, and hold your hand as we stroll through Times Square. I'm not tired. I'm just glad I don't have to do any more presentations."

"Good," Matt said, ruffling Hagen's hair. "We'd rather you were with us, too. Now are you ready for some really great news?"

"Always."

"I spoke to my father this morning. He said he got a call from Ken yesterday afternoon. They set up a conference call for

Monday afternoon, and he said you should plan on leading it."

"What?" She bolted upright. "Are you kidding?"

"Nope. See, sunshine? You're a miracle worker."

"A *miracle* worker," Hagen mimicked.

"When did my little boy turn into such a tease?" She tickled Hagen's ribs, earning a stream of giggles. "That's incredible. We might actually pull this off after all. Can you imagine?"

"There isn't a man alive who can resist following your lead," Matt said with more than a hint of heat. During their trip, they'd stayed in either two-bedroom suites or adjoining rooms, and after Hagen fell asleep they'd sneak into the other bedroom for some secret sexy time. They'd perfected the art of quiet orgasms. As much as Matt wanted to get Mira alone and make love with reckless abandon, he wouldn't trade the time the three of them had together for anything. He cherished every moment, and spending so much time with Hagen made him realize how much he wanted to be part of Mira and Hagen's family.

She pressed her palm to the center of his chest and said, "I think that's only you, Mr. Lacroux."

Damn he loved her. If there weren't a set of six-year-old eyes on them, he'd carry her into the bedroom and show her just how much.

"Good answer. He also said my family's getting together for dinner at his place Saturday night. I know we have a long drive home tomorrow, but if you and Hagen are up to it, I'd really like you to come along."

"Please?" Hagen begged.

She tapped the tip of his nose. "Of course we can. If Hagen gets tired, we just won't stay too long."

"I won't get tired," Hagen promised.

"Maybe Mommy will get too tired," she teased. "Or maybe

Matt will."

Hagen laughed. "Matt never gets tired. He gets up before us to work and goes to bed after us."

"Matt does have amazing stamina," she said in a dreamy voice.

Only for you, sexy girl.

She pushed to her feet and lifted Hagen from Matt's lap. Then she took Matt's hand and pulled him up to his feet. Their bodies grazed, and his flooded with desire.

"Come on, boys," she said. "Let's go hunt down that pizza."

"We're *guys*, Mom." Hagen grabbed his Princeton baseball hat and carried his robot into the bedroom. "I hope it's better than the pizza in Connecticut. *Blech.*"

Matt swept an arm around her waist, pulling her against him, and whispered, "After a certain little guy goes to sleep, we'll have our own private celebration, and I think you'll remember I'm all *man*."

"I'm going to need a *lot* of reminding."

"I'll remind you so long, and so *thoroughly*, you'll never forget again. And then I'll remind you again and again, for however long it takes, until every breath you take brings a memory of just how much of a man I am."

IF MIRA THOUGHT Matt was protective of her and Hagen before, then he'd gone full-on Brink's Security in New York City. He kept a secure hold on both of them, scanning the crowded streets as they navigated the city and made their way toward Central Park, as if at any moment a villain might swoop down and steal them. She'd come to accept that he was also watching out for the safety of others, and he always would be. That was Matt, and she loved his protective nature as much as she loved everything else about him. Over the last two weeks she'd thought about Cindy Feutra often. As much as she wished he'd track her down so he could apologize and hopefully find a modicum of peace from that horrible incident, she knew he was right about it drudging up horrible memories for Cindy. Even though she worried that not having closure would leave that layer of guilt on his shoulders forever, she fell even more deeply in love with him for putting Cindy's well-being first. That incident was his burden to bear, but at least now he didn't have to bear it alone.

"There it is!" Hagen dragged them toward the Maine Monument at the entrance to Central Park. "That's a statue to remember the sailors that died when the battleship *Maine* exploded in Cuba."

Mira looked at Matt and sighed. "I owe you five dollars."

When they'd visited the New York Public Library, which was every bit as elegant as the Boston Public Library and as interesting as the Beinecke Rare Book and Manuscript Library in Connecticut, Matt and Hagen had taken out a book all about Central Park, and they'd read about the history of the monuments, the castle, and the carousel. Mira had bet Matt five dollars that Hagen was too excited and exhausted to remember any of it, even though Hagen's brain was usually like a vault. Her brilliant boy had proven her wrong.

"We'll have to figure out some other means of repayment," he said for her ears only. "I don't accept cash."

MATT'S HAND SLID south and he gave Mira's ass a squeeze. She tipped a smile up toward him, her eyes bright and eager. He couldn't resist leaning in for a quick kiss.

The park was bustling with families, businesspeople, joggers, and young lovers walking hand in hand. So much of life had been passing Matt by while he climbed his academic ladder toward an unattainable goal. It was wonderful to finally step back down to solid ground and take it all in. He thought he'd been fulfilled as a teacher, but spending time with Mira and Hagen, and reconnecting with his family, made him realize he hadn't been anywhere near fulfilled. He'd been intellectually stimulated, but all the other parts of himself had fallen by the wayside.

The red and white striped brick carousel building came into view, and Hagen pulled Matt toward it. "Come on! Look!"

Like Mira, Matt wanted to experience everything *with* Hagen, to soak in the first moment of excitement when he saw something he'd read about, or sat on a carousel for the very first time. Sweet calliope music rang out from inside the building. He stepped up his pace, squeezing Mira's hand a little tighter as they headed for the ticket booth.

After buying tickets, Matt draped an arm around Mira's shoulder and they watched the carousel circle the platform. Colorful horses frozen in various states of excitement carried smiling riders around and around.

"This is beautiful," Mira said with awe. "I'm so glad we made this trip."

She was gazing at the carousel with a thoughtful expression, and as Matt drank in her perky nose, that sweet spray of freckles, and her deliciously kissable lips, his mind traveled to their future. He imagined coming next year, or the year after, with Hagen and his little brother or sister. He carried that thought with him throughout the afternoon, expecting it to rattle around and find an exit in his mind. But it didn't rattle. It settled.

They rode the carousel five times, and by the time they headed for Belvedere Castle it was near closing time. Matt gave Hagen a shoulder ride, and they made it just in the nick of time to take a quick walk around the grounds of the majestic stone castle. They had dinner in Times Square, and much to Mira and Matt's surprise, Hagen stayed awake through the entire production of the *Lion King*. But the minute they got in the cab, he closed his eyes.

"That was the best day he's had in his entire life," Mira whispered. "And it's in my top four, too."

"Top four?"

She glanced at the cabdriver, then whispered in Matt's ear, "The day Hagen was born, the day you and I shared our first kiss, and the first time we were intimate."

"Man, do I ever love you." Matt tipped up her chin and kissed her.

"We love you too, Matt," Hagen said in a sleepy voice.

Matt's heart swelled, and he kissed the top of Hagen's head. Catching a glimpse of Mira's surprised expression, he realized Hagen hadn't heard either of them declare their love for each other yet.

"Sorry," he whispered to her.

She wrapped her hands around his arm and leaned in to him, adoration replacing the surprise in her eyes. "Don't ever be sorry for loving us."

And he knew he never would.

CHAPTER TWENTY-SIX

MATT LAID HAGEN on his bed in the hotel room he and Mira shared and kissed his forehead. "I love you, buddy. Sleep well." He slid a hand around Mira's waist and kissed her softly. "Do you want help getting him into his pajamas?"

I love you, buddy. Could Matt possibly know how much those four words meant to her? Mira had never thought too hard about how she would feel if a man loved her son, because she never fully believed *she'd* fall in love. It wasn't part of her plan, her *mommy bucket list*. But Matt's love for her and her son was so pure, so real and natural, it felt tangible, and hearing him tell Hagen he loved him was even more powerful than when he told *her* he loved her.

Tonight she was starting a new bucket list. A *family* bucket list, filled with all the things she'd like to do with Matt and the things she'd like to do with Matt *and* Hagen. Maybe she was getting ahead of herself, which she'd warned herself not to do just a few days ago, but their life was coming together, and Matt was staying at the Cape. She didn't want to hold back any longer.

"Baby? Do you want help?" Matt asked again, pulling her from her thoughts.

"No," she whispered. "He's out like a light."

Matt nodded. "I'm going to take a quick shower. See you

afterward, or are you wiped out, too?"

"Oh no, Mr. Lacroux. You're not getting off that easy." She wrapped her arms around his waist, went up on her toes, and kissed him. "You have some *reminding* to do. Let me rinse off all this city dirt, too, and I'll meet you in your room." As he walked out the bedroom door, she whispered, "Wear your glasses!"

Mira showered and dressed in the sexy lingerie she'd bought from a cute boutique while they were in Rhode Island. The sheer and lacy pink nighty had a halter-style top and a skimpy, flowing body that just barely covered her goodies. She put on the silk kimono she'd splurged on as a special gift for her man and tried to ignore the butterflies fluttering in her stomach as she walked through the dark suite toward Matt's bedroom. She carried her panties in her hand in case Hagen woke up and she needed to cover up. She pushed open the door, revealing a dimly lit room, candles on the nightstands, and Matt, wearing only black briefs and the glasses that made her want to page through *him*, sitting in the center of the bed. Music floated softly from the radio into her ears as she closed the door and went to him.

He reached for her, his stare bold and inviting. She crawled up the bed on all fours, feeling sexy and naughty as they embarked on their secret tryst. She dangled her pink lace panties before his eyes, then tossed them on the nightstand.

"How's my beautiful, sexy girl?" he whispered as she strad-dled his lap.

His hands slid beneath her lingerie, warm and strong against her skin as they laid claim to her waist, his long fingers brushing over her ass. Somehow she knew that even if she were wearing a sweatshirt, the look of love and devotion in his eyes would be just as strong. Her heart was already in take-me-now mode, and she loved the feel of him growing instantly hard beneath her. If he were covered head to toe in mud or wearing armor, her desire for him wouldn't diminish. He was always so loving toward her, sensual and caring, pleasuring her first multiple times before letting go himself. Tonight she wanted to return the affection and let him know exactly how much she appreciated his sinful talents and generosity.

She ran her finger down the center of his chest, holding his gaze. "I'm filled to the brim with happiness."

When she leaned forward to press a kiss to his lips, his erection twitched against her sex. His fingers pressed into her skin, and when he spoke, his voice whispered over her lips.

"Me too, sunshine." He leaned in for another kiss, his scruff scraping enticingly against her cheek. "I kind of hate going back to the real world and sharing you with everyone else."

"Do you, now?" She kissed his neck.

He made a low, sound of appreciation, spurring her on. She nipped at the ridge of his jaw. "Which part of me do you hate sharing the most?" she asked daringly, her hands playing over his pecs, feeling them jump beneath her touch.

"All of you." His hips rose beneath her in a delectable rhythm as his hands pressed down on her hips, the exquisite friction carrying oceans of lust to the far reaches of her body. "Your sassy, tenacious personality, your charm and intelligence."

He slid one hand to the nape of her neck, claiming her in a demanding kiss.

"Your gorgeous face and stunning body." He tangled his hand in her hair, tugging her head back, and sealed his mouth over her neck, sucking and kissing and chipping away at her resolve to be his temptress.

She closed her eyes and grabbed hold of his shoulders, giving in to his seduction. He dragged his tongue up the column of her neck and took her earlobe between his teeth. Spikes of pain and pleasure raced to her core. She dug her fingers into his hard flesh and heard herself moan.

"My girl likes that. We're going to have to keep quiet, remember."

Her brain could hardly hold on to that warning as he crashed his mouth to hers in another penetrating kiss. His tongue stroked hard and eager over hers, around her mouth, over her teeth, until she abandoned all control, relaxing her jaw for him to take everything he wanted. And *take* he did, loving her cheeks, her jaw, her neck, and when he tugged her head further back, she didn't resist. His adept fingers untied the top of her nightie, and it puddled around her middle.

"Off, baby." When he released her hair to lift her nightie over her head, the air left her lungs. "How did I get so lucky to be the man you picked?"

Her eyes fluttered open and he kissed them closed. "Close your eyes. Let me love you."

So different from his usual command of her eyes open, it intrigued her, but she wanted desperately to give him a memorable night, and she forced her eyes open again. "But I wanted to treat you tonight."

She pushed her hands into his hair, but he had other ideas. With both hands, he reached beneath him. Lifting his hips with her on them, he pushed out of his briefs. The base of his arousal pressed deliciously against her sex. He reached for his glasses next, and she stuck her lower lip out in a pout. He chuckled and left them on.

"Look who's got the seduce-the-professor fantasy now." His

eyes narrowed, their heat consuming her.

Feeling empowered by his desire, she said, "I just want you to see me clearly, so you never forget this night."

His smile turned sinful as he locked his hands behind his head, giving her complete control. *Oh Lord, where to start?* Her eyes swept over his chest, down all those glorious ripped abs, to the head of his cock poking out from beneath her.

He rocked his hips, jolting her eyes to his and spurring her body into action. She kissed his chest, her fingers drifting over his hard nipples. He smelled fresh and virile, and as she moved lower, laving her tongue over each hard nipple, down his stomach, and following the treasure trail south, his scent changed to one of love and affection, safety and passion.

She teased him with feathery kisses all around the tuft of dark hair at the base of his cock and along his inner thighs, which flexed beneath her lips. She felt his penetrating gaze eating its way through her, making her wet and hungry as she wrapped her fingers around his length and pressed a kiss to the tip. She slicked her tongue over the slit and lifted her eyes to his.

"Watch," she said, as he'd once said to her so demandingly. The control was addicting. She wanted to see him untethered, to have all the heat in his gaze, all in the tension in his body, unleashed upon her.

As she took him to the back of her throat, his hands dropped to his sides, fisting in the sheets. She drew him out of her mouth and in deep again, punishingly slow, earning a heady groan.

"Ah, my man likes that," she teased, loving it when he cracked a smile through all that passion. "Mine?" she whispered tentatively. She wanted to roar it out to the world from the rooftops.

"All yours, baby."

Oh, how she loved hearing those words, and knowing he was staying at the Cape made them even more *real*. She loved him with her mouth and hands, stroking and licking, then taking him deep until she felt him swell in her hand. His head craned back, the veins in his neck pulsed through his tanned skin, and his knuckles blanched against the sheets. Oh yeah, she loved seeing all that fire roaring for her. She moved lower, slicking her tongue over his tight sac.

"Holy hell, baby." He grabbed her head, holding her mouth exactly where they both wanted it as she teased and sucked him into a tightly wound bundle of need.

"Fuck," he ground out, surprising her. He rarely cursed, and hearing it turned her on, because she knew she'd taken him to the brink of his control.

In the next breath she was beneath him, her arms pinned over her head, Matt's big body perfectly aligned with hers. His face was a mask of pure rapture as he drove into her until she felt all of him—his love, his sex, his greed. She reached up and removed his glasses with a shaky hand.

Matt stilled, breathing hard, his body trembling as much as hers was.

"Feel that, baby?" he said with heated breath. "That's the moon and the stars and the sun all coming together. That's *us*. How did we miss out on love like this for so long? Why couldn't I have found you ten years ago?" Before she could respond, he said, "No, not ten years ago. *Six* years ago."

His words cut straight to her heart. He didn't want to change Hagen's lineage, he just wished he'd have been there for her during that difficult time. When he gathered her in his arms, their bodies moving in perfect harmony, she whispered,

"The moon and the sun and the stars were waiting for all the pieces of our lives to align. They trusted us to know when that time came."

They made love for hours, fast and frantic, then slow and passionate. Mira lay in Matt's arms long after they were done, reveling in the feel of his legs twined with hers, his heart beating against her cheek, and his fingers trailing through her hair. She needed to return to her own bedroom in case Hagen woke up, but she loved being in his arms too much to move. Matt kissed the top of her head.

She tipped her face up, taking in his sated gaze. "I have to go back to my own bed."

He kissed her again and rose to his feet, bringing her up beside him, and lovingly helped her put her nightie and kimono on. "I'll walk you to your door."

"Mm. Sexy *and* a gentleman. Aren't I the lucky one?"

"I want to spend every second I can with you."

He kissed her again, then tucked her beneath his arm. Her favorite place—when she was *vertical.*

As they walked through the quiet suite, with the lights of the city shining in through the curtains, she wondered how she'd ever step back into her real life again, where nights were spent at different houses instead of separated by a short walk across the living room.

In her bedroom, Matt pulled the covers up around Hagen, and she realized she was no longer a do-it-yourself woman patching holes with concrete. She was part of a team of two and a half, building a foundation out of love.

CHAPTER TWENTY-SEVEN

AFTER A LONG drive home Saturday, Matt dropped Hagen and Mira off at their house and spent the next few hours trying to concentrate on work and feeling like he'd misplaced part of himself. The cottage was too quiet. The hum of energy Mira and Hagen added to his life were markedly absent. Matt had done laundry, gone for a run, hammered out a few pages of writing, and *finally*, after giving Mira time to reconnect with her brothers and Serena and get the million things done that she'd talked about on the way home, he picked her and Hagen up for dinner at his father's house, but those few hours apart had felt like a lifetime.

Matt and Pete carried plates of steaks and burgers across their father's backyard to Hunter and Grayson, who were manning the grill.

"Hey diddle diddle the *Matt* and the fiddle, *Pete* jumped over the moon," Sawyer sang from his perch on a lawn chair where he was playing his guitar and making up silly songs for Bea and Hagen, both of whom giggled wildly.

Jana, Parker, and Jenna were standing by the big shade tree, fawning over Jana's new haircut, which didn't look much different to Matt, but what did he know. Matt glanced across the yard at Mira, who was checking out the art studio their father had built for Sky when she was younger. She looked beautiful in a light green skirt and white blousy tank top. He swore she got more stunning with each passing day, and knew there was a direct correlation to his growing love for her.

Sky noticed him staring and said something to Mira, who looked over her shoulder with a killer smile that made his IQ drop about a hundred points. He blew Mira a kiss as he handed the plate to Hunter and their father joined them by the grill.

"She's something, isn't she?" his father said, draping an arm around Matt's shoulder.

"Pop, she's *everything*. I'm giving my resignation and I'm moving back for good. I left a message for my boss earlier in the week."

Neil's eyes filled up and he pulled Matt into an embrace, holding him tighter and longer than he had in years. "Thank you, son. Your mother would be so happy that the family will be together again."

"Hear that, Grayson?" Hunter said. "Matty's been bitten by the love bug. He's back for good."

"Seriously? Life just got ten times better." Grayson slapped Matt on the back.

"Yeah," Matt said, his eyes landing on Mira again as she crossed the lawn toward the kids. "Best decision I've ever made."

"Sing about Poppi!" Bea squealed, grabbing everyone's attention with her high-pitched voice.

Sawyer glanced at Neil and began strumming out another tune. "Poppi be nimble, Poppi be quick. Poppi jump over a candlestick!"

The kids laughed and laughed.

"Maybe you can sing at the wedding," Jana said, and grabbed Hunter's hand, dancing around him. Hunter, who was *not* a dancer, pulled Jana against him and swayed to the beat of Sawyer's silly song.

Sawyer sang out another verse. "*Pete!* Row, row, row your boat gently down the stream."

"Merrily, merrily, merrily, merrily," Sky sang as she came to Sawyer's side. "Life with *Sawyer* is a dream."

They took turns making up silly songs, and just as Matt got his arms around Mira, his cell phone rang. He dug it out of his pocket and squeezed Mira's hand. "My boss. Excuse me, sunshine."

He headed inside and answered the call. "Hi, John. Thanks for returning my call." John listened without interruption as Matt paced his father's living room, explaining why he was submitting his resignation.

"It's a hell of a book deal, Matt, and I know how important family is to you. But before you make any rash decisions, you need to know that Jacob's wife has just been diagnosed with stage four cancer. Jacob is stepping down as dean of the School of Social Sciences to be there for her, and we're considering you for the position."

"EVAN, BELLA'S STEPSON, is an aspiring cinematographer, and he's videotaping the wedding, and Lizzie is taking care of all the flowers," Sky told Mira. "And her friend Brandy is catering. Brandy just moved here from Virginia, and Lizzie's helping her get her wedding planning and catering business up and running."

Mira and the girls were standing on the patio talking about their upcoming wedding, and Mira was trying not to focus on the fact that Matt had been on the phone with his boss for more than half an hour. She knew how big a decision it was for him to resign, and she imagined his boss begging him to reconsider. They'd talked about it on the long drive home from New York, and although Matt had been adamant about having made the right decision, she knew there were many aspects of his job that he loved and that he was proud of his accomplishments. She also knew that it was a lot to walk away from and not something many people would do.

"Wait until you taste the wedding cake," Jenna said. "It's to die for."

"I wish I could cook like Brandy," Parker said. "I'm really good with the microwave."

Everyone laughed.

"She's talking about giving cooking classes," Jana said. "If she does, I think we should take them."

"*After* the honeymoon, of course," Sky said.

Hagen tugged on Mira's shorts. "Mom? What's a honeymoon?"

She crouched beside him and brushed his hair from his eyes, noticing that he needed a trim. "Remember when we talked about how when people get married there's a ceremony and a party?"

He nodded.

"Well, after the big party, the bride and groom go on a special vacation with just the two of them to celebrate. That's called the honeymoon." She saw Matt step outside, heading in her direction with a serious look in his eyes, and her thoughts stumbled.

"Oh," Hagen said. "Like when Molly's daddy got married and she stayed at her grandma's for a week?" Molly was a little girl in Hagen's class.

"Yes, exactly." She rose to her feet, and Matt put his arms around her from behind and kissed her cheek.

"How'd it go with your boss?" Grayson asked him.

He glanced at Hagen and said, "Jacob's wife received some very bad medical news, and he's stepping down. They want to consider me for the dean of the School of Social Sciences position."

Mira's heart nearly stopped. Matt's family began peppering him with questions, and in Mira's head, worries took flight, turning everything else to white noise. She was elated and concerned. This was the chance Matt had worked for. It would be his greatest achievement. The pinnacle of his career, and she was so very proud of him, and happy for him. But would this change his decision? Was he going back to Princeton after all? Would she and Hagen upend their lives and go with him? She wanted to be with him, and one look at the way Hagen was hanging on to Matt's shorts told her he did, too.

She turned in Matt's arms, and he smiled, an easy, sexy smile that was miles away from the swarm of bees swirling inside her and silencing her voice.

"Matt?" Hagen said.

"Yeah, buddy?"

"When people love each other, they get married and they go on a special vacation."

Mira's mind spun. She was vaguely aware of her son's voice, of Matt crouching beside him. She searched Matt's face for a clue of what he was thinking, but he was completely focused on her little boy, intent and thoughtful. *Where is the worry?* She looked around at everyone else, none of whom seemed to be choking on worry, as she was. Was she alone in this whirlwind of concern? Maybe she shouldn't worry. They had options.

She glanced at Neil, who was looking at Matt with pride in his eyes. She'd already received two email confirmations from her meetings with business owners who wanted to move forward with the co-op. She couldn't just dump that on Neil. That wasn't fair, and he wouldn't know how to run the co-op. She loved Matt to the ends of the earth and back, but she loved his father in a different, though equally as important, way. Neil needed her here more than Matt needed her in Princeton. At least to get him through the co-op setup and find someone to help him run it.

"A honeymoon?" Matt asked, bringing Mira's thoughts back to his conversation with Hagen.

I'm getting too far ahead of myself again.

Hagen nodded. "I love my mom, but I can't marry her because she's my mom."

"That's right, buddy," Matt said. "But one day when you're older you'll meet a woman and fall madly in love. A woman you can't imagine living without for a single day." Matt's eyes found Mira's, warm and loving. "*That's* the woman you'll marry."

"So?" Hagen said matter-of-factly. "When are you going to marry my mom?"

"Hagen." She shook her head. "Honey, that's not the type of—"

Matt reached for her hand, repositioning on one knee, and said, "As soon as she says yes."

Ohmygod. Mira felt dizzy. "What…?"

He unfurled his other hand, presenting a light blue Tiffany's jewelry box, and draped his other arm around her little boy, who was looking at Matt like he was his whole world.

She reached for Matt's shoulder to steady herself. She was

completely flummoxed by the new information about his dream job and this proposal. A collective gasp surrounded them, but all Mira heard was the thundering of her heart.

"Your brass ring," she said in a shaky breath.

"Never even a consideration," Matt said confidently.

A sob escaped her lips, and as she went to cover her mouth, Matt took her hand in his. The smile she'd fallen in love with during that amazing day at Parker and Grayson's engagement party almost a year ago spread across his handsome face.

"You and Hagen are my brass ring. My *gold* ring. The *pinnacle of my life*. You have become my whole world. I want to carry Hagen on my shoulders until I can no longer manage it, and answer his litany of questions until he knows every fact there is to know. I want to know he's safe and loved, and if you'll let me, I want to adopt him so he knows he'll have a father who will always love him, through good, bad, and frustrating days. A father who will build boats and read about anything his heart desires."

Tears tumbled down her cheeks.

Matt rose to his feet. "And I want to love, honor, cherish, and adore his beautiful mother. I want to follow your whims and chase your dreams until every one of them has been achieved—and then I want to make more and continue chasing them until Hagen has to push us around in wheelchairs and chase them for us. I love you, sunshine. You and Hagen. Will you marry me?"

Sobs stole her voice, and all the girls said, "Yes!" as she nodded.

"I'm not marrying the girls," Matt said.

"Oh yes you are," Hunter mumbled, and everyone laughed.

Matt opened the Tiffany's box, revealing a gorgeous canary yellow diamond ring. "I need to hear your answer, baby," Matt said, stepping closer and curling his hand around hers. "I want to remember this moment forever. Are you ready to start our next adventure together, as a family?"

She fell even harder, which she didn't think was possible.

Hagen tugged on Mira's skirt. "Say *yes*, Mommy! I helped pick out the ring when we were at the *apple*."

More sobs burst from her lungs.

"I swear I didn't ask him to keep it a secret," Matt said. "I know how you feel about that."

Matt had become her anchor, her lover, her partner, and a father to her son, but not once had he tried to become her savior, and she was madly, passionately in love with him.

She nodded vehemently, forcing her voice past the lump in her throat. "Yes, Matt. I'll marry you. *We'll* marry you."

He slipped the sparkling diamond ring on her finger, and she threw herself into his open arms. Their friends and family cheered as they were passed from one set of loving arms to the next.

"A quadruple wedding!" Sky yelled.

"Yes! Please!" Jenna bounced, which started a flurry of hopeful coercion.

Neil embraced Mira and said, "Looks like the business will stay in the family after all. Maybe you'll consider letting Poppi watch Hagen when you and Matt take your honeymoon?"

Fresh sobs engulfed her. "Of course." She hugged her future father-in-law again, the man who had treated her and Hagen like family since the very first day they'd met.

"May I?" Matt drew Mira from his father's arms and gazed into her eyes, making her body melt and thrum at once. "Are you ready to begin our next adventure, sunshine? Want to join the Lacroux wedding party?"

"More than you'll ever know."

Chapter Twenty-Eight

A GENTLE BREEZE swept off the bay as the sun began its slow descent from the sky, leaving ribbons of colors in its wake. The perfect backdrop for the quadruple wedding. Matt pushed his glasses up the bridge of his nose, a secret smile tugging at his lips as he waited for his future bride to appear on the crest of the dunes. He'd worn the glasses just to catch that brief moment of surprise, followed by the entrancing lust he knew so well in his bride-to-be's eyes. It had been five weeks to the day since Matt had asked Mira to marry him, and one week since she and his father finalized the preliminary paperwork with their new business partners for the co-op. Matt and his siblings each put in an equal share and bought a stake in their father's business to further ensure it would never leave the family.

Matt was about to become a husband and a father. Wow, did that thought hit him square in the center of his heart. Standing beneath the driftwood arbor Grayson and Hunter had built for the wedding, Matt had no qualms about his decision to leave teaching. His writing was going well, and his editor was making noises about a second book deal if the first sold well. More importantly, he was back among family and starting a family of his own with the woman and child he adored. He'd snagged his brass ring and so much more.

Theresa, who was officiating the wedding, stood at the head

of the altar wearing a simple and elegant navy dress. Matt had never seen her in a dress. She was even wearing makeup, and she looked beautiful.

Beside him, donning matching tan linen slacks, rolled up at the ankles, and a button-down short-sleeved shirt the color of each of their bride's dresses, Grayson, Hunter, and Sawyer waited anxiously for their beautiful brides to make their way down the candlelit aisle. The girls had spent the last few nights filling mason jars with sand and decorating them with shells and rocks they all had gathered from the beach. In the center of each jar was a candle, illuminating the path leading from the dunes to the altar. Pete and Neil stood with them as Matt and his brothers' best men, while Sawyer's father, who had Parkinson's disease, sat proudly beside his son in his wheelchair with his wife at his side.

"I wish Mom could have been here," Grayson said to Matt.

Matt nodded, emotion pooling inside him. He gazed at his father and imagined he was thinking the same thing. He looked up at the stunning sunset, which seemed to suddenly get brighter and more vivid.

Their mother had strived for one thing their whole lives, to see her children happy and loved. Today was her birthday and it was only right that they honored her with the best gift of all—by marrying their forever loves.

Matt put a hand on Grayson's back, and his brother's lips tipped up in a thoughtful smile. "I think she is here, Gray."

"Yeah," Grayson said. "I imagine she is."

"Can you believe we're getting married?" Sawyer asked.

Matt, Grayson, and Hunter exchanged a knowing glance. "Yes," they all said, and laughed.

"I never thought it would happen to me," Hunter said with

a smirk. "But Jana's..." He shook his head. "Man, she's like no other woman on earth."

"I think we could each say that about our woman," Sawyer said.

Matt knew he could, but he wasn't in the mood to debate whose future bride was hotter, smarter, funnier, and whatever else they could think of. He was ready to say the two words that would make Mira his forever. He looked out over the group of friends and family who had come to celebrate with them. All of their friends from Seaside were there, including Jamie's grandmother Vera, who had known Matt for many years. Mira's family, Jana's brothers and parents, Parker's grandmother, and the rest of their friends were chatting by the tables, while the Seaside girls, as well as all the kids, were somewhere over the dunes with the brides-to-be. Matt wished he were up there with them. He couldn't wait to see Mira in her wedding dress and Hagen in his tan linen pants and blush-colored linen shirt, which matched Matt's.

"Cue the music!" Evan hollered from the far end of the candlelit aisle, where he stood with a video camera in his hands and Serena and Jana's sister Harper by his side. Matt hadn't even seen the two women come over the dunes.

His heart rate sped up as the "Wedding March" rang out and Serena and Harper took their places on the brides' side of the altar. They'd modified the procession to suit their group, and Bea, Summer, and Hannah appeared at the crest of the dune in their pretty seafoam-green dresses, each carrying a basket. Matt hoped to one day have a little girl who looked just like Mira. Their mothers stepped up behind them and reached for their hands. Jenna, Bella, and Amy wore similar knee-length dresses. As they made their way down the aisle, the little girls threw rose petals into the sand.

Sloan and Dustin, both two years old, appeared on the dune in their tan pants and white button-down shirts. Leanna and Jessica took their little boys' hands and led them down the aisle. Each little boy also carried a small basket, which they'd deemed safer than a pillow with a ring on it.

Matt squared his shoulders, trying to calm his breathing as he waited for his bride to appear. He dug his toes into the sand to keep from sprinting up the dune to find Mira—the entire wedding party was barefoot. The wait felt interminable. Just when he was sure he'd stop breathing or take off in search of her, she appeared with Hagen at her side, smiling like he was the happiest little boy in the world. He beamed up at his gorgeous mother, holding tightly to her hand and gripping the handle of a basket, which Matt knew contained their wedding bands. Mira's beautiful dark hair fell in loose, natural waves over her shoulders as she leaned down and kissed Hagen's cheek. Her short, blush-colored, shimmery wedding dress blew in the breeze. The tank-style dress gathered at the waist in silky layers, accentuating her feminine curves. A ruffle of chiffon danced behind her, delicate and transparent, and as she and Hagen walked down the dune, he noticed pretty white beaded flowers that seemed to sprout from her toes and snake and swirl over her foot to her ankle. When they reached the sandy path that would bring them to the altar, her eyes traveled to Matt's, and his heart turned over in his chest.

MIRA WANTED TO remember every second of this evening, from the scent of her gloxinia bouquet and the feel of Hagen's hand in hers, to the glimmer of happiness in his baby blues. She inhaled the scents of the sea—*and our future*—and listened to the *ooh*s and *ahh*s of their family and friends as she and the girls made their way down the aisle. She'd already memorized the layout of the pretty white tables layered in seafoam green and peach, with pretty shell and flower centerpieces Lizzie had made. And as she approached the stunning altar that Matt's brothers had made and Lizzie had decorated with streams of white, peach, and seafoam-green silk, with greenery and flowers decorating the corners and the peak at the center, it wasn't any of those things that were etching into her mind. It was the love and bottomless happiness emanating from the man of her dreams, who had worn the sexy black-framed glasses that made her insides go hot. Her heart was clawing its way through her chest to reach him as they took their place across from him. Matt blew her a kiss and mouthed *I love you*, then winked at Hagen and mouthed the same. If Hagen weren't holding her hand, she thought she might float right up to cloud nine.

The brides had each worn short, summery dresses in chiffon and silk, though none of them wore white. Jana wore lavender, and Sky wore teal. Parker's dress was sky blue, which looked amazing with her long blond hair. Mira had chosen blush, to signify what happened to her every time she looked at her handsome groom.

Serena stepped up and took Hagen's hand, bringing him beside her, a step behind Mira. Mira's heart was beating so fast. Matt's riveting gaze held her in place throughout the ceremony, until the very moment Theresa said, "You may kiss your brides."

Matt swept Mira into his arms and said, "Hold on tight, sunshine. I'm going to kiss you for the rest of your life."

They kissed and danced and kissed some more. Mira had never been so happy, and as she and Matt danced for the hundredth time, Hagen and the children played with Sky's friend Cree, who'd offered to help entertain the kids. She caught sight of Rick and Harper chatting by the buffet table with Theresa and Neil. Matt's father had a coy look about him, a *flirtatious* look. The Seaside girls danced with their husbands, and Matt's siblings were right in the thick of it. This was her new family. *Their* new family.

"Think love is in the air?" Matt asked, glancing in the other direction, at Serena and Brandy talking with Brock, Dean, and Dean's brother Jett.

"Which couple?" Mira asked.

Neil led Theresa to the area where everyone was dancing, and they blended right in.

"You tell me." Matt smiled, eyeing his father, and then he nodded toward Drake, who was watching Serena talking with Jett. Drake looked like he was chewing on nails.

Mira laughed. "What is it about guys wanting what they can't have?"

"I don't know, sunshine. I've got more than I ever dreamed of."

As the music played and the evening took on a magical feel, Pete and Jenna sidled up to Matt and Mira, followed by Bella, Caden, Amy, and Tony.

"Check out Pop," Pete said to Matt.

"He looks happier than he's been in a long time," Matt said. "Did you know he could dance?"

Pete shrugged.

"Well, I'm happy for him," Mira said. "He looks so…"

"Comfortable?" Bella offered. "It looks like they've been

dancing together for years."

Jenna wrapped her arms around Pete's waist. "They're cute together. Don't you think, Petey?"

Pete smiled and kissed her.

"She told us she didn't know how to dance, remember?" Amy said. "When we asked her if Jana could use the recreation room for her dance studio."

"That's right," Bella reminded them. "Jana even offered to teach her."

When the song ended, Hunter, Grayson, Sky, and their new spouses joined them.

"How long's this been going on?" Hunter asked Pete.

"How do you know there's anything going on?" Sky asked.

Pete shushed them as their father and Theresa headed their way.

"You guys looked great out there," Mira said. "Theresa, you didn't tell me you were an ordained minister *and* an amazing dancer."

"I thought you told me you didn't know how to dance," Jana said to Theresa.

Theresa raised her brows. "Did I? *Hm.* Maybe I'm not an ordained minister either." She walked away with a slight smirk on her lips, leaving them all slack-jawed.

"Wait, what?" Mira said. "She's not a minister?"

"Oh my God. We're not really married." Jenna gasped and glared at Bella. "This is all your fault. You had to prank her for all those years."

Not married? No. No, no, no. Mira's heart sank.

"I...but...*ohmygod.*" All the color drained from Bella's face. "I'm so sorry."

"You guys," Amy said, her eyes wide. "If we're not married,

then we have children out of wedlock. Holy fudgenuggets! My family's going to flip out. Tony?" She grabbed his arm, her eyes imploring him to fix this mess.

Tony gathered her in his arms, leveling a serious stare in Theresa's direction. "We'll figure this out, kitten. Don't worry."

"We're not really married?" Mira turned to Matt, feeling lost and on the verge of tears.

"I've got this." Matt took a step toward Theresa, but Theresa turned and headed back toward them. He put an arm around Mira, and she was glad, because she thought she might crumble to the ground in a million brokenhearted pieces.

"Theresa…?" Jenna's voice hung in the air.

A slow smile crept across Theresa's lips. "Gotchya!"

There was a collective exhalation.

"Of course you're really married!" Theresa put her hands on Bella's shoulders and stared into her eyes while the rest of them tried to put their hearts back in their chests.

"You know you scared the shit out of us, right?" Bella said flatly. "That was cruel."

"Bella, my dear girl, you have been pranking me since you were a teenager, and then this summer…*nothing*." Her face went serious. "My summer has been excruciatingly boring without constantly waiting for your clever mind to figure out just how to prank me."

Neil hiked a thumb over his shoulder at Theresa. "I like this one." He reached for Theresa's hand, guiding her into his arms for another dance.

"Someone's got to keep them on their toes." Theresa shook her head. "Kids these days. They have no idea how to do a prank, do they?"

Matt lifted his brows. "What the hell…?"

Pete patted him on the back and said, "Welcome to Seaside, bro. Get used to it. There's never a dull moment."

He pulled Mira into his arms, both of them finally laughing at Theresa's prank. "What would you have done if we weren't really married?"

"Cried and eaten half the cake. What about you?"

"Gotten you and Hagen on the next flight to Vegas to tie the knot. You're mine, sunshine, and no prank in the world can keep us apart."

Ready for more seaside fun?

Get ready for *Bayside Desires*

The first book in the Bayside Summers series!

Fall in love at Bayside, where sandy beaches, good friends, and true love come together in the sweet small towns of Cape Cod.

Bayside Desires releases May, 2017, and may be pre-ordered prior to that date.

Meet your next book boyfriend, Dylan Bad

Dylan is one of four fiercely loyal, sinfully sexy, uber alpha brothers, about to fall head over heels for their leading ladies.

Everything's naughtier after dark...

Sinfully sexy bar owner Dylan Bad has a thing for needy women. He's a savior, a knight in shining armor, and his mighty talented sword has no trouble bringing damsels in distress to their knees. Enter Tiffany Winters, a gorgeous cutthroat sports agent who looks like sex on legs, fucks like she's passion personified, and wouldn't let a man help her if she were dangling from a ledge and he was her only hope. One night and too much tequila might change their lives forever. The question is, will either one survive?

Have you met the Ryders?

Get ready to fall in love with Jake and Addy in Rescued by Love

As the daughter of a world-renowned fashion designer, Addison Dahl enjoyed a privileged life attending the most sought after parties, traveling around the world, and having anything she wanted. Until she broke free and went against her father's wishes, needing to prove to herself—and to him—that she could make it on her own. Now she's ready to take her adventures in a new direction and sets her sights on roughing it in the wilderness.

Jake Ryder followed in his father's footsteps as a top search and rescue professional. He spends his days saving those in need and his nights in the arms of willing women who offer nothing more than a few hours of sexual enjoyment. Just the way he likes it.

When Jake's sister-in-law calls and reports her best friend missing, it's up to Jake to find her and bring her home. But Addison isn't lost, and she sure as hell isn't going to be told what to do by an ornery mountain man with whom she'd spent one torrid night after her best friend's wedding. Jake has never left anyone behind—will Addison be his first failed rescue?

The hot, wealthy, and wickedly naughty Bradens are waiting for you! The Bradens, like all of Melissa's books, are a series of stand-alone romances that may also be enjoyed as part of the larger Love in Bloom series.

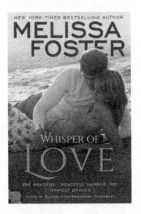

From New York Times bestselling author Melissa Foster comes a new sexy romance, WHISPER OF LOVE, in which Tempest Braden, a music therapist, sets her sights on Nash Morgan, a reclusive artist, and single father, with a secret past.

MORE BOOKS BY MELISSA

THE BRADEN NOVELLAS

Promise My Love
Our New Love
Daring Her Love
Story of Love

THE REMINGTONS

Game of Love
Stroke of Love
Flames of Love
Slope of Love
Read, Write, Love
Touched by Love

SEASIDE SUMMERS

Seaside Dreams
Seaside Hearts
Seaside Sunsets
Seaside Secrets
Seaside Nights
Seaside Embrace
Seaside Lovers
Seaside Whispers

BAYSIDE SUMMERS

Bayside Desires

The RYDERS

Seized by Love
Claimed by Love
Chased by Love
Rescued by Love
Thrill of Love

BILLIONAIRES AFTER DARK SERIES

WILD BOYS AFTER DARK
Logan
Heath
Jackson
Cooper

BAD BOYS AFTER DARK
Mick
Dylan
Carson
Brett

SEXY STANDALONE ROMANCE
Tru Blue
Wild Whiskey Nights

HARBORSIDE NIGHTS SERIES
Includes characters from the Love in Bloom series
Catching Cassidy
Discovering Delilah
Tempting Tristan
Chasing Charley
Breaking Brandon
Embracing Evan
Reaching Rusty
Loving Livi

More Books by Melissa
Chasing Amanda (mystery/suspense)
Come Back to Me (mystery/suspense)
Have No Shame (historical fiction/romance)
Love, Lies & Mystery (3-book bundle)
Megan's Way (literary fiction)
Traces of Kara (psychological thriller)
Where Petals Fall (suspense)

Acknowledgments

One of my greatest joys is writing about Cape Cod, and when I told my Fan Club that the Seaside Summers series might end after *Seaside Whispers*, I had to run into a closet and hide from the backlash. The series is *not* ending, but, my dear readers, you have my awesome Fan Club members to thank for our Seaside Summers spin-off, Bayside Summers! Bayside Summers promises to be fun, flirty, and sinfully sexy—you've met a few of the daring cast of characters in *Seaside Whispers*. And of course you'll also see our Seaside Summers friends in the Bayside series—they are neighbors, after all! **For information on Bayside Summers, be sure to follow me on Facebook and sign up for my newsletter.**
www.MelissaFoster.com/Newsletter
facebook.com/MelissaFosterAuthor

There's nothing more exciting for me than hearing from my fans and knowing you love my stories as much as I enjoy writing them. Please keep your emails and your posts on social media coming. If you haven't joined my Fan Club, what are you waiting for? We have loads of fun, chat about books, and members get special sneak peeks of upcoming publications.
facebook.com/groups/MelissaFosterFans

I am indebted to my meticulous and talented editorial team. Thank you, Kristen, Penina, Juliette, Marlene, Lynn, Justinn, and Elaini for all you do for me and for our readers.

Having sold more than a million books, Melissa Foster is a *New York Times* and *USA Today* bestselling and award-winning author. Her books have been recommended by *USA Today's* book blog, *Hagerstown* magazine, *The Patriot*, and several other print venues. She is the founder of the World Literary Café, and when she's not writing, Melissa helps authors navigate the publishing industry through her author training programs on Fostering Success. Melissa has painted and donated several murals to the Hospital for Sick Children in Washington, DC.

Visit Melissa on her website or chat with her on social media. Melissa enjoys discussing her books with book clubs and reader groups and welcomes an invitation to your event.

Melissa's books are available through most online retailers in paperback and digital formats.

www.MelissaFoster.com
www.MelissaFoster.com/Newsletter
www.MelissaFoster.com/Reader-Goodies

CPSIA information can be obtained
at www.ICGtesting.com
Printed in the USA
BVOW03s1127111116

467592BV00001B/6/P